The Pillad

FRANCIS STUART

New Island Books / Dublin

The Pillar of Cloud
is published in 1994 by
New Island Books,
2, Brookside,
Dundrum Road,
Dublin 14
Ireland

Copyright © Francis Stuart, 1948, 1994
Introduction © Hugo Hamilton, 1994

ISBN 1 874597 09 X

New Island Books receives financial assistance from
The Arts Council (An Chomhairle Ealaíon),
Dublin, Ireland.

First published by Victor Gollancz in 1948.
Republished in 1974 by Martin Brian & O'Keeffe.

Cover design by Jon Berkeley
Printed in Ireland by Colour Books, Ltd.

CONTENTS

INTRODUCTION

Hugo Hamilton

Berlin, October 1991. it was my first meeting with Francis Stuart, in the newly reopened, hastily stitched together city of Berlin. At a literary festival in Pankow, a district in the Eastern half of the city which had formerly been sequestered as a residential reserve for high ranking GDR officials, the tall, boney figure of Francis Stuart made its way into the auditorium of a stately home which had since been taken over by the Literatur Werkstatt Berlin. *"The great are not great now, the good are not good..."* he read in his unmistakable voice, dismissing all sense of merit and honour, undermining all forms of judgement, punctuating a century of upheaval in which this unmistakable city had revolved right back to the beginning.

In a drab and colourless suburb of North Berlin, he appeared to acknowledge with mute satisfaction that history was just starting over again. The slow shock of assimilation had begun to set in in the lacklustre East. I remember the faint chiming of the trams and the pale yellow light of the surrounding streets. Inside, the fake East German grandeur of chandeliers, the blonde ash veneer panelling everywhere and the oddly square, blockey, locked-in-the-fifties furniture. Francis Stuart and I sat in armchairs only recently vacated by the GDR leadership and Stasi personnel, drinking tea from the cups they left behind, both of us taking a sneak look back at our former adoptive city, both of us acutely aware of how yet again, another ideology had been wrong-footed and discredited.

Of course, Francis Stuart was looking so much further back, at the whole of the century, back to a time long before the Berlin wall, back to his time before, during and just after the war. He was able to tell me how much more open the city looked now, how so many green parks had replaced the bombed out blocks of apartment buildings, and how he remembered a far more densely built up city.

1

There were humorous recollections too, vividly brought back by the sudden exposure to the past, like the night he came home and stumbled into the landlady's china cabinet in the dark. And there were also the inevitable, haunting memories of his presence in Berlin during the Nazi regime and the unspeakable sense of internal uneasiness at being, like most Germans of the time, caught on the wrong side of the worst crimes of the century. But that was something we spoke little of. It is not something that is likely to be explained by words alone.

Perhaps this should be cleared up, before I can say anything about *The Pillar Of Cloud,* Francis Stuart's first postwar novel, set in the moral ruins of Germany after the war. *The Pillar Of Cloud* represents Stuart's attempt to understand at a fictional distance, though not quite as an unmarked outsider, that era of horror in which he chose to remain. Even as an artist and a writer, Stuart would not take the easy route, change sides or line up with the righteous where he would have been saved from attack. Nor did he stand aside and join the chorus of denunciation, or the easy triumphalism of the victors. If anything, by making no attempt to stage-manage his past, he became a target. But even if the logic of his presence in Germany during the war years has remained ambivalent, his prose remains entirely honest, as honest as song. It's what made Francis Stuart such an inspiring writer to read in the seventies, when I began to think seriously about writing myself. It's what made me think how impossible it is to be false in fiction. The last thing you would do in order to hide is to write novels like *The Pillar of Cloud.*

As a fellow Irishman, of Irish/German parentage, I can begin to understand the alien status once given to Francis Stuart after the war. Brought up in Ireland in the fifties myself, I quickly understood the sweet air of victory all around me, and the stench of defeat too. Pounded by a culture of anti German heroism in the British and American cinema, from "The Dam-busters" to "Von Ryan's Express", I had to run the gauntlet and allow myself to be called a Nazi; all through my childhood, even as recently as in my thirties, I endured the taunts of Hitler and Eichmann shouted after me by locals. The funny thing was that we never denied it. I never spoke out and said: sorry lads, but you're mistaken – I wasn't a Nazi, I wasn't even alive then. It would have made no sense. It would have been, what they now call the non-denial denial, and in any case, like others with German connections here, we silently understood that those who hurled these accusations, were hardly likely to recognize a real racist.

This is not a protest. This is not some kind of counter-accusation, or some diversion in order to diminish the facts. This is not a defensive revisionism. It is merely an acknowledgement of the power of postwar cliches. I have always felt, much like Francis Stuart at the time of writing this novel, that victors would be the last to really understand the events of this century. Indeed, in Pankow, Francis Stuart and I were bearing witness to the very same high-moral stance of the capitalist triumph over communism at the end of the Cold War. Even now, at the beginning of a new wave of entertainment starting up around the Holocaust, I feel it is always important to acknowledge how brutally wrong you can be, how awkward biography can be, and how little it sometimes has to do with the art and the true, dissident expression of the intellect. The fact remains that Francis Stuart gave his greatest allegiance to his art, to his poetry, to the tightly spun craft of his prose which still leaps up from the pages of *The Pillar of Cloud* today. This novel continues to deliver the strong and passionate narrative of an Irishman in Germany, a fascinating precursor to his masterpiece, *Black List, Section H*.

Set in the postwar landscape of southern Germany, imprisoned in the "vast graveyard" of ruins in the small town of Marheim, unable to escape the Nazi legacy, unable or unwilling to get back to the quiet "pig swill" beauty and safety of his own native land adrift on the periphery of Europe, the main character, Dominic Malone, tries to extract sense from this scarred universe in terms of love and sexual expression. Dominic mistrusts the terms "innocence" and "guilt". He mistrusts religion; Christ is a super-Ghandi; God is the chief executioner. He feels he "needed a war" to discover fraternity and to be able to lie down with the victims. In a newly defeated Germany of hunger and food parcels, American cigarettes and French silk stockings, a blackmarket of sexual opportunity where everything has its price, he battles with his own motives and clings to an Irish sense of purity, defying even his own desires.

Only through the selfless act of marrying one of the "Truemmerfrauen" can he be redeemed. Only by rescuing the consumptive Lisette and taking her to Ireland, can he liberate himself from the rubble of evil. Even though he does not love Lisette, even though he loves her sister Halka, the "*magic of flesh...*

and the luminous pull of her belly," he must take on this doomed sacrifice. During an arrest by the French, he is shown pictures of concentration camp victims and meets up with a camp guard and yet Dominic is less eager to proclaim his own innocence rather than to express his sexual love for the victim Halka.

Stuart's achievement is to place his characters – victims, villains and saviours alike in a world of desire and longing, love and lust, which will ultimately explain everything and nothing in the end. His intellectual terrain is one of intense moral conflict, a conflict which links the Irish obsession with purity to the postwar guilt of Germany. The moral awareness of *The Pillar Of Cloud* is perhaps long outdated by the new European awareness of duty towards pleasure, but it does pitch us perfectly back into that "Stunde Null" – Zero Hour sense of catastrophe in 1945. It portrays his uneasiness with organisation of any sort, his mistrust of order and justice, even of marriage. "*Marriage is mostly an arrangement, to make things easier with papers, with getting out or with getting a room or extra rations...*"

As an intellectual anarchist or writer-as-rogue, positioning himself at a distance from society and from the righteous, Stuart's view is that nothing but the intensity of human love can ever put things right. Losing all faith in ideologies, the prose of this novel bears a stark, uncivil beauty. There are passages, like "The Wedding Night", where Stuart is brilliantly inventive in describing the failure of love, using a device of shadow-characters, or supporting characters in order to represent different visions of the same emotional chaos, eventually bringing the narrative back to the main character again. His attitude towards love and sexual desire makes the position of this unquantifiable Irishman in Germany unique.

The Pillar of Cloud stands as a compelling and courageous attempt to understand the procession of dark events in this century. It is an important book for a younger writer to come across. If we can be as honest in our exposure of the new, totalitarian ideologies of fun and entertainment into the next century, if we can approach the blindspots of consumerism and the culture of exclusion, if we can be as much an intellectual "contra", then we have learned from Francis Stuart, his work and his life.

TO
MAGDALENA

CHAPTER I

HUNGER AND COLD

SNOW HAD FALLEN in the night and covered the ruins. It was bitterly cold as the tall, thin man, who, by his loose and lanky movements, by the very way his worn winter coat hung on him, could be seen to be a foreigner, entered a large undamaged building at the corner of the street. He had been here the previous day enquiring about the long-awaited food parcel from Switzerland, and he knew the way up the stairs and down a couple of passages to one of the many offices in the "Good Samaritan" building. But, of course, the official whom he sought for was not yet back after the lunch pause; he was too early. There began the hanging about, the wait in dusty passages that he knew so well, pressed to the wall while men and women bustled past with an air of persistent activity.

He was weary from cold and hunger. He had not much hope that he would get hold of the parcel that had been sent him by his uncle in Ireland. He had suffered in the last years so much disappointment and humiliation, had spent such endless hours of waiting in dusty corridors, in queues of every kind, in snowy streets and dark, half-ruined entrances, that he seemed to himself to have grown sceptical and wary.

At last a red-headed man came hurrying down the passage, full of the air of importance that all these officials gave themselves. He disappeared into the office outside of which the man waited.

"I will give him a moment to take off his overcoat," he thought. Now that the moment had come, he wanted to delay it. He was afraid of an empty-handed return to his unheated room with the long afternoon before him and a meagre supper of three slices of dry bread.

When he entered the office, the small red-headed official

7

on whom his fate hung was standing by his desk talking to a woman secretary. Dominic could not help giving a swift glance around the room for any sign of the food packets lying around. And sure enough on a table in a corner there lay an opened carton of the sort that he had imagined.

The official did not immediately turn to him, but finished what he was saying to the woman. When he did notice the stranger it was with that slight expression of reluctance which Dominic knew so well. The official read the note of introduction that he had managed to get from the owner of the flat in which he had his room. He had some connection with the "Good Samaritan Society" and had finally written the note after much thought and hesitation. Without a note of some kind it would have been no use coming here, as Dominic knew from much bitter experience.

He watched the official reading what was written on the half sheet of paper. His expression was furtive and wary. "As mine perhaps is too," Dominic thought. In this place and time of famine and desolation every man was an enemy. And it was this that gave such an atmosphere of hopelessness to the ruined towns.

The red-haired official began to repeat the usual phrases about the difficulties of doing what was being asked of him. If the parcel was there, Dominic would have received notice of it through the post.

"It is here," said Dominic. "I saw the slip myself yesterday."

"It is possible. It is possible," said the official with a hint of irritation. "The letter notifying you of its arrival may be among those waiting to be posted."

Dominic followed him into another room, where rows of addressed envelopes were packed into the lids of cardboard boxes. He flipped over the envelopes; and this movement of his finger going slowly over the low row was painful for Dominic to watch. He stood there a little in the background with that now-familiar sensation of hollowness just beneath where his ribs ended and he knew that the hand would not pause and draw out the fateful envelope from the row. All the same, he could not take his eyes off the crooked, moving finger. The official skipped over a section of envelopes,

8

muttering something unintelligible to Dominic, and began again from the other end of the row. But, of course, the fatal envelope was not there.

"I will enquire in our despatch department," said the official. "But there is no doubt the letter has been posted. Let me see, what was the name?"

"Malone."

He scuttled after the official, whose very back seemed to radiate irritation and suspicion.

To have waited four months and then to know the parcel is here and not to get it! "But, if the letter has really been posted, I'll even go round to the Post Office and see if we can't get it," Dominic decided.

He was dreaming of the feast he might still have that afternoon or evening. Not alone; there were one or two others as destitute as himself whom he meant to invite.

The official returned and told him that the letter with the receipt which must be signed and handed in in order to get delivery of the parcel had been posted with a batch that morning at nine o'clock.

"So it must certainly be in the General Post Office?" Dominic asked.

The official glanced at his wrist-watch. "Of course. It is now there. It has by now been sorted and, if you like to go there, they will no doubt give it to you." It was obvious to Dominic that he was simply anxious to get rid of him.

Once out in the snowy street again, he hurried along towards the Post Office.

"If they will only give it to me!" he mused. "If I can only get hold of it!"

Everything depended for him on his getting the parcel to-day. That, if it had actually been posted, the letter would be delivered by the morning post was no comfort to him. In the extreme of prolonged hunger from which he suffered, it was almost impossible to take that calm and objective view of the affair. He needed the joy and comfort of the meal he had so long dreamed of, not to-morrow, not with another night of hunger and dreams in between, but now, some time between now and night. These long nights of hunger had their own peculiar horror. In the nights, the lust for food took hold of him and there was no escape from it. He lay prostrate in the darkness and hungered for the fruits of the earth with a burning, sensual longing out of which were spun feverish, almost palpable visions of food. He had never so longed for a woman. Hunger was lodged in his innermost bowels like a fire there that must be fed if it was not to consume him and waste him away.

There was terror in these visions of foods, in these dreams. Their sterility was a kind of nightmare. It even seemed to him that the more he was possessed by these visions, the longer the day on which he would receive a parcel would be postponed. All this ghostly food by which the nights were haunted seemed to him in his feverish vigil to bode evil for his chance of soon feeling the blessed weight of solid food in his hands.

In the damaged building that had been converted into a Post Office he was sent from one counter to another. He climbed the wooden stairs dripping with snowy slush from the street and in a large room on the first floor was confronted by some kind of overseer. He actually got up from his stool and, going over to the sorting tables, began looking through rows of envelopes. But again Dominic knew that nothing would come of this. The big room with its crudely rigged-up benches and rows of pigeon-holes was full of letters piled here and there, and large baskets, like those used in laundries, filled with letters, stood on the floor.

After a bit, the official strolled back and told him that if the letter had really been posted at nine that morning it had been by now doubtless sorted and was already in its appointed pigeon-hole on the second floor. Dominic climbed another flight of stairs. He entered another large room, conscious of being an intruder, knowing in his heart the hopelessness of the search. He had to begin all over again in his faulty German his explanation to a young man in an alpaca coat. The latter reached up and took a few letters from a pigeon-hole. It took only a moment to look them through. He shook his head, smiling sceptically.

"But where can it be?" Dominic asked in desperation. "If

it was posted this morning at nine, where can it be?" The young man shrugged his shoulders.

"It is probably still unsorted. Or it may be already sorted and transferred to the District Postmaster's office."

"If I come back shortly before you finish sorting it might be here by then?" Dominic asked.

The young man nodded, returning to his work.

With that faint hope still before him the afternoon would not be so empty. There was still the chance that in the evening he would spread the small table beside his bed with all the good things he had not seen in years and that then he would run round to Lisette with the good tidings.

But walking back through the ruins to the tall house in which he had his room he knew that it would not be so. All his running around and struggling against his fate would not alter it. All this unaccustomed exercise and nervous tension only added to his hunger and deepened the hole in his famished body.

The air in his room seemed to him even colder than in the street and, without undressing, he got into bed and covered himself with the eiderdown and the thick feather coverlet. How sick he was of these endless afternoons spent in bed, lying stretched out, too cold to move his hands out from under the bedclothes to read, waiting for the day to pass over! He lay this afternoon as usual and listened to the landlady jingling her bunch of keys as she locked and unlocked other doors in the flat. She kept everything under lock and key for fear her lodgers should pilfer from her stores of potatoes or apples which she got from relatives in the country.

He began to think of the past, of how sometimes on a warm summer morning after breakfast he took a couple of clubs and went out on to the sand-hills where there was a small golf-course. "But wait," he thought. "What did I have for breakfast?"

In those days he had thought little of food. What he had had was toast and butter and marmalade and coffee. Plenty of coffee.

And that was then "nothing special," he thought in amazement.

"But then it was nothing. All those good simple things were as nothing. Then I was blind. But to other things, to Nature, I was not so blind. When I stood alone in a gentle hollow between the low sand-hills with the feathery grass under my feet and with the tiny wild violets and the yellow-and-purple vetch among it and felt the great throb of the sea through the clear, salty air and through the sandy earth, then for those moments I was really happy. I would strike the small white ball and send it soaring up, up into the blue sea air and see it hover, white and shining, high against the wind and then begin to drop into the hollow over the next hill exactly as I had aimed it. Then if, when I had strolled on after it, I found it lying on the green, that was a little shock of pleasure. Because I had made a good shot; but even more because of the sudden sight of the very fine, close-cropped and rolled grass of the green that lay like a smooth carpet spread in the hollow between the dunes. So perfect in its tender greenness and so beautifully had it been mown and rolled that I would hesitate to step on to it.

"Golf," he mused. "How incredible it seems to me now. Even the word sounds strange!

"To stroll around the sand-hills with a club or two, alone; that was for me a way of musing, of greatly enjoying myself, but it hadn't much to do with playing golf."

But then he remembered that he had not usually played alone.

"Mostly I played with Uncle Egan." Uncle Egan brought him back to the parcel. It was he who had sent the money to Switzerland.

He began once more to try to get plain why he had ever left those sand-dunes with their wild flowers, and the country house in which he had lived with his uncle. He had made many pictures for himself out of his past life. And these visions were never the ones that he would have expected to recall. They were strangely inconsequent, but moving and revealing. And what they revealed was, among many other things, a life of such outward peace and plenty that it was a mystery to him that he had ever left it and come here where there was, even then, the beginning of the great desolation.

He had promised to make this mystery once clear to himself, but not yet; he must have time; all must become gradually clear in its own time. As yet, all was still too near, too unripe.

He kept an eye on the watch on the table by his bed. It was time for his second pilgrimage to the Post Office. Again he trudged through the snowy streets. He kept as far as possible to the less ruined streets, though he hardly knew why. He would certainly see nothing to buy in any of the shops. There was nothing to be hoped for in making this detour; but he was distracted by the passers-by and the traffic from the increasing ache of emptiness in his stomach that always began to make itself felt at this hour of the late afternoon. He entered the Post Office and climbed once more to the big sorting-room on the second floor. But before he asked the fair young man with whom he had spoken earlier, he knew his quest was hopeless. Long and bitter experience had taught him to understand the mysterious flow of events. As birds sense the coming weather through the faintest indications in currents of air, so Dominic seemed to be able to tell from the feel of each day or hour what there was to expect from it. Perhaps hunger had given him back this primitive instinct. The letter was not there.

In the dusk he returned home, and when he came into the room he could not but imagine how it would have been if he had brought the parcel with him. These vain imaginings were a symptom of his state of extreme nervous tension and physical exhaustion. He imagined himself opening it, laying the table and tidying up the room in preparation for the tea. As it was, he sat down and turned on the small heater which his ration of electricity allowed him to burn for an hour or two every day.

From the half loaf of bread that he kept in the ugly glass-faced cupboard, he cut three slices. The heater could make no change in the iciness of the room, but, by crouching over it, a faint warmth reached his hands and face. It was at least a spark of living warmth, a bright little bud of fire in the endless waste of winter around him. But suddenly and quietly, as he was eating his second slice of the dark bread, tasting in it the flavour of the corn—in his present state all his senses

13

were supernaturally acute—there was a momentary white incandescence inside the heater and immediately the red glow dulled and faded and there was darkness inside the tin cylinder.

This breaking of the electric stove was a further sign to Dominic that there was to be no lightening of the misery that lay over him. He knew that what he must do was simply to take up the still hot, cheap little contrivance, put it away in the corner, and creep back into bed. But, no, he could not leave it at that. He wanted to force events into another shape; his will was set against the quiet and humble acceptance of his present lot, which his heart knew as the only course of wisdom. He immediately began to tinker at the stove. Without tools, with nothing but a pen-knife, and with freezing hands, he started trying to unscrew the bolts that held the jimcrack heater together. But, of course, the bolts would not turn; the first loosened, but the nut turned with the second and he had nothing with which to grasp it. He took a tin-opener and rent the case of the heater asunder. With great trouble, he managed to join the two ends of the fused wire. And in the midst of his impatient struggle with broken wire and recalcitrant bolts he tormented himself with thoughts of the sand-dunes, the return to lunch, or tea-time at home in winter.

There was a moment of intense expectancy when he plugged the stove connection back into the contact in the wall. He peered into the polished tin cylinder and after a moment saw it take on a faint flush. He experienced a pang of joy and relief. He had rekindled this beacon that was his last light in the darkness around him. He wrapped himself in a blanket and began to read. But it was not long before there came a vicious little hiss from inside the heater, there was the same momentary incandescent flare as before, and then again the warm flush quickly faded from the polished metal.

This time he took the heater and put it away in the corner and climbed into bed. Then began the interminable night of hunger, the lust for food burning in his blood and in his bowels.

He thought: "In those halcyon days with the mornings spent in writing and the afternoons in playing golf or fishing

14

with Uncle Egan I knew none of the great fears, nor the great lusts. I knew nothing of the fear of being without shelter, without a bed and a roof; and that that is a great abysmal fear in the midst of which all peace of mind is shattered. Oh yes, that *is* a fear that I have seen face to face and have had to bow down before. And then its corollary, the longing for a bed. What is that for an ache! Something that after a few weeks of homelessness and sleeplessness grows into a smouldering lust before which all the little peacetime lusts pale. All these years when I ate my regular three or four meals a day, when I lived in a house whose kitchen and larder were stacked with supplies I knew nothing about food! Without hunger, without starvation, you cannot know what food is, you cannot really know what life is or what your body is. Wait till the hole beneath your ribs comes to ache and to have no bottom to it," he went on—he had got into this way of addressing himself through times of great loneliness, "and then you begin to know what it is to be burdened with a body."

In the morning before he was up there was the triple ring at the door which was the sign that it was someone for him. He jumped up and found an acquaintance of his, a French soldier belonging to the Army of Occupation, Robert Descoux, at the door. With Descoux was another Frenchman, wearing a leather jacket and beret and with one side of his face disfigured by a scar.

This visit was not altogether agreeable to Dominic. He had previously only met Descoux in the company of a mutual acquaintance, and Dominic's French was not good enough to keep up any sort of prolonged conversation. Also, he always felt ill at ease in the presence of the French, who were here as conquerors.

But about Descoux there was nothing of the conqueror. He had a lean, reddish face. He was a peasant's son who had worked in a factory during most of the war and now he was beginning to enjoy life.

He had noticed a gold ring that Dominic wore and that a few weeks before he had mentioned wanting to sell. Now he had brought his friend, who wished to buy it.

But Dominic had the ring no longer. He had only the day before given it to a friend who had promised to sell it for him. He needed money because the savings that he had had at the end of the war were almost exhausted and he had no desire to do any work other than his own writing, which for the present brought him in nothing.

He began to explain in his very halting French that he had the ring no longer, but that he would get hold of it later in the day and bring it round to Descoux' flat.

"Come round after lunch to drink a little wine," Descoux suggested. Dominic was grateful for the invitation, though he had much more need of bread than of wine. But it was something to look forward to, something to break the long, meal-less monotony of the day. And then, one never knew; there might well be some cheese and biscuits or a piece of cake left on the table from lunch which Descoux would offer him.

The other Frenchman offered Dominic a cigarette. He began to take mark notes from his pocket which he wanted to pay on account of the ring.

"No. It is not yet certain. Wait till I see if it is not yet sold," Dominic said.

"It doesn't matter. Here's two hundred marks."

He stuffed them into Dominic's hand. He had a good-humoured, sensual face with very small eyes and an air of being all the time somewhere else with his thoughts that certain heavy drinkers come to have. Dominic did not want to take the money, though he thought it pretty sure that the ring had not yet been disposed of. But after they had left, he felt uneasy about the transaction. What did he know of this friend of Descoux? Nor of Descoux either for that matter? They could easily denounce him for having dealings on the Black Market. He had an instinctive distrust of the French, though at the same time he preferred their company, their casual and nonchalant airs, to that of the German bourgeoisie of this provincial town.

He hurried round to Frau Arnheim.

She was out, and he found Lisette alone, her thin, still childish legs sprawling out of an armchair, with a cigarette in her mouth. She was a protégée of Frau Arnheim, and he remembered hearing that her elder sister, with whom she habitually lived, was away—an expression that might mean anything these days.

"Have you had breakfast? Ah, what a stupid question! Wait. I will make some coffee," the young girl said. She was proud to be able to offer him some real coffee. And later he found out that she took it from a private supply of Frau Arnheim's. She busied herself with an electric pot and cups. He told her of the visit of Descoux and explained the object of his coming.

She turned quickly to Dominic and the swift, defensive expression that he had before remarked passed over her face.

"I don't know. I think Aunty has found someone to buy it and has gone out to see him," she said. She called Frau Arnheim "Aunty," although she was no relation.

"It can't be helped. I'll simply say it's already sold. Descoux asked me to come round after lunch for some wine. You can come too if you like."

How he hated this business of the ring! There seemed to him a subtle poison in it by which even Lisette was affected. She had turned away again and was bent over her cupboard, getting out cups, but he sensed in the very poise of her shoulders something defensive, nervous.

"Did you take some money from them?" she asked.

"I didn't want to. The other Frenchman kept pushing it into my hand. But we will simply say it is sold and give it back to him."

Between him and the little Lisette there had sprung up a kind of understanding. He had told her about Ireland, speaking to her in a way that he had spoken to no one else in all the years of his exile. He made pictures for her very much as he did in the long wakeful nights. She would listen for hours, fascinated; she was never tired of asking him to tell her more. Now, as he drank the coffee, he began to speak of one of the many mornings he had spent fishing with his Uncle Egan on the lake.

"On our way to the lake," he began, "we had to pass

through the old graveyard and there we came on the grave-digger, Hand, who was a great croney of my Uncle Egan's. He had just finished digging a grave for a girl who had died in the glen and whose funeral was to take place the following morning."

Lisette had heard few other tales in her life, books being scarce, children's books especially being unobtainable in the demolished towns in which with her elder sister she had grown up.

"It was very silent on the lake," he went on, "except for the little watery whisper of the oars and under us the dark depths of the water. And I hardly knew what might not come out of that great shadow of water. There was such expectation in the silence and in the heavy cloudy morning over the water and in our hearts.

"Uncle Egan never went fishing without taking with him some whisky, and we passed it from one to the other, taking a shot straight out of the bottle. We grew a little excited, but not noisily, you know; very quietly because of the coming funeral. The presence of Hand, the grave-digger, made this fishing trip of ours a ceremonious business. I could see that he never forgot the funeral in the morning, and it made him row with a slow and solemn sweep of the oars. And that was just what my Uncle Egan wanted. He liked funerals and he liked fishing and he liked drinking, and here was something as near as could be got to combining them all."

"Did you like them all?" Lisette asked.

"I was taught to appreciate them all by my Uncle Egan," Dominic said.

"Drinking and fishing," mused the girl, "and what else? What was the other?"

"Funerals."

She was musing. She liked it when he came. His words gave her a prickle of warmth in her flat little breast. He saved her from the horrible monotony of this existence with Frau Arnheim. If only she could persuade him to take her away, she thought. But she was so pale and ugly. If she had known he was coming, she could have made herself up a little. But she forgot herself in the fascination of the tale.

18

"Did the fish come?" she added.

"Yes."

"How did you know when it came?" She was eager, attentive, her whole soul concentrated on the tale.

"I felt the slight pressure, like that," and he put his fingers on her thin wrist and pressed it. The blood came into her small face at his touch.

"Where did you feel it?" she asked. She was confused.

"In my wrist. It came up the line, down the rod into my wrist. And from my wrist all over me, into my heart and into my head that was already half turned with the whisky."

"How big was it?" she asked.

"It wasn't big," he went on. "It was small and wild. It was wild with the dark water- and rock-wildness, wilder than any beast that lives under the sun."

"What did it look like?" she breathed.

"Like a shadow. I hardly saw it; I only felt it in its wild leaps and tugs striking through my wrist. It was the touch of all that is wild and least human on my heart."

"Like that demon," she said, "in the prayer."

"What prayer?"

"'Save us from the shadow of death and the demons that fly by night,'" she repeated. It was part of a prayer she had learnt, a relic of the war years, of the time when the coming of each night was full of the dread of destruction and sudden death.

"What happened when you caught it?" she asked, and waited in suspense.

What could he say not to disappoint her, not to shock and outrage her? The heavens had not fallen, no veil of no temple had been rent.

"We ate it," he said bluntly.

He saw a little spasm of disgust pass over her face.

"We made a fire of sticks on the shore of the lake," he went on, "and we grilled the fish over it and ate it with potatoes roasted in the ashes."

"You should not have eaten it," she said.

"There are several ways of eating," he told her, "though now we only know one way, that of gobbling down all we can get. But it was not like that. Our little meal was very solemn and ceremonious. Hand did the cooking, and he did all very solemnly, making it into a kind of funeral meal. Before we began to eat, he made the sign of the Cross over the grilled fish. We drank the rest of the whisky and eat the fish."

"Without being hungry?" Lisette asked. Not to be hungry; on that she had to ponder a while. To eat without being hungry; that was beyond her. How would food taste if you weren't hungry?

"That eating of the fish we had caught ourselves was a kind of ceremony. It had nothing to do with hunger. It was a consummation."

"Consummation? What is that?"

"That is a thing you can't know," he told her. "You are not yet consummated; you are only in bud."

Yet was she in bud? Was not there something already bruised in the bud?

They talked on. She sat beside him and her dark eyes kept creeping back to his face. She was puzzled over the words: "You are not yet consummated." All his words had a life of their own; they penetrated into her and caused a stir in her, sometimes of joy, but sometimes troubling her.

"Where is your sister?" he asked her. After all, they were close enough for him to ask her such a question, although he knew it was one not asked these days, when so many people had a good reason of one sort or another for being "away"; which meant that they were not to be found at their registered address.

"She has entered a convent," Lisette answered unexpectedly.

"Then you will live on here permanently with Frau Arnheim?"

The girl looked at him appalled.

"Oh, no!" she exclaimed.

"What will you do?"

"I will take a room for myself. But for God's sake don't mention this to Aunty."

Dominic shook his head.

"Not that I have any money," Lisette added quickly. He saw the defensive look come into her face and he realised that that was her habitual expression with other people. With other people she had a small, closed, rather ugly little face. Only while they had been talking had it altered; it had opened out, flower-like for these moments.

"Are you going to have lunch?" he asked her.

"No."

"I neither. Then we can start for Descoux'," he said. "It's time. With luck, we might get something there."

CHAPTER II

THE ANGEL

DESCOUX AND HIS FRIEND were sitting at the table in the small parlour of the furnished flat in which Descoux was quartered. An iron stove was glowing in the corner. They had finished lunch, of which the remnants remained. Dominic kept his eyes from the table-cloth lest his glance might betray his hunger. The lean, dark face of Descoux had a heightened colour and the other Frenchman, with his ugly, scarred face, sat back in his chair, smiling and drinking white wine.

Lisette could manage to look at the table indifferently. Her small face was set defensively; her dark eyes seemed to become smaller and her nostrils pinched. She spoke some French, her mother, who had died when she was still a small child, having been French. Her father had been a Pole. The two Frenchmen were pleased at her coming with Dominic.

Descoux brought another bottle or two of wine from the big glass cupboard and filled glasses for them.

When Dominic got into difficulties explaining about the ring, Lisette helped him, talking her quick French that Dominic found it difficult to follow. But he gathered that she told a somewhat different story about it to that which she had recounted to him. He saw that in these ways she was capable of slyness and deceit, and it astonished him—this mixture of childishness and slyness.

He took out the money that he had been given and wanted to return it, but the Frenchman laughed and waved it away, saying something to Lisette that Dominic did not catch. So that in the end he was still left with it and not sure what arrangement about the ring Lisette had made. He saw for all her chatter how nervous and on the defensive she was. But soon her cheeks began to glow with the wine and minute drops of sweat appeared on her forehead and upper lip.

"Haven't you a little friend who would like to come here and look after Descoux?" the other Frenchman asked Lisette.

"The town is full of girls who would come in return for eating here. Don't you know that?" Lisette said.

"Yes. I know it. But Descoux doesn't know how to set about arranging these things."

Descoux smiled, and his whole lean, lined face with his black eyes had an almost wistful air. He was a little drunk, but quietly and with that air of indifference that Dominic could never quite make out. He sat drinking the white wine, and agreeing with all that was said, exclaiming from time to time, "*Ah, oui,*" or "*Bien sûr.*" He agreed in the same casual way when his friend, with a laugh and a curious glance at Lisette, asked him a question that Dominic did not catch. The other then went into the adjoining room and returned with a small folder in his hand. He pushed past Dominic and sat down beside Lisette on the sofa. Dominic supposed he was going to show her photographs of the woman with whom he lived in France and their child about whom he had just been speaking. He laid the folder on Lisette's thin knees and opened it for her. Dominic had only time to glimpse a picture of bodies. Before he even saw the picture, at the moment of the Frenchman opening the folder, he had known what would come. Lisette closed it quickly. He saw her hand tremble.

The Frenchman laughed. "A fellow countrywoman of yours, a Polish girl, gave it me." He opened it at another picture. This time Lisette's glance rested on it, as though she

22

was too tired to close it a second time, as though not knowing, in her hunger and the weariness brought on by the wine, how to hold out against the smiling, casual insistence of the man. He seemed to fill the tiny parlour with his animal dominance. Dominic was conscious of it too. He was conscious of his own empty stomach, of his hollowness, of his thin, pale face beside those of the two Frenchmen. They were so much more solid than he and Lisette.

"Don't look at it," he told Lisette in English. She immediately turned away, as though this single word from him gave her the power to do so.

Descoux had taken no part in the little incident. He sat at the table, quiet and evasive, waiting to see what would happen, as Dominic thought. He refilled their glasses. Dominic would have liked to have left. The atmosphere in the little room was oppressive to him. He felt humiliated. And each time he saw the small eyes of the Frenchman fixed lecherously on Lisette it was he who suffered the humiliation. She was chattering again and always still pale.

From shock she seemed to find a certain fascination in being there, and when Dominic suggested that they should leave she did not appear to hear him. But when he got up, she followed his example and, wrapping themselves up in their scarves and overcoats, they escaped out into the snowy street.

"Ah! how good to be out in the cold again!" Dominic said. "I am sorry I dragged you there all for nothing. They might have offered us a piece of bread and cheese."

"They don't know we're hungry," Lisette said. "They don't know anything about us."

"But what did you arrange about the ring?" he asked.

"It's all right. I said that a friend had it and that we would get it back from him."

"But supposing Frau Arnheim has sold it?"

"She won't have sold it," Lisette said. But she did not want to talk about the ring. Neither of them mentioned the pornographic pictures. She began to speak of her sister, Halka.

"Without her I feel so lost," she said. "But it is right that

23

she went into the convent. She was too good to live here in this world."

She began to tell him about her sister. Of how they had lived together in Poland after the death of their mother and the disappearance of their father. That had been at the beginning of the war, under the German occupation. But she had been too young for her to find anything unusual in the conditions in which they had lived. She had known no others. Halka had been ten or twelve years old, and had looked after her until she had been taken away for having harboured a Jew in their room and put in a concentration camp. Then Lisette had spent some miserable years being looked after, or neglected, by an old woman who had been living in the same house, until the return of Halka. The latter part of the war they had spent in Germany, where Halka had had to work in a factory.

All this she told Dominic for the first time. Probably because of the wine she had drunk on an empty stomach, she chattered to him about things of which she had never spoken before.

They travelled on the crowded tram through the completely devastated centre of the town back to Frau Arnheim's, and got off in a more or less undamaged suburb.

Frau Arnheim was a tall, stately woman with black hair beginning to turn grey. She had a very quiet manner and she received Dominic with a subdued kind of warmth.

They sat in the old-fashioned room with its big, tiled stove, into which Frau Arnheim put several more logs.

"Don't waste your wood on our account, Aunty," Dominic said. "For me it is warm enough here."

He was glad of the quiet, simple atmosphere without tension after the hour or two in Descoux' flat.

When Lisette went out of the room, Dominic asked Frau Arnheim about her sister. He thought it strange that she had entered a convent and left her alone in the midst of so much hardship.

"She isn't in a convent. That is what they told the child," Frau Arnheim said. "The fact is she's in an asylum. They say she went through frightful things when she was in the

24

prison camp during the war, indescribable horrors. And her mind must have been affected."

Frau Arnheim lost much of her air of stateliness and aloofness as she talked. She liked sensational gossip. But her gossiping was never malicious; she was always ready to open her heart to all those who came to her.

She went on talking about Halka Mayersky until Lisette came back into the room. Then she got up and disappeared into her tiny kitchen and Dominic heard the welcome clink of plates.

"What has Aunty been telling you about me?" Lisette asked.

"About you? What is there to tell about you?" Dominic said, laughing.

In a few minutes, Frau Arnheim returned, bringing them each a plate of thick potato soup.

"I don't know whether you will care for this, but I have nothing else to offer you," she said. "On such a cold day something warm is a comfort."

Dominic was strangely affected. It was not only the intense pang of physical joy of at last having a plate of good food in front of him, but the simple goodness of this woman after all the indifference he had met with at the "Good Samaritan" house, at the Post Office and at Descoux was nearly too much for him.

She brought up a small table for them by the stove at which they ate the soup. These were for Dominic blessed moments after the desolate weeks that had just gone by.

They sat on in the twilit cosiness of Frau Arnheim's room. There were two or three slices of dry bread that he could eat for supper, but there was no comfort in the thought. Almost any meal is a comfort and a joy to the starving, as he knew. Out of the simplest scraps it was possible for him to make a little meal that gave him renewed courage. Only from dry bread came no new faith. With dry bread alone it is impossible to make a little ceremony out of eating. And without ceremony nothing is real, as he had tried to explain to Lisette.

Back in his room he crept into bed with his three slices of bread and munched them, pulling the bed-clothes up over

25

his head against the cruel cold. Then slowly he was drawn into the vast solitude of these sleepless nights. There began the long nightly torment of the ache of hunger beneath his ribs. He tried not to think of food, to become obsessed by visions of the common meals of the past, which he now saw as miracles which should have turned each day into a day of rejoicing. He tried to banish all these sterile thoughts. He began to repeat the *Pater Noster* over and over very slowly to free himself from the lust of food which burnt in him like a fever. And in his struggle to keep his attention on the words of the prayer, he finally went to sleep. In the morning there was again the anxious waiting for the post in expectation of the letter. He was aware that it would not come, that this very waiting for it in some way precluded the possibility of its coming, but he was powerless to let the morning go over as it might, to leave all to take its own shape. It was all very well to understand the final wisdom of saying, "So be it," but to be able to act on it in the actuality of living was often beyond him.

When the letter did not come, he went round to Frau Arnheim, as they had agreed the previous afternoon, to fetch her to accompany him to the "Good Samaritan" House. But she was not at home. In his impatience, he had arrived earlier than they had settled. He knew that it was hopeless for him to go and speak to some official of the charitable society alone.

"She has probably gone out about the ring," Lisette said.

"Better she had waited and come with me to get my parcel," Dominic said. "Didn't she say anything about me, about what we arranged yesterday?"

"I don't think so. She said something about you, but not about that. She said she couldn't make out why you had ever left your home and come here," Lisette told him. "And I don't know either," the girl went on. "Because you have not told me that. You probably don't want to tell me."

"No. On the contrary, you are the only person I could tell. Because only you would accept what I told you, simply, and believe me."

"You can tell me, if you like," said Lisette.

"Yes. But not in a word. It is hard to explain. I lived with my Uncle Egan in security and comfort. But that wasn't really what I wanted.

"Although there were times when I seemed to have a glimpse of the secret of how to live, the mornings in the sand-dunes or the evenings on the lake, still I saw that those were only accidental interludes. I was blind. My eyes were not opened. I lived for myself, cut off from others, even from my Uncle Egan who loved me and was infinitely patient with me. Nothing touched my heart."

"If I had been there," said Lisette, "I could have touched it."

"How?"

She considered. "You would have had to care for me. I would have been small then and you would have had a lot of trouble getting food and clothes for me and looking after me."

Talk as he might of his home, she would never grasp that all had been plentiful there. A state of plenty was something that she could not imagine and did not believe in.

"But you were not there, and I lived on in my blindness. I don't mean to say that life was not often very pleasant. I wrote my books, played golf and went fishing with Uncle Egan. How glad he was when I would go with him; he was so glad and proud of the least attention I showed him. He looked up to me; he thought I was immensely clever and gifted. But in his company I was more than half the time bored. I became soon bored with the fishing trips and even the sand-dunes began to lose their fascination for me. I believed that happiness lay elsewhere—in fame, in riches, in the cities, in the company of certain young women of fashion. Had I had a guardian angel, he would have seen it was desperate with me, and that it had come so far that I could only be saved by some desperate remedy."

"Perhaps you did have a guardian angel," said Lisette, "as Halka was my angel. She is still. Even in the convent she will pray for me. If it was not for her there praying for me it would be much worse for me."

"Yes. Perhaps I did have such an angel. That is one way

of putting it," said Dominic. "And such an explanation comes as near to the truth as any other. He came to me and touched my eyes and they were opened for a moment. But it wasn't pleasant; it was a horror to see myself for a moment as I was."

"Did he come in the day or the night?" the girl asked.

For her all mysteries, all horrors had come out of the sky and were of two sorts: those that come by day and those that had come by night. His words were referred by her to those memories of her childhood of night skies lit by fire or midday darkened by palls of smoke in the horror of the air-raids through which she had been.

"He came in a very different way to what you think," Dominic told her. "Not with noise or flashes, with the sounding of sirens or the blowing of trumpets. He stole up beside me, like a thief in the night. He was beside me in my room, and on the lake and at the strand. When I went fishing with Uncle Egan and all was at its quietest and most usual, Uncle Egan sitting with his rod and his whisky flask in the back of the boat and I rowing slowly and noticing nothing but the dark water and the dark mountains closing in over the lake, then, looking back, I know that he had already signed me with his sign."

"What sign is that?" Lisette asked.

"The sign of pain. All these last terrible years were at that moment foreseen and prepared for me. That was to be my cure."

"Couldn't he have found a quicker cure?" Lisette asked. "And not such a complicated one?"

"No. It was the only one, apart from death, that would really work. But that is a later part of the story. Now I have only got to those days when I still lived a quiet and undisturbed life in our house by the sea with my Uncle Egan.

"I lived largely in the future. I was always promising myself great success and happiness in a few months' time. I dreamed of writing a very successful book which would take the public by storm, of having riches, of escaping from what seemed to me the miserable country life to which I was bound. I became blinder and blinder and it was more and more impossible for me to escape from myself and my desires and

28

to be simple and humble and at peace. Many incidents I can recall of those days with shame and remorse. I would never confess them to anyone but to you, Lisette," Dominic told her.

"One night I drove home from the city with two or three of my fashionable friends. There were a couple of young women and perhaps a man. I cannot recall the details. I brought them into our big sitting-room. It was a summer evening, just dusk, and I did not light the lamps. Like that, the bad taste of the house was not evident and our old-fashioned furniture and bookcases showed to the best advantage. Uncle Egan had already gone up to his room. He was naturally retiring and did not care for company except of a few country people like Hand, the grave-digger.

"But when he heard us, he came down. And this he did out of a kind of delicacy. He did it for my sake, not wishing me to think that he disliked me bringing my city acquaintances to the house or that he did not like them.

"He came in and it must have cost him a great effort to appear like that before us. I suppose I introduced him to the visitors. But I did no more. I ignored him and so did they. Perhaps the youngest of the two women took a little notice of him and exchanged a word or two with him, because she was not a bad sort. As for me, it was one of those many hours of darkness in which I was sinking more and more.

"I would never even have realised what I had done, had not Uncle Egan given a hint of the way I had denied him to old Hand. It was very seldom that he ever made the slightest criticism of me, and that he did so this time surprised me so much that I had to realise that I had wounded him more than ordinarily."

Dominic stopped. He thought that for the moment he had told Lisette enough. He knew that it was an effort for her to listen to and follow him and that his words produced a kind of inquietude in her when he told her too much. It seemed to him at times that if he told her too much, she might awake out of her dream and that she might begin to doubt the tale of Halka having entered a convent. She had very little idea of what a convent was; she thought of her sister whom she adored as being already a being removed far above this miserable world and, from the heights where she dwelt, smiling down upon her, Lisette, like a picture she had once seen of St. Thérèse of Lisieux casting down on to the earth a shower of rose petals.

Frau Arnheim returned from a long wait in a queue with nothing more than one small and bruised cauliflower out of which she would make a soup for Lisette. And then she was quite ready to start off with Dominic to the "Good Samaritan" House.

She was very worried, because, when she had gone that morning to take the ring from the little box where she kept it since Dominic had given her it to sell for him, she could not find it. But she did not mention this now. She meant to have a thorough hunt for it later.

They reached the "Good Samaritan" building and went up to the office that Dominic had been in previously. Here it was the same tale as before. The letter had been posted. Without the receipt, it was impossible to give out the parcels and so on. But this time Dominic had come determined to fight to the last. Slow to be roused, lethargic in many ways, yet a point finally came where his patience failed. Somewhere in a room in this building there was the parcel of food that belonged to him, containing such things as bacon and tins of pork. It was the image of the bacon that roused him to the point of combat. This it had been that had haunted him in the night. This it had been that had appeared in the darkness, a slab of fat bacon. He had a lust for it that seemed to radiate from the hole below his ribs and invade his being. To actually have the cardboard packet in his hand, that was a joy that they would try to deny him. He felt, standing here in the office, that it was a struggle between him and these officials whose task it was to delay and diminish all joy. Because their own hearts were too constricted to really encompass joy in its full shock they wanted to deny it to others. Therefore they made difficulties, delayed letters and would have liked only finally to have delivered a parcel when the recipient had become sick at heart through the struggle and procrastination. Perhaps these ideas of Dominic

30

were childish, but he was in a state of nerves brought on by prolonged starvation.

Frau Arnheim had a good way with these people. She could speak to them in their own dialect and at the same time she could play the great lady of other days, smiling a little haughtily and insisting her way from office to office until they reached the bureau of one of the chiefs.

He was a pugnacious-looking little man with brusque movements and gestures. When at last he finished telephoning, signed some letters that a secretary handed him, and swivelled suddenly round towards them, Dominic's heart momentarily failed him. It was the old tale of the individual *versus* the organisation, the machine. But he was not going to submit to all this display of mechanical power, to this show of officials, bureaux, typewriters, telephones. He heard Frau Arnheim putting on her airs in vain and he saw that her white hair had become disarranged and she looked old and defeated. Dominic began to speak.

He spoke quietly and slowly in his bad German. The fury in him was a quiet, soft fury, like that of a wary, savage beast.

"The money has been paid by my uncle, the parcel has been bought and it has been delivered from Switzerland here to your society. By what right do you refuse to deliver it to me?"

"My dear sir, you cannot come here and teach me my own business. Do you realise that we have already distributed thousands of parcels and no one has made any complaint? You are merely one in ten thousand and must await your turn like the rest," the official said. He spoke rapidly. His words were a formula, the same old appeal to numbers, to masses.

"It is not a question of numbers," Dominic said. "It may be that among all these miserable wretches no one has yet dared to come to you and make a complaint. But I am not one of them. I am a foreigner, an Irishman, and organisations have no divine rights for us as they seem to have here."

Dominic felt a relief at having vented some of the smouldering passion within him against the tyranny of the organised mass. It made no difference whether it was the small mass of a charitable society or some other mass. It was all hateful to

31

him with its air of having rights far beyond those of the individual human creature. His heart felt already lighter, he was almost content, although the outcome was still undecided. But he felt that the official was unsure, a little uneasy. He had been assailed from a quarter where he did not feel himself to be on sure ground. And Dominic, in spite of the hard words that had passed between them, felt no personal hostility to this man. He did not despise him as he did the sly, anxious little red-haired underling on the second floor.

Now suddenly all went smoothly, quickly. The man rang up another office and a clerk with an envelope came in, which he gave to his chief. From it the official extracted the receipt.

"Here you are," he said to Dominic. "Your letter had not yet been posted. With a little patience and common sense these things can be cleared up. I am here at my desk twelve and sometimes fifteen hours a day working for the good of the populace. I know the need and the misery, but nothing can be achieved by excitement and accusation."

Dominic was now ready to be conciliatory. He had no more rancour against the other. He had lightened his heart and it was enough. Now he did not want to argue any more. The official had to have the last word and Dominic conceded it to him.

With the precious piece of paper in his hand, Dominic turned to the store-room on the ground floor from which the parcels were distributed.

CHAPTER III

HALKA

LISETTE BEGAN TO COME and see Dominic often and sit with him, wrapped in blankets, in his cold room. He was a little surprised at her coming, but he soon saw that she was not so much lonely as bored at Aunty's.

She did not talk much. He knew she came because she felt
that the things that happened would happen here and not in
Aunty's warm and comfortable flat. She would sometimes
even bring her lunch or supper with her and eat it with him.

"What will Aunty say? Won't she be offended?" Dominic
asked.

"*Ach*, Aunty! I don't always tell her where I am."

And indeed one day Frau Arnheim told him that Lisette
had begun to take music lessons and spent many hours at a
place where there was a piano on which she could practise.

Sometimes she spoke of her sister. Her sister had been to
her an angelic being against the background of misery and
disaster. She had appeared and disappeared again; there
had been the long time when Halka had been in the prison
camp. And then suddenly one evening she had appeared at
Lisette's bed. Lisette had woken up and there her sister had
been standing, pale and thin, but to the child like an angel
by her bed.

"I couldn't bear to look at her," Lisette said. "She was so
beautiful and all that I had had to look at for all that time
was so ugly, so mean and miserable. I turned and hid my
face in the bed-clothes."

Sometimes Descoux came round to Dominic. At first
Dominic did not know why he came and felt uneasy at his
presence. But there was something so quiet and unexacting
about him, he would sit in the armchair with his illustrated
papers so contentedly, that Dominic soon got used to him.

"He comes and goes so quietly, like a thief," Lisette said.
She did not like him. She was still afraid of him.

"And he never brings anything. He has everything and he
comes and sits here and never brings a thing," she said.

"It doesn't matter. Let it be so," said Dominic.

But one day, with her small face set and her nose pinched
in anger, she said to Descoux: "What do you do with all your
potatoes? I think they must be rotting in your cellar?"

Dominic signed to her to be quiet.

"Do you need potatoes?" Descoux asked Dominic. Next
day he brought a bag of potatoes and put them down in a
corner of the room without a word.

Dominic was glad. Not only because of the gift of the potatoes, but because he had thought that after Lisette's words Descoux would perhaps come no more and, strangely enough, he had begun to like and look forward to his visits. And even Lisette gradually lost her fear of him and began to talk to him a little. The three of them spent much time together in Dominic's room.

And now, as though the ice had been broken, Descoux sometimes brought with him a loaf of bread or a couple of chops. He gave these things without seeming to give them, leaving them on the table, saying nothing. But when Dominic offered to pay him for the bread at the Black Market price he would take the money.

Dominic came to like the rather mysterious, quiet nonchalance of Descoux. He came and sat in the armchair and read his French newspapers and sometimes stayed to drink a cup of coffee and eat one of his own chops, and he did not impinge on Dominic. He came and went, really "like a thief in the night," as Lisette said. When he rang, it was a quicker, softer ring than anyone else's, and when he came into the room, swarthy and lean in the rough khaki overcoat and black beret, there was no sense of strain, nothing altered.

Dominic had cleared the snow from the window-sill and crumbled some bread on it for the birds. Descoux, who never seemed to take much notice of anything, watched the birds with an air of attention that Dominic had never seen on his face before. When once a crow came and, without daring to perch on the sill, swooped down with a beat of black wings and took a piece of bread in its beak, Descoux seemed for once to lose his nonchalance and spoke animatedly to Lisette.

"You won't often see a crow come to a window," he said. "Sparrows, *bien sûr*, but not a crow. A crow is *un oiseau sauvage!*"

And after that Lisette always called him "*l'oiseau sauvage.*"

One day he arrived towards evening with a three-litre bottle of wine in a wicker cover, a *bon-bonne* as he called it, and a piece of pork. He put down the *bon-bonne* on the floor and the meat on the table, saying something about there being a glut of wine in the French *économats*, the shops reserved

34

for the French troops and their families. He always liked to make as little as possible out of what he brought.

"Then I'll make supper and we will have a little celebration," said Dominic.

As Descoux said nothing but began to open a French magazine devoted to lurid illustrations of police news, he went on:

"But you don't have to stay if you don't want. Perhaps you have an appointment."

"*Ah, non,*" said Descoux, looking up. He stayed for supper, pouring the wine for them, eating quickly and hungrily what was set in front of him as though he was as ravenous as they, but then suddenly stopping, pushing away his plate.

"He must be a peasant," exclaimed Lisette in German. "He is like them in the way he eats and his knowledge of birds!"

"Let him be a peasant," said Dominic.

"You come from the country, from the peasants?" Lisette suddenly asked.

"*Ah, oui.* My parents had a farm. But I, I did not have much interest in staying there. I wanted to see something of the world. And I was lucky. I have seen many parts of France, and now I am seeing Germany. It interests me very much, Germany. And all that is thanks to the war."

He began to tell them about how his life had been affected by the German occupation of France. He had never spoken so much to them before.

"Sometimes in our town, during the night, Communist posters were pasted up in the streets. The Germans searched our house one morning and found some Communist documents hidden in my brother's room. They did not get him, but they arrested me and my wife Antoinette. I was sentenced to two years and Antoinette to six months." ·

"You spent two years in prison?" asked Dominic.

"*Bien sûr.*"

Dominic looked at Descoux with a new regard. Those two years might explain a lot of what he had found mysterious in him. He listened attentively.

Descoux seldom spoke much, but now Dominic was

conscious of a strange power in his words. It was almost as if an animal could speak, telling of its fears, its pains and its joys.

Descoux described his cell and his life in it. He told how every evening he had climbed up and with great difficulty managed to look from the small window down into the square. And one evening he had seen his two children, "*mes deux gosses*," playing out there in the street.

"That night I wept," Descoux said. Dominic was touched by these words. He looked at the lean, swarthy face of Descoux, at the dark muzzle. On it he saw reflected a mixture of animal lust and animal shyness and timidity, and over that, as though imposed on it afterwards, a little spark of watchfulness, of cunning in the dark eyes.

But they had caught this *oiseau sauvage* too, Dominic reflected. And it moved him to think of that lean, swarthy face with its dark undertone of animal placidity, reduced to human tears.

One morning Descoux came round and invited them to dinner that evening at his flat.

"Who will cook it?" Lisette asked.

"I have got a *bonne* to come and cook for me and clean the flat."

"So you've got a *chérie* at last? Does she look nice?" Lisette asked.

"You will see her this evening," Descoux said, with his dark, wolfish smile.

With the dinner to look forward to, the whole day was lit for them from within.

"From our stomachs," Lisette said.

"I feel like one of the beggars invited to the marriage feast," Dominic said. But she had never heard the story and she did not know what he was talking about. He hardly knew himself. The seduction of a *fräulein* for food had not very much to do with the marriage feast of the parable perhaps.

From the moment they entered the house in which Descoux had his flat, it was like stepping back into a vanished world. The house had been requisitioned by the French and the stairs were polished and smelt of wax, electric bulbs burned

36

over each landing. Descoux opened the door of his flat himself and they took off their overcoats in the tiny hall. Lisette, out of curiosity, had to peep into the kitchen. Dominic only caught a fleeting glimpse of a woman busy at the range, of an unexpectedly white face with an overpainted mouth. At that moment he was less conscious of the woman than of the smell of rich food being prepared. But then he was aware of something happening in the kitchen that put the hunger and expectation quite out of his mind. Lisette had thrown herself at the other, elder girl and was clinging to her. Dominic could see the face of the woman lowered over Lisette. She was trying gently to unloosen the girl's arms from around her. Her face was full of pain. She had pale eyes, strangely pale and tranced, under full lids.

Dominic went into the small sitting-room where the table had been laid. He did not want to overlook the scene between the two sisters, for he guessed the girl cooking in the kitchen was Halka.

Descoux had lost none of his habitual nonchalance by the discovery of the relationship between his newly acquired *chérie* and Lisette. He poured himself and Dominic out a glass of *apéritif* while they waited, and he said, with a shrug of his shoulders: "Lisette thought her sister was in a convent, eh?"

Dominic nodded. At that moment what he hoped was that nothing would spoil the dinner that they had been promised. Let them first eat, let them eat all that they could, and then afterwards this business of Halka turning up here could be dealt with, if it had to be. But he need not have feared. Quite soon the girl he had caught a glimpse of appeared with the dishes and Descoux introduced her to him as Halka Mayersky.

"Don't let our touching family reunion spoil the meal," she said to Descoux. "You had probably brought your friend to inspect your new *chérie*. And so he can. He can see she's no beauty." A moment later Lisette came in; she said nothing, but took the place her sister indicated at the table.

At first the meal was a rather silent one. It was only Halka who did not seem to feel any reason for being ill at ease.

She was not pretty and had not the air of seductiveness that would have fitted in to the picture. But Dominic knew that in reality no picture was ever as he would have painted it, that his imagination, even at its most daring, could never reach the strange contradictions and apparent disharmonies that made up the sum of reality.

She had a very pale face—pale with a ghostly whiteness— and the eyes were also very pale. This pallor and her straight, rather colourless hair gave her at first glance an almost ugly appearance. She was like a hag, a witch, who had appeared uninvited at the feast. She was talking with Lisette in German, explaining her presence here.

She had met Descoux the evening before as she had been wandering in the dusk by the bank of the river that flowed through the town.

"What were you doing there? Why didn't you come to me? You knew where I was," Lisette said.

"I couldn't come to you. I had nothing to bring you any more, only my misery," she said. "Ah, you don't know what they did to me."

"Where? In the convent?" asked Lisette.

Halka smiled. Her too red lips stretched a little without parting. "What convent?" she asked. "In the convent where I was, instead of crucifixes, we wore canvas belts in which our hands were strapped. I could not come back to you from there as the angel that you expected and needed. It couldn't have been like the other time. I had meant it to be like that, in the first days I was there. I meant to hold out, no matter what happened, and to come back to you. But then I didn't know the ways they had of dealing with me."

"I stopped her throwing herself into the river," Descoux said.

There was a momentary silence, and then Halka said to Dominic:

"If a condemned criminal in America had by some miracle lived through the horror of being brought again and again to the electric chair and executed violently and publicly, don't you think that, if afterwards they released him, he might well make his way to some lonely river bank in the evening and, standing there alone under the trees, far from

38

the abomination of men and their cruelty, long for nothing more but a quiet refuge in death? Wouldn't such a death be almost sweet to him after all the public obscenity of the other mock deaths?"

"That may be," said Dominic, "if there is anyone in the world who has really been through such things as this resurrected criminal of yours."

"Oh yes, there are such people," she said. "And I am one of them. I have been through these mock deaths, many times. And how easily can these things happen to one! It is so terribly easy to fall into the hands of the executioners, *les bourreaux*."

She told of her existence in the asylum and of the electroshock treatment to which she had been submitted. She told of being strapped into the chair, of the apparatus being fitted to her head, clamped to her temples, and of the moment when the current was switched on.

"I learned what it was to be executed. We all learnt the electric death in which we lay in our beds on rubber sheets, because when we came back to life, hours later, we were always in a filthy mess. Oh yes, when you must suffer this killing every Friday and Tuesday, there's not much of the angel left in you. You're publicly executed and it's like a kind of public rape and you wake up in your own excrement. So you see, Lisette, I couldn't come back to you when they released me. I couldn't be your angel. They had cured me of all my angelic fancies.

"That same evening, as I was wandering down by the river, this fellow here"—she nodded at Descoux—"came up and spoke to me. He walked along with me and asked me to be his *chérie*. He was so gentle, so simple and a little stupid that I was not at all afraid of him. I thought: why not be his *chérie* for a little? Is that not a good deed? And then afterwards, there is still time."

As she had been speaking, Descoux had been watching her. He could not follow what she said, as she had spoken in German, but he watched her with curiosity and desire. There was the misty look of desire in his black eyes, on his swarthy, "robber's" face.

Dominic looked at her, at the play of the tiny muscles beneath the skin of her forehead and brows as she spoke, so that it seemed that he could see there the quivering of the raw, tortured nerves. He wanted to kiss her brows and forehead, her face, not as he had kissed other women, but in a new way. He wanted to put his arms round her. But he did nothing. He looked at her and she was not ugly any more. But in the end it was time to go and to take Lisette back to Frau Arnheim's.

CHAPTER IV

THE DUNGEON

NEXT MORNING, SOON after Dominic had finished his scanty breakfast, there was a triple ring for him at the door of the flat. He thought it was Lisette and he hurried to the door to let her in. But when he opened it, there was a German policeman who told him that he must present himself at the French *Sûreté* in the Nietzschestrasse before midday.

He went back into his room and sat down. The very word Nietzschestrasse had a dread sound. It was where political suspects were taken and kept while being interrogated. He tried to convince himself that the summons was of no special significance, but there was a darkness over his heart that could not be banished by any of his arguments.

Touched by an impulse that he could hardly account for, he got up and went round to Descoux' flat to find Halka. She was alone in the flat preparing Descoux' lunch, and she did not seem surprised to see him.

"Have you come about your ring?" she asked.

"My ring?"

"I have it. See," and she held out her hand. He saw the gold ring on one of her fingers. "Lisette slipped it into my bag last night. She said I should sell it to Descoux, that he had already offered a lot of money for it and that then we could take a room together again. But I guessed it came from you."

"Keep it," he said. He had no feeling about the ring. What were two thousand marks when they would not buy him freedom?

He told her of the summons he had received to appear at the Nietzschestrasse. The name was familiar to her.

"Sit down," she said. They had been standing beside the electric range at which she had been cooking. They sat down at the kitchen table.

"What have you done?" she asked.

"Nothing!"

"Really nothing? Me you can tell all."

"Of course. If I had not known that, I wouldn't have come to you."

"Why was it to me you came?" she asked.

"I wanted to tell you. I don't quite know why. Perhaps because of some of the things you said last night."

"No. Don't explain it; that would be a pity," she said. "You came and that is the main thing. But now let us consider. First, is there nothing of which they can accuse you; if not now, before?"

"Who knows of what they cannot accuse me? That is just it. Does anyone know what is guilt and what is innocence any more?"

"Wait a moment till I put on a skirt and blouse," she said, "and I'll come round with you."

"Oh no, Halka," he said. "I don't want that. In one way I am not afraid. Now that I've told you I'm not really nervous any more. It was only the thought of disappearing, or being cast into a cellar and kept there and no one knowing. But now I've told you. Someone knows. After all, I dare say they simply want to have a look at my papers."

"Good. I'll expect you back at lunchtime," she said.

"Yes. At lunchtime."

He reached the house in the Nietzschestrasse in which the Sûreté was lodged. It was a villa standing in a garden. He was received by the policeman who had brought him the message and was led into a room that had once been a parlour, to wait. The policeman reseated himself at a table. Dominic had not expected this postponement of the decisive moment.

Ah, this waiting in uncertainty and anxiety! How well he knew it with its own peculiar form of torment. Nevertheless, his first forebodings had largely gone. Had it been serious, they would not have sent him a message to come round; they would have simply arrested him. He only hoped that there would not be too long a delay. Whenever the outer door banged, Dominic hoped it heralded the arrival of the officer dealing with his case. He asked the policeman whether he thought it would still be long.

"They are usually here by this. Though they are not early risers, the French," the policeman said. He had the reserved, colourless way of speaking that those adopt who are in the habit of being asked many anxious questions.

Suddenly, when Dominic was least expecting it, when for a considerable time he had not heard the banging of the hall door, a thick-set little French soldier came into the room, regarded Dominic from grey eyes in which there was a slight evasion. Then he looked round the room before turning to the policeman. Dominic had the impression that his entrance had nothing to do with him. But the Frenchman suddenly said to the policeman, with a nod in his direction:

"Is this Malone?"

And when the policeman nodded, he went on in a louder voice, turning back to Dominic and staring at him: "Take everything out of his pockets!"

It had come, the deathly blow had fallen. In the stare of the soldier and his words all the horror of what was before Dominic was already contained. He had lost his anonymity, the precious veil between him and the world was being rent. He stood there stared at, once more a man singled out, exposed and violated.

He took from his pockets the keys of his room, some money, his pocket-book, in which were some notes he had been making for a novel, letters, among them his Uncle Egan's, and other scraps of paper that were in one way or another precious to him. He laid them on the table.

"Is that all?" aked the policeman.

"Search him," said the soldier. The policeman put his hands into the pockets of his overcoat and although there were still a few other odds and ends, he did not take them. He tapped the pockets of Dominic's jacket perfunctorily. Taciturn and uncommunicative, he was not, however, officious, nor had he a lust for humiliating and bullying.

The French soldier pointed to Dominic's shoes, and Dominic stooped and took out the laces. Then, accompanied by both, he was led down the stone stairs of the cellar. In the room it had been warm, the whole villa was well heated, but down here the air was icy. The policeman unlocked a door and Dominic passed into his dungeon. He heard the door relocked on him with a kind of relief. At least the first violation was over and for a time he was alone.

Ah! how well he knew this place in which he had never before been! All these cellars and cells, all these places of despair, were they not the same? There was a whole world of cells and dungeons, cold and damp and bare, a dim and silent nether region whose shades had been creeping over the world of the living in the last frightful years. This cellar was like all the others with its one tiny, dirty barred window, high up in the cement wall, its straw sack and the sanitary iron bucket that stank, not so much of excrement, not of the warm manure-smell of excrement, but with a cold, acrid smell, that seemed to Dominic, when he lifted the lid, the very stench of hopelessness.

There were three or four plank beds in the cellar, and he began to busy himself making himself a corner, shaking out the straw mattress, selecting blankets from the grey pile that lay on one of them. He made what defence he could against the cold, and, huddled up on the bed he had chosen, started the long waiting. It was a waiting whose duration he could not calculate; it was the beginning of the other time, of the time that obtains in this netherworld and which is shapeless, measureless.

And now it was incredible to him that the days that had gone by, the days of freedom, had been filled with so much anxiety and unrest. The delay in the delivery of a parcel, the failure of a stove, some business over a ring, how could it have been that these things had all had power over him, subtracting from the blessed gift of freedom? He had not

43

yet learnt how to be free, how to pass through the days of his life, be they hard or in ease, in the quiet of his spirit.

There was the jingle of keys, which is the captive's angelus, often the only sound that breaks the long tomb-like silences of the day. The door swung open and the policeman stood there and beckoned him. He was taken up to a small, well-heated office in the villa. There were two tables in the room and Dominic was given a chair in front of one at which a big, fair-haired official in civilian clothes was sitting. He glanced through some papers before him and then looked up at Dominic.

"Your name is Malone, nationality Irish?"

There were the usual questions as to his place of birth, parentage, profession. Then the official read out the fact of his previous imprisonment under the Germans during the war, the dates of his arrest and his release.

"What were you arrested for?" the official asked him.

Dominic hesitated. If he was to state the simple facts, he would probably not be believed.

"I will be frank with you," the official went on, "we have information about visits you made to prisoner-of-war camps here in Germany during the war. And very shortly after you had been making these visits you yourself were sent to a camp, not a prisoner-of-war camp, it is true, but a concentration camp. And there you remained only a month, after which you were let out again. You must see yourself that these facts, taken together, threw a certain suspicion on you."

"I suppose it creates the suspicion that I went into the camp as some sort of spy or agent. Is that it?" he asked.

The official did not answer. He was again turning over papers.

"Tell me first, what was your object in visiting the prisoner-of-war camps," he asked.

"Because there were many of my fellow countrymen in them."

"Yes. That is stated here. But what did you talk to them about?"

"I gave them cigarettes, and once I brought bread for

them. That was in the early days of the war before they began to receive the Red Cross parcels."

"Yes. Quite so. But you talked to them, too."

Dominic saw to what all was leading. Another of these nightmares was beginning in which he would be questioned, accused, suspected, until he himself came not to know whether he was not in some way guilty, whether he too in some mysterious way was not culpable for the war, for the new horror which he had hated most.

"I spoke to them of Ireland, of their home, but not much, there was not much time. And I listened to their complaints, about the conditions in which they suffered."

"You went there in company of a German officer, a major," said the Frenchman, glancing at the typescript on the table.

Dominic assented, and his interlocutor began to question him about this major and his relationship to him. Dominic began to feel that his answers were like the answers that someone would have given in trying to hide his guilt.

"Perhaps I went to the first camp more out of curiosity than anything else. But the other visits I made because I was drawn to see and speak to those suffering in them. All this was seven or eight years ago and I did not then know what I know now——"

"Yes? What is that?" his interrogator interrupted him. He was listening to Dominic without looking at him, playing with a pencil, and Dominic could read neither belief nor distrust in his small blue eyes.

"I did not yet understand that the crucial events in Europe would take place where people suffered most in long-drawn-out despair—that is to say, especially in the prisons and prison-camps. But I had an instinct that this was so, and when I had a glimpse of these prisoner-of-war camps I had a strange feeling. (You must remember that this was all in the first year of the war. Later, I believe the conditions in these camps, at least for British prisoners, greatly improved; but then they were, in the three or four I visited, to my mind, very bad.) I had the feeling, as I was saying, that I was on the wrong side of the barbed wire. I don't mean that

I regretted not having been a combatant. I never regretted not fighting. I am not a fighter. But I saw that the fighting with weapons wasn't the only part of this war. I was not even sure that through the fighting there would come a new peace and a new justice. I began to see that it was out of pain and suffering that, if there was to be a new peace, it would be shaped. My eyes were opened by these visits I made to the prisoner-of-war camps in the early days of the conflict. From then on it was obvious to me that if I was to remain outside the great stream of suffering that was flowing across Europe, if I had no real part in it, then I might as well have remained at home in Ireland in comfort and security. This will probably appear to you unlikely, Captain," Dominic went on, "but I gradually had a stronger and stronger desire to be among those who were suffering most."

"Go on," said the officer. "Tell me how it was that you actually got into one of the concentration camps."

Dominic went on with his confession. It seemed to him a confession. It was something of which he had never before spoken. The officer did not interrupt him, did not try to bully him, did not make ridiculous accusations. Whether he believed what Dominic told him, whether he accepted it, that was not yet clear.

He kept looking through the typescript before him, reading short extracts from it that appeared to be transcripts of statements made by prisoners-of-war. The interrogation was interrupted by the German policeman. The officer went out of the room with him and Dominic waited. He was keyed-up and tense with the effort of defending himself in a strange language against a charge that was, in a sense, no charge. For this question of guilt, what was it? There was no serious accusation made against him, that much he began to suspect. But there was for him something even more vital in all this questioning. Let all be said or supposed against him, only against one charge was he vitally concerned to defend himself. That he had ever, in any way, in thought or deed, sided with the captors against the captives, with the executioners against the victims.

The officer came to the door and called him out. Dominic thought that he was to return to his cellar, that the interrogation was over for the moment. He went to the stairs, but the officer indicated another door on the same floor. Dominic entered a room and saw in front of him Halka awaiting him.

Never had he been so glad to see another human being, never had a face been so beautiful to him as her face at that moment. Her coming to him here, her following him, was something that moved him more than anything that had ever happened to him.

They were left alone in the room. Dominic took her hands and kissed them.

"How is it? Is it bad?" she asked him, regarding him, trying to see in his face what he was enduring.

"No. I don't think it is bad," he said.

The fact that Halka had been let see him and that they were being left alone together was reassuring. There was always a small unaccountable element in these people, so that there was no ultimate telling what they were really thinking about you.

"How did you get in? Wasn't it hard to get in here?" he asked her.

"When you didn't come back, I knew they had kept you. I ran round here and told the policeman I wanted to see you, but he said it was impossible. I went on begging him and finally he agreed to go and ask a Captain Renier. I waited, and the Captain appeared and called me up, and here I am! Look. I have the money for the ring. I ran round to a gangster I know on the way. We will need the money when you come out."

She opened her bag and, delving into it, brought out a bundle of notes and some loose cigarettes in one grasp. He took the notes in his hand, not knowing what to do with them, trying to grasp what she meant by saying they would need them. But he did not worry over this problem; he stuffed them back into her bag.

"To-morrow I'll bring some bread and what else I can get. But now I didn't wait. Luckily, I knew where there was butter being offered and I grabbed it and ran on." She

47

began to look in her bag for the butter among a confusion of papers, keys, all sorts of odds and ends.

"Never mind about butter," he said. "That you have come, that is what is so extraordinary that the long hours down in the cellar will be filled now by my contemplating it. It will be something with which to fill the long emptiness."

"I shall come back every day," she said, "whether they let me see you or not. And I can always manage to bring you something, even if it's only a few slices of bread. Something coming in from outside, that is always a little link with the world, isn't it?

"How good it was that Descoux came across me the other evening; not because of him—he'd have found another girl half an hour later—but because of you. There is still something left for me to do that I can do better than most other girls—to come here and be with you for a little. Ah! it is so easy to be with you now that you are a prisoner. Now I am close to you; but with others, with free and happy people, I feel lost. I am no good as a *chérie* for Descoux. I don't know any more how to live with a man like that, in a warm flat, with four good meals a day and a clean white bed and a shaded bed-lamp at night. But I could come here and be with you in your cellar, if they'd let me, and be a comfort and a companion to you in your cold and loneliness. That is what I've learnt, that is all that I really know any more."

Not only what she said, but her very body was a balm to him. She had taken off her shabby overcoat in the warmth of the office, and he was conscious of the shape of her body, the balm of her breasts and her belly like a well of tenderness. Her flesh, that had borne so much pain, was like a healing fountain to him. He put out his hand and laid it on her knee.

"Lisette was round and she wanted to come with me," Halka said. "But I did not know how it would be. I thought they might keep me too, so I did not bring her."

Captain Renier opened the door. Dominic and Halka took a hasty farewell of each other. They thanked the officer for allowing her to visit him.

"That's all right," he said to her, "but don't hang round here or try to talk through the window. We'll continue in the afternoon," he added to Dominic and went back into his office for his overcoat. The morning's work was over. Dominic followed Halka down the stairs. The policeman was awaiting him to conduct him back into his cellar. He took another farewell of Halka at the hall door. She waited as he disappeared down the cellar stairs.

Another prisoner had been delivered into the cellar in his absence, a thick-set youth who was sitting on his bed eating the dinner of bread and soup. Dominic's bread and soup stood on the floor by his bed. He took the butter out of his pocket and spread some on the two thin slices of bread and offered it to his fellow prisoner. There was the same easy acceptance of each other that Dominic· remembered from his previous captivity. There was none of the forced cordiality that arises on two people being introduced to each other in the world. The coming together of prisoners was a quite different thing. Thrown together by their common fate, they accepted each other gratefully, for almost any companion was better than complete solitude. They introduced themselves briefly. The newcomer was a Czech. He had been studying English at a technical school in Prague and was glad at finding someone with whom he could speak it. For English was the language of hope, of ease and plenty, and the very speaking of it seemed to be a propitious sign.

"I came back to Germany to look for my fiancée," he told Dominic. It was such a tale as Dominic had often heard before. There were still people searching for each other all over Europe, slipping secretly over frontiers when they could not get the necessary papers.

His fellow prisoner had come back after years to try to find a Ukrainian girl with whom he had spent the latter part of the war when both were working in the same factory. He had failed to find her and had been arrested for being without papers and would be sent back to Prague.

He was not kept all day in the cellar, but was allowed to work in the kitchen of one of the villas occupied by the French. He had already spent the morning at work and now he was waiting to be fetched out again. So that he was no real prisoner, and Dominic felt at once that he would not get close to him in that communion of pain which he knew. He did not belong to the real communion of prisoners, shut off from life, set apart, signed with the sign of captivity.

He was under no suspicion and would never be interrogated, and, above all, he was not a prey to the time monster that is the ultimate horror of captives. For it was not hunger or cold or filth, it was not being shut away in a cell or a cellar that filled the heart with despair. Dominic knew that all these things could be borne with tranquillity as long as they had limits in time that he could grasp. The spirit could deal with a certain measure of time according to its patience, its courage and its faith. But when there was no measure to time, or when the measure was so great that the spirit could not grasp it, then there was this fear and this horror; it was the horror of a slow drowning in timelessness.

The Czech had not been touched by this horror. He was waiting impatiently to be taken back again to the villa across the street where there was furniture to be moved. He could dare to be impatient.

"Did they say they would fetch you again?" Dominic asked. He could not help hoping that they would not come for him.

"Of course."

Dominic saw that this expression, which was continually on the lips of the other and which had begun to irritate him, was used through a misconception of the nuances of English. The Czech avoided a simple "Yes," probably out of some idea that his "Of course" was more colloquial, betrayed a greater familiarity with the language. All these "Of courses" and all this impatience irritated him. But Dominic was glad of the company of the other and he was afraid of the long afternoon hours if the Czech was taken for work.

But it was Dominic who was first taken. The policeman came for him and conducted him up to the office of Captain Renier. Dominic was surprised. He had not expected the interrogation to be so speedily resumed; his former experience had taught him that the French, in this way like his own people, took things very easily, did not get through much in a day.

But Captain Renier sat at his desk with the papers in front of him, the pencil in his hand.

With his tightly shut mouth and small, watchful blue eyes there was something almost prim about him. There was something old-fashioned in this French officer, reminding Dominic of he did not quite know what—of times long past, of an aunt of his, a sister of his Uncle Egan's, now dead. And he was a little reassured; he began to know a little where he was. There were, then, still such people in authority in the world, with this unexpected sense of duty, of being responsible.

Dominic explained to Captain Renier the circumstances of his arrest and imprisonment.

"It was not very difficult to get myself suspected and finally taken and put into a camp," Dominic said, "but I was not kept long because friends of mine, fellow countrymen and other neutrals, soon managed to get me out again. I hadn't reckoned with that, or I might have taken other steps. But, on the other hand, I don't know. The short time I spent there was bad enough."

"Did you feel you had achieved anything by your imprisonment?"

"I had been there. If only for a very short time, I too, if only as one of the last and the least, had been at the heart of what was happening. Because it was there in the prisons and prison-camps that some great change took place, rather than on the battlefields. But I don't have to tell that to you as a Frenchman," Dominic went on. "It is the French above all, French writers, who brought back with them from the concentration camps the words of life. I was not there long, but I had time to see that it was in such places that a new world was taking shape; in the hearts of the tormented a new world was born. A world in which there would be no more victims and no more executioners, without prisons and dungeons. Nowhere else was there such faith in a new peace, in the coming to earth of a liberty of spirit that would be like a new sun shining on men and women. No more suspects, no more hunted."

Captain Renier was again looking through the papers on his desk. Dominic began to think of Halka. Perhaps in a world of complete equity there would be no such women as she. Perhaps she could only come out of such a time, moving like an angel through the midst of the furnace.

CHAPTER V

FRATERNITY IS NOT A MYTH

EACH MORNING AND afternoon Dominic was brought up to Captain Renier's office and interrogated. All went very slowly. Dominic had often difficulty in expressing himself in German, and at times he felt that what he had to say was of such importance that he dare not run the risk of using the wrong words by giving hasty answers. Perhaps the importance of what he said was often more for himself than for his interlocutor; perhaps the interrogation might have been curtailed had he not introduced the question of his inner attitude, of his *penchant de l'âme* to the events about which he was interrogated. The fact, too, that all had to be transcribed by Captain Renier into French was another cause of delay. There were also many interruptions while the officer was called away to another office in the villa or when a subordinate came in to discuss some other case with him.

Captain Renier showed Dominic the greatest consideration. He came early and stayed late. He even came on Sunday and continued the interrogation. And all this gave Dominic hope that he would not be held prisoner long. But he was afraid that the final decision did not rest with Captain Renier, but with some other official elsewhere—in Paris, perhaps. He knew the whole slow grinding of the official machine.

Every day towards evening Halka came and brought him coffee in a thermos flask that she had procured from he knew not where and bread or boiled potatoes, and often they were allowed to see each other.

She sat beside him on the couch in the empty office and she brought him the breath of life. He sat there, turned to her, his dirty, captive flesh turned to her, his pale face, yellowish now and strained and covered with a stubble of beard, turned to her and drawing from her the balm of fraternity. It came to him through her breasts and her belly and her shoulders and arms out of the deep source within her. It was something that he had only felt faintly before at times under the night sky, his face and breast turned to the night sky, to that other mode of being, feeling its great mystery touch him and change him a little. And now her breasts were luminaries and her belly was a dark luminary from which flowed out the tender, invisible rays to him, so that the dusty web of captivity fell from his unshaved face and his hands. His brows and his mouth were bathed and anointed in the balm of her companionship.

"If we had only met at dinner in Descoux' flat or at Frau Arnheim's, I would not have known you as I do now," he said.

"You would have had no need of me," she said.

"It is prisoners who can see clearly! More clearly than the so-called free. For prisoners, there are no distractions and pretences, they see life as no one in the midst of it can see it, and wherein its sweetness lies."

"Yes, I have learnt that too," said Halka. "And it seemed to me if the dead could think, it would be they who would see life clearest of all and know best of all wherein its sweetness lay."

"And what would that knowledge be, I wonder?" he said. "But I don't really wonder any more. I begin to know. Oh yes, Halka, I begin to see that they would think as I do now. They would see, as I do now from my dungeon which is the nearest thing to their graves, that life is communion."

It seemed to him that there was no end to the communion that he might have with this woman. What secrets on secrets might not be shared with her!

She began to speak again of the ring and of how she had

sold it for two thousand marks and had managed to get a room for herself and Lisette. She had spent the whole day running round, but now there was this room, and she told him the address of it in case he should be unexpectedly released. Then he was to come direct to her. "Because you will have been alone enough," she said.

It was very cold that evening in the cellar. When the Czech returned from work, bringing with him a packet of French cigarettes and a candle which he lit and stuck on the end of one of the bed posts, Dominic was glad of the company. There was almost a sense of homeliness in the cellar. But he knew this came from the joy that Halka's visit had given him. Now he could enjoy the long evening talk in English with his fellow prisoner while they smoked endless cigarettes and drank the hot coffee that Halka had brought.

In the isolation of their cellar, all topics had an interest, everything that brought the breath of the outer world to them had a fascination. This exchange of the simplest words, the lighting of a cigarette at the candle, the swallowing of the warm, strong coffee from the thermos flask, were comforts that for Dominic all radiated from the great central fact of Halka's visits.

But the horror was for Dominic never completely overcome. In the end, nothing could fill up the icy emptiness of the long hours of waiting. When he heard the rattle of keys as the policeman came to open the door there was a pang of dread tinging the expectation and relief in the monotony. There was always the knowledge that one morning or one evening he could be taken and sent off to some strange place. Some higher official had only to get it into his head to question him personally, and he could be shipped off to a strange cellar in a strange town where Halka could never find him.

He gossiped with his fellow prisoner about the few things that they could gossip of: food and prices in Prague, food and prices here in Marheim. The thing nearest their heart they did not speak of, or hardly at all: the probable length of their captivity.

At last the interrogation was finished. Captain Renier had

asked Dominic to write him a short history of the time he had spent in the prison-camp, of his conversations with his fellow prisoners in so far as they bore on his outlook and belief. The officer had spent all an afternoon translating Dominic's bad German into French and had come down a couple of times to the cellar for the exact explanation of a word.

Dominic waited. The Czech returned from work with a friendly grin on his face that had grown plump on the good food from the French kitchen and whose jaw was beginning to be circled by a dark fringe of beard. In answer to his usual question, Dominic told him that his interrogation was finished.

"Then your time is up. You will be going free."

"I don't know."

"Of course. To-morrow you'll be released."

But Dominic did not dare to give in to any such hope. He must wait and let all shape itself for him as it would.

An hour or two after their evening meal of soup and two slices of bread there was again the jingle of keys and the moment of almost intolerable expectation before the opening of the door. The policeman and a French boy of fifteen or sixteen whom Dominic had noticed in one of the offices stood in the doorway. The boy came slowly into the cellar, looking around him, throwing that casual French glance around the room that is so different from the close German scrutiny. The boy strolled about the cellar, never actually letting his slightly prominent eyes rest on the faces of the two prisoners, and tapped the small suitcase that Halka had brought with clean clothes to Dominic with his foot. The policeman told Dominic to open it. The boy had passed on and was looking with disapproval at the array of cups and dishes on one of the beds.

"All that stuff must come out, too. Everything must come out except one mug and one spoon for each man and his personal washing things."

The boy picked up some English newspapers lying on Dominic's bed.

"And no books or newspapers are allowed in the cell," said the policeman. "How did these get here?"

But Dominic did not answer. He took the few clean things out of his suitcase and left it, as directed, outside the door. Meanwhile the policeman was busy extracting a nail from one of the bed-posts on which the Czech had been in the habit of hanging his jacket at night. The boy blew out the candle and took it gingerly between his finger and thumb, careful not to let any grease fall on his dark suit. With the newspapers under his arm and the candle in one hand, he strolled out of the cellar as he had entered it. The policeman followed him. As the door was shut, the French boy switched out the light.

The two prisoners stood in complete darkness and for a moment after the door had been re-locked said nothing. Each was shocked by the apparition of this youth, he was little more than a child, with his sly lust of persecution.

"That is mean. My God, that is nasty!" said the Czech after a moment.

In his secret heart, Dominic had been expecting something very different. But now all his hope was gone. Had they believed him, had they been intending to release him in the morning, they would not have sent this office-boy to persecute and humiliate him. For he felt that it was against him rather than his fellow prisoner that the little scene had been enacted. Now he saw himself doomed to many such small persecutions, to being an object of suspicion and hatred. He had let himself too easily be reassured by the friendliness of Captain Renier, by the privileges he had been at first allowed. That had very likely all been to produce in him a condition of trust and open-heartedness in which he would be more likely to speak out. And how right they had been! He had spoken to Captain Renier without reserve, not only of facts, but of his own innermost attitude.

"Better I had lied from beginning to end," he told himself. "Better I had denied everything that it was possible to deny."

The Czech struck one of his precious matches and lit a cigarette for himself and Dominic. He looked at his watch. It was half-past six.

"Our young friend will now have dinner in the *Popotte*

and then go into the town to pick up a German girl," he said. "And the thought of us sitting here in the dark and the cold will give a zest to his love-making. His power over some *fräulein* and his power over us—that must be very sweet to him."

An hour went by and again there was the jingle of keys and the opening of the door. The light was switched on. "What is coming now? What new little horror?" Dominic thought.

The policeman stood in the doorway. The policeman in his dark uniform standing there and looking into the cellar, always waiting a moment before saying what he had come to say, had become for Dominic like an apparition, like an annunciator from whose lips could come words either of life or doom.

Now in his slow way he pointed to Dominic.

"Pack up your things and come upstairs," he said.

"There you are," said the Czech before Dominic could compose himself sufficiently to say anything. "You are being released as I told you."

"Not necessarily. I can be taken somewhere else."

"He's being released, isn't he?" the Czech asked the policeman.

But the policeman was noncommittal as always: "He is to come upstairs with his things."

Dominic gathered the few things that he had left into the blanket that Halka had brought him. He could not think nor calculate. What lay ahead of him he did not know. The Czech was talking to the policeman, asking why their things had been taken and why they had been left in darkness. The policeman shrugged his shoulders.

"Am I to sit here in the dark?" asked the Czech.

"Oh, no. As far as I am concerned, you can have the light on all night," the policeman told him.

Dominic had got his things bundled into the blanket. He shook hands with his fellow prisoner.

"Good luck; and may you find your girl!"

"Good luck! Good luck!"

Dominic went up the stairs and into the bare room in

which he had waited on the day of his arrest. He moved in the same blindness and deafness to outer things in which he had first descended these stone stairs. "In all intensity of feeling one dies a little," he thought, "whether the intensity is one of hope, of pain or joy." And in this state he walked into the empty parlour like a sleep-walker, carrying his blanket.

He heard the policeman address him and looked round at him. The other was leaning against the table in that air of always being a little withdrawn, with a half-sceptical detachment from all the small dramas that he constantly witnessed.

He was making one of his annunciations and Dominic felt it enter into him as though the three words was each a barbed arrow. Strange, strange words: "You are free," overcoming him with the almost unbearable annunciation of life.

The policeman brought his confiscated suitcase out of a corner and Dominic began bundling his things into it. He did not try to pack them in any order; he could not wait to begin to breathe the cold night air that would be the air of freedom.

Captain Renier came into the room in his long, leather overcoat, pulling on his gloves, ready to leave. He shook hands with Dominic, and the pressure of his small lips against each other, his "old-maidish" mouth, relaxed into a smile.

"I'm sorry you were kept here, but it had to be looked into. And perhaps this time, too, you got something out of the experience."

"At least I had an understanding and intelligent interrogator to whom it was possible to speak," Dominic said.

"Well, perhaps. But I won't keep you. You will surprise Mademoiselle Mayersky."

He regarded Dominic's pale, unshaved face with a half-puzzled sympathy in his small blue eyes. Then he turned and went out and Dominic heard the hall door slam after him as he had so often heard its muffled slam down in the fastness of his dungeon, and as it would very soon slam after him too.

He brushed off the pieces of straw still clinging to his overcoat from the prison mattress and quickly smoothed down

58

his hair in a small mirror hanging on the wall. It was the first time he had seen himself in a looking-glass since his arrest. But he had no time to be startled by the pale, yellowish face with its stubble of beard which he glimpsed. He did not wait to put back the laces in his shoes which the policeman had laid out on the table with his pocket-book and papers. He held out his hand to him.

"Goodbye. And thanks."

He was not sure for what he was thanking the policeman. But he was ready to thank the whole world for the inestimable gift that had been given to him.

"Good luck, but not *auf Wiedersehen*. I won't say *auf Wiedersehen*," said the policeman in his slow, noncommittal manner.

Dominic passed out through the door and into the suburban street. It was not particularly cold. The weather had turned damp and misty, the snow was all gone and the few street-lamps hung haloed in the winter evening. He breathed in the night air, the blessed air of freedom and the blessed wet pavement under his feet.

He hurried and yet did not hurry. This hurry was not like the ordinary haste to reach a goal, because much as he longed to stand before Halka's door and press the bell, every step of the way there was precious, every step through the damp night air that was touching his face with an infinite sweetness, as it only can touch the face of an ex-prisoner.

He did not know whether Halka had already moved into the room whose address she had given him or whether she was still at Descoux' flat. Strange that he had not asked her that. Yes, that was really singular of him that he had not thought to find that out. But he would go first to the room.

He turned the corner, walked up a second street and at the next corner got a tram. The long lit chariot of the tram looming before him in the mist was something that he had never seen before, or not since long ago when as a child trams and buses and cars had all had something of this air, had been new and full of the mystery of an unknown power. He climbed into the tram and made his way through it to the unlit back platform. With his bundle and his stubble of beard, he did not want to stand in the lit interior. Not that he was ashamed of being a newly freed prisoner, but he could not bear that others might guess his secret exaltation. That must be cherished and not exposed even to the sympathetic glances of the world.

He stood on the back platform and the tram began to move, clanging slowly down the street. Short and familiar as this tram-ride was to him, it was now a strange journey—a journey through the immense night of endless possibilities towards this woman with whom there would be no limit to the secrets he could share.

He descended at the corner by the bridge and walked along the busy street until he was at the house where she had told him her room was. He did not go in immediately, but crossed over to the other side of the street and looked up to see if there was a light in her window. She had described to him exactly where the room lay. He saw the glow of light behind the curtains. He went in and climbed the stairs. Trembling, he put his finger to the bell. Through the frosted-glass panel of the door of the flat he saw the door of Halka's room open, letting a gleam of light into the dark corridor. Then the door opened in front of him and there she was, peering out, for a moment not recognising him in the darkness of the landing, from which the bulb had been long ago stolen.

Then she uttered a little cry—more a cry than a word—and drew him in quickly, drew him in through the door and across the yard or two of corridor into her room.

"Are you free? Have you escaped out of their hands?" she cried, as though imploring him to speak to her, to make his presence felt in words and in touch.

"It's good. It's good," he said to her, looking round the bright room, a room without bars.

Lisette was in her bed in the corner. She held out her arms to him and he noticed how thin they were; the sleeves of the nightdress fell back from them and they were like white stalks.

"She's been ill. That's why she didn't come to visit you," Halka said. "She has pains in her chest."

Dominic stooped to kiss the young girl, but his stubble

of beard pricked the pale, tender skin of her cheek and she drew back into her bed.

"I've something to tell you. Something bad. I stole the ring," she said to him. "It was I who took it out of Aunty's box."

It had been worrying her all the time since his arrest, this business of the ring. She had taken it, meaning to sell it and with the money take a room for herself and so escape from Frau Arnheim's. And in the end she had given it to her sister that evening at Descoux'.

Since that evening she had been ill. The shock of the unexpected meeting with Halka had brought on a fever and the doctor had told Halka that she must take care of her chest.

Dominic washed and stripped off his clothes, to which clung the faint nauseous prison smell. He dressed and sat down by Lisette's bed while Halka prepared a meal. He was gradually taking in the room, growing accustomed to the new night that had begun in a cold dark cellar without hope and had been changed into this night with the two girls in a bright room in which a table was being laid with cups and plates and knives and forks.

"There is a couch in the corner that you can have if you like," Halka was saying. "That is if you want to stay here with us. If you think it will be quiet enough for you."

"It is beautiful here," he said.

"And there is enough separation everywhere. Surely there has been enough being alone," she went on a little enigmatically.

"Oh yes, Halka. There has been too much loneliness. Now let there be something else."

They ate the meal that she had prepared with such care. They did not speak much. Lisette lay in the bed that she shared with her sister and watched Dominic out of her dark eyes. It was the fulfilment of her dream that he was coming to live with them. Now she had both Halka and him and she was happy as she had hardly ever been before. Even the fact of Halka having gone to the river on her release from the asylum with the intention of committing suicide no longer oppressed her. All that was forgotten, even the asylum, in her new happiness. Even the cough that kept her awake at night was easy to bear.

After supper Dominic and Halka went to Frau Arnheim's. She had been very kind, Halka told him, during his imprisonment, giving her coffee and cigarettes to take to him and lending her the thermos flask.

They found a Rumanian called Petrov sitting in the corner by the stove. He was one of Frau Arnheim's protégés, and since Lisette had left her she had begun to take him under her wing.

He was interested when he heard that Dominic had just come out of a prison cellar.

"You see, even a neutral like Mr. Malone must suffer from the continuing hate and vindictiveness," Frau Arnheim said. "They tell us we have peace, but the war is not really over. All the worst passions of the war are still rife. I know what the war was. I went through it all and I lost my husband in it. And I tell you it is not really over, there is no sign of real peace."

"But don't blame the French," said Petrov, speaking from his corner for the first time. "The French of all people have been least to blame. They more than all others know what the war was; they had to go down deepest into its shadow."

"How can you say that?" Frau Arnheim exclaimed. "Have you travelled through Germany since the war as I have? Have you seen the devastated towns and cities? But you have only to look out of this window and what you see there is what you see everywhere. Rubble! And that wasn't brought about in one night or one day. It took night after night and day after day of bombing." She turned to Dominic and Halka. "You know what it was. You must have gone through it, too."

"But it is not a question of going through air-raids," said Petrov. "People who only experienced the war as air-raids or soldiers who only experienced it as a battlefield were never really touched by it and changed by it in their inmost beings. Those who looked into its visage were those in the prisons and concentration camps."

"*Ach*, Herr Petrov, haven't we heard enough about the horrors of the concentration camps? Has not that been publicised in every possible way so that no one is likely to forget it?" said Frau Arnheim.

"But, like everything else that is publicised, the whole story has been made unreal. The more some significant event is talked about and written about by people incapable of really grasping it, the more danger there is of it being in the end overlooked and forgotten," said Petrov. "It is so diluted with a flow of mediocre words that its original taste is lost."

"But to get back to your contention," said Dominic. "The French were not the only ones to suffer in the concentration camps." He wanted to keep Petrov to the theme that interested and concerned himself.

"The French were not the only ones?" Petrov repeated in his slow, careful German, raising his voice at the end of the sentence so that it became a question. This was a way he had when he became involved in a conversation that affected him. He repeated others' sentences in the form of questions, as though picking them out as something strange and unexpected that must be examined before being answered. And these sentences were usually those that their speakers took for the most self-evident, so that Petrov had come to be looked on in Frau Arnheim's little circle as a bore with a love of contradicting. Nevertheless, Frau Arnheim mothered him along with the others who sought a refuge in this bitter winter by her stove.

"The French were those capable of suffering most. For a great tragedy two protagonists are needed: the inflictor (whether Fate or man) and the afflicted. Like the word of God, suffering must be sown in fertile ground or it bears no fruit. And the French were the most fertile soil into which the seeds of all that suffering fell," Petrov went on, his long, rather swarthy face with its slightly oblique, Asiatic eyes seeming to turn inwards, so that its ugliness was accentuated. The effort it was for him to find the correct German words for what he wanted to say made him grimace until his face was like a fantastic mask of ugliness. But perhaps it would have been the same had he been speaking in his own Balkan tongue; perhaps he would always have gone into a half-trance of ugliness. Dominic knew that Frau Arnheim felt this trance, too, out of which Petrov spoke, and was impatient of it. She disagreed with him profoundly and even disliked him, but she would not cease mothering him.

"But what, for instance, about the Poles and Jews and many Germans themselves? There were many Germans who must have suffered torments in the prisons," Dominic said. He wanted to come at the end of the strange, slow process of Petrov's theme.

"There were many Germans who must have suffered torments?" Petrov repeated with the unexpectedly high, questioning, almost querulous note at the end of the repetition and a further grimace of his long sleepy face. "But these torments have not borne fruit."

"How can torments bear fruit?" asked Frau Arnheim.

"In art, in a few poems, a few books and pictures," said Petrov. "But the pictures I cannot judge. I haven't seen them. It is in the French literary periodicals that I have made this discovery. Scattered through little magazines and reviews that are only read by a few people are the new words of annunciation formed out of loneliness and despair. These poems and stories are signed with mostly obscure names—names that will mostly never be famous because many of them, like Benjamin Fondane or Boris Wildé, died in the night of their captivity. And we know they went down to the uttermost end of desolation by the words they have brought back with them—words that could not have been spoken before, words that have been formed in this particular world-darkness, and the only words that have encompassed the darkness and not been encompassed by it."

But Frau Arnheim could not bear these views of Petrov's. She could not believe that anything but evil had come out of the war, nor could she bear to hear his praise of the French. All the things that had happened, all the loss and destruction, all the disaster that had overtaken the once peaceful town of Marheim were often too much for her. She did not believe there could be any meaning in such things. She would go

64

on doing what she could out of the warmth of her heart, but she knew that it was nothing in the great night of misery.

She began to cry. The tears ran silently down her sagging cheeks. The day had been a bad one. She had stood for hours in a queue and had got nothing in the end.

"Don't take what I said too seriously," said Petrov, his long hand nervously gripping his knees. "I only meant that it took all these years of death and pain to open our eyes and our hearts."

"On the contrary," said Frau Arnheim, "we have lost our belief in man and in civilisation."

"Yes," said Petrov, his ugly face thrust forward out of his corner by the stove; "and now we have seen this image of 'civilised man' stripped of its last illusion. We are so much nearer the truth. And the truth is that we can never become civilised in the old sense. We can only become spiritualised."

"And will you be so good as to explain to me the difference?" said Frau Arnheim.

"Ah! explanations!" exclaimed Petrov. "Explanations are useless! But there is one great difference that is surely clear. The ideal civilised man whom, as you justly say, was believed in some years ago had, as one of his proudest attributes, a so-called sensitivity to death. He looked on death as the supreme calamity. When he read in the paper of an accident involving eight people he was shocked. The papers even in those days devoted several columns to such things. I remember myself as a boy reading of a tramway accident that took place in my native town. But now thousands can be wiped out by a single bomb and no one minds very much—or at least it will soon be so. But is that really callousness? No, it is not. It is, at least for many of us, that we are no longer so certain that worldly existence is the one supreme good and death the one great calamity. We are less civilised in this sense, but already a little more spiritualised, more purified in our hearts!"

"Well, that is a very strange conclusion," said Frau Arnheim. She was obviously deeply resentful of Petrov and his outlook. She spoke as she might to someone who had made a personal attack on her. She was hurt and defensive. She turned immediately to Halka.

"I often wonder what a young girl like you must think of this world that you have grown up in. What a cruel and heartless place it must seem to you!" she exclaimed.

"*Ach*, Aunty," said the "young girl." "I would like to have seen the town when it was full of streets and shops!" The simplicity of her answer surprised Dominic.

"And when people were kinder," said Frau Arnheim.

"Were they kinder?" Halka asked.

Petrov promised to come round and visit Dominic and to bring with him some of the new French literature. Then Halka brought out some cigarette butts she had gathered in the office in which she and Dominic used to be allowed to meet, and gave them to Frau Arnheim out of which to roll herself a cigarette. Frau Arnheim regained her composure. She lit the cigarette and sucked in the smoke and then went over to the mirror and dabbed some powder on her cheeks. Soon they said goodbye to her. They were anxious to get back to their room, to the beginning of this life of theirs together.

CHAPTER VI

PARABLE

BECAUSE THEY HAD passed through the night of dungeons and prisons, of prison-cellars in which time stagnated and air-raid shelters which trembled and filled with smoke and glowed with reflected fire, they could be together in this room, happy in a singular fraternity.

Dominic slept on his couch in the corner and Halka and Lisette slept in the bed, and each morning there was the beginning again of the adventure of their communal life. Outside were the ruins, the hunger, the suspicion and hopelessness, but in their room high up above the street there was another mode of living. All was new, intense and tender. The simplest things were like small, living flames in the old, faded light of day. Eating their meagre food together at the small table, sitting there on the couch at the table in the midst of the long, quiet hours, each time that was like a little ceremony, a celebration of their communion. When Halka sat down on the bed and pulled on her old shoes, one after the other, a flame flickered through him, through his blood to his heart.

They read together the poems in the French periodicals that Petrov brought Dominic. They read the poems of Antonin Artaud, who had spent years in various asylums in France, and of Benjamin Fondane, who had died in a concentration camp, and they found here the words of those who had gone down into the final depths of the night and who had not been overcome by it. Perhaps others in other countries were singing a new song too, but they could not get any other foreign books or periodicals. It did not matter; what they had was enough, this room and this communion. But sometimes as she sat on her bed in the evening, brushing her colourless hair, and he caught a glimpse of her body as she got into her nightgown he was disturbed by her presence.

He waited. Let her flesh, to which so much violence had been done, heal in solitude. Let her be healed again from having fallen into the hands of men; to that he could bring her by a non-demanding and gentle fraternity.

Besides, with Lisette always there in the room it was easier. He and Halka were seldom alone together. He did not touch her. Once when he had touched her on the breast with his hand he had felt a shudder go through her and he saw that she was not healed of the horror of exposure.

She had been brought to the edge of doom, and the shadow of doom had touched her flesh and blood and was not yet thrown off. He was appalled when he thought of the enormous weight of pain that she had had to bear alone and which had encompassed her. He recalled what Petrov had said: "Either we must encompass the night or be encompassed by it."

Besides reading together, they went sometimes to the cinema, the three of them. Mostly they saw some heavy German film. Alone he would have been oppressed and bored, conscious of the audience around him, drinking in the dull, pretentious fare. But with Halka and Lisette he formed a little centre of resistance; they were not going to submit to these old tricks by which the bud of new life was nipped. For even a film could serve truth, could in its way show some awareness of the miracle of being alive, of people being alive and free and together. It was an insult to go on serving up this old defamation of the sweet breath of life, this befouling and dulling of everything. "My God!" Dominic would whisper. "After all the death and destruction and horror, can't they see the simple beauty in a man, in a woman, and make something of that, anything? Must they go on with all this stupidity, these stale, stale love stories?"

And then Halka would get even more indignant and there would be so much whispering that someone in the row behind or in front would object.

"Good heavens!" she would say. "Do they really think that things go like that? Nothing goes with that slow, ponderous tread outside of German films."

It was good to feel her sharing his hatred of all the mediocrity, staleness, the tame, stale sentiment, of all this belittlement and diminishing of the heart. And he did not tell her that it was not only a matter of German films, that there were other films just as bad, and books too—many books and pictures and music. He did not want to oppress her with a knowledge of all the mediocrity that there was in the world. He would not burden her with the knowledge of all the mediocrity that she did not yet know of.

And it was the same with religion, with what they had made out of religion. That much she had grasped already.

"Whatever I was told about Christ as a child," she said, "made Him and His life into something rather like one of these German films. A pretentious, sentimental sort of drama. Oh, how I hated this Christ that they showed to me preaching all the old idealistic moralities! And for them and their Christ the simple sincerity of my heart that was looking for a real morality seemed to be a closed book."

He laughed. And he did not say anything, for he had a deep, instinctive dislike of all preaching; even the amount of talking that Petrov did in his queer spasms of prophesying

68

was alien to him. He must not lay hands on her, one way or the other, not even in love. Too many hands had been laid on her, and she was still seared by the violence of their touch.

Although they had the money for the ring to live on and could now and then buy some extra food, they often went hungry. Sometimes Descoux came round and brought them bread or meat. He came as quietly as ever, sat in his chair, reading his police papers, watching for the birds at the window-sill, speaking little, and went again. Dominic did not know why he came. Whether he still had his eye on Halka or whether it was merely out of a desire for companionship. He seemed to have few friends among the French troops. His friend who had wanted to show Lisette the pornographic pictures had been transferred elsewhere. Nor had he found a *chérie* to replace Halka, as he admitted when she asked him.

"*Ah, non,*" he said, smiling with his habitual insouciance that always charmed Dominic.

"But why not? There are so many girls who would like to come and look after you."

He shrugged his shoulders.

"It goes, too, without girls."

Then for a time, they did not see him. It was a time of extreme hunger. Lisette lay much in bed and her arms seemed to get thinner and thinner. They waited day after day, but no new rations were distributed.

One very cold afternoon Dominic was sitting, struggling against being obsessed by the thought of food, on the side of Lisette's bed and Halka had gone out and did not come back. Lisette had made a full confession about the business of the ring, though he had tried to stop her. But he saw that it weighed on her, and in the end he let her open her heart to him.

"I took it out of Aunty's bag," she said. "I was so afraid that when Halka came out we would have no money and could not get this room back again, and even if Aunty would have had us, it would have been frightful for Halka there, because Aunty could never understand her. To Aunty it was a disgrace to have been in the asylum."

"If you had asked me, I would have given you the ring," Dominic said.

"Have given it? For nothing?" asked Lisette, incredulous.

"For what then should I have given it if not for nothing?"

"I don't know. But nothing can be given for nothing," said the girl. She had grown up in this world of barter and Black-Marketeering and had never known times of plenty, of the giving of gifts.

"Where can Halka be?" he asked. "Did she tell you where she was going?"

But she had said nothing to Lisette. He was very anxious when she stayed away longer than he expected. He kept thinking of what she had said that first evening at Descoux' little supper-party: "It is so terribly easy to fall into the hands of the executioners." Outside of the small oasis of this room, he felt there lurked all sorts of dangers. He knew that there were dungeons and cellars; there was also the river at which Descoux had met her wandering, and there was even Descoux himself.

The helplessness of this waiting! He kept going to the door and opening it and listening for her footsteps on the stairs. There were plenty of others, for it was a large house in which they lived, with much coming and going, but not hers. Not the light tap-tap of her wooden-soled shoes that he knew so well. He settled himself in his corner of the couch and determined not to go to the door again. He knew that Lisette was very hungry, though she said nothing, but there was only a little dry maize bread and some *ersatz* coffee and he did not want to prepare that until Halka returned.

At last she came. She came in and put down a parcel wrapped in newspaper on the table. He knew at once that something had happened to her. He had become used to her pallor, but now it struck him afresh, and he saw it was greater than usual, as though the last drops of blood had been drawn out of her face. Her pale eyes into which there had come back a look of serenity were again too bright, with a pale, bright fire, as they had been the first time he met her.

"My God, witch, where have you been?" he asked her.

"Look!" she said, not answering, pulling the paper from

the package. It contained butter, flour, sugar and even a small blue-paper bag of coffee beans.

In the midst of his foreboding he could not prevent a leaping of his heart at the sight of these things. But he said anxiously:

"Where did you get them?"

"Ah, where do you think I got them?" And she smiled that smile of hers with stretched, unopened lips. Could she come from Descoux and still smile to him with that sweetness, he wondered? But was there not something in that smile that he had never grasped? Had he not been astonished at it that first evening when it had followed on the account of all the horrors she had given him?

"I don't know."

Why should she not go to Descoux and get these so vital things from him? Had he, Dominic, any right over her? He had never indicated to her that she should not go to Descoux. But now that it seemed that she had done so, he was tormented.

"So you did not fall into the hands of the executioners, but into the arms of Descoux!" he said brutally.

He saw the flinching of her breast and the ripple of pain that passed over her brows. She had sunk down on the bed beside her sister, exhausted and overcome. She was there before him, defenceless and exposed to him, and he remembered something he had said to Captain Renier during his long interrogation: "Never for a moment have I ever sided with the strong against the weak, against the victims."

Whatever she had done, had not been done out of malice or lust or even out of calculation. He knelt down by her. "Ah, poor witch," he said. "Go where you please, but only let me know. Don't leave me without knowing."

"I am so hungry," said Lisette impatiently. She could not take her eyes off the things on the table. He noticed a thin bandage round Halka's arm; the sleeve of her dress had slipped up her thin arm as she had stretched herself on the bed and he saw the white cotton.

"What is that?" he asked.

"Nothing."

"Where were you?" he asked again, but gently, without reproach.

"I was at the hospital, where they take blood transfusions. I went there and gave my blood."

He said nothing. He went back to the table and looked down at the little packet of food which she had got in exchange for her blood.

"I had only to sit in a deck chair and put my arm through a hole in a wooden partition. It did not take long, but afterwards I had to lie down. I wanted to come straight home, but they said I must rest. Ah, how I hated having to stay there in a room with beds—it reminded me too much of the asylum."

"Go to bed now in your own bed," he said, "and I will make supper."

He made dumplings with the flour and fried them in butter. It was the only way he knew of making a meal with the things she had brought. He brought the small table that stood beside his couch to the bed in which the two sisters lay and they ate the first solid meal that they had had together for a long time.

"It really is solid," said Halka, referring to the dumplings, which were leaden and grey.

"But they fill one up," said Lisette; "and that's all I want, to be filled up once again below the ribs."

The night was very cold. They had had to let the stove out early to save their dwindling supply of wood, and soon after the meal Dominic tucked the feather coverlet over the sisters and retired to his couch with his blankets and overcoat.

Halka and Lisette could not sleep. They talked together in whispers. Lisette threw her arms around her sister and pressed her to her.

"Wasn't it frightful for you? How could you do it?" she asked.

"Oh, it wasn't so bad; the loss of a little blood is nothing; it was the being in their hands."

"Was it worse than being Descoux' *chérie*?"

"To be in anyone's hands, that is always more or less of

a horror. Because they all seem to me to belong to the executioners."

"Our *l'oiseau sauvage* too?" asked Lisette curiously. "He seems so gentle."

"They were gentle enough in the asylum, too," said Halka. "When you made no trouble, they were quite gentle setting you in the electric chair. And even the poor mad girls who came and violated me when my hands were strapped into the straight-jacket were gentle in their way. Of all those into whose hands I have fallen, it was only the guards in the concentration camp in 1943 who exulted in being executioners, and of them only one or two."

The next day, Descoux came and took the two girls into town. With him they could go into the French *économats* and buy those vegetables which were not on ration cards. Halka let Lisette go in with him to do the buying, and herself waited outside. It was an ordeal for her to venture in and know that at any moment she might be asked for her identity card. And even although nothing could be done to her when she was with a French soldier, she felt she could not have borne just now even a shadow of the old horror of suspicion to have fallen on her.

As she waited in the snowy street she saw the wives and maidservants of the occupation troops coming out of the shop laden with fruit and bottles of wine. She remembered that it was almost Christmas. And suddenly as she waited, she recalled a dream that she had had last night when she had at last fallen asleep after the long whispered conversation with Lisette. She had been standing almost exactly as she was now in a snowy street outside a large shop with windows full of all kinds of luxuries and hung with Christmas decorations. And although the *économat* had no shop windows and no decorations, she knew that this was the street and that this was the shop that she had seen.

In her dream a large black car had driven up and stopped at the shop and a woman, elegant in furs, had stepped out and gone into it. This woman had had her own face, but her face as it might have been had she lived in a world in which there had been no concentration camps, no bombs, no hunger, no asylums, no dungeons. She had waited in a fever of impatience for this woman to come out again. At last the woman had appeared with her purchases and had been about to step into the car when Halka had addressed her. What she had said to her she did not know, but the woman had stopped, surprised, and looked at her.

"Don't you know me?" Halka had asked her anxiously.

The woman had looked at her out of her pale, clear eyes set in a serene brow.

"No," she had answered, but uncertainly, as if she could not quite remember. "What do you want?"

"Only that you should recognise me," Halka had said.

"Come," the other had said. "We can't stand here." And they had got into the car together and had been driven off in it.

"Don't you see how we resemble each other?" Halka had asked.

As the car had sped through the snowy streets (and in the dream it had sped in silent flight through so many streets, passed so many ruined buildings that Halka had never seen before) the woman leant close to her, taking off her fur cap and letting down her long hair. Her hair covered them both and Halka smelt its scent that was like the smell of spring. She looked into her face. It was not beautiful any more than her own was. The eyes were pale like hers, the lids heavy, the lips colourless. She laid her hand on Halka's breast and her heart beat quickly.

"Fear not, Halka," the woman said. Her voice was low and she spoke Polish.

The car had stopped at a big building, and at first Halka had thought it was one of the palatial villas at the undamaged outskirts of the town which had been requisitioned for the most important French officers and their families. But then she saw that it was the Cathedral.

They had entered it together, the woman in her furs, her hair loose, and Halka had followed her to the dark corner of the nave in which the crib with its painted plaster figures had been set up.

Then she was kneeling alone by the crib and the woman

was not with her any more. She knelt on and repeated an *Ave Maria*. And as she prayed, Dominic was beside her and, seeing her distraught face, he had said to her:

"We must suffer it, too, that we can only make our prayers in parables."

Now she stood in the street and recalled it. She was afraid. She was afraid that a large, dark car might come and stop in front of the shop and a woman in furs get out of it. If she should see that she would believe she was suffering an hallucination. She would know that she was really mad, that when the doctor had signed that slip of paper and given her an injection and put her into the hands of the nurses he had been justified. She dare not wait here. She turned away, afraid to raise her eyes, and began walking back up the street.

She had not gone far when Lisette came running after her and overtook her.

"Where are you off to? Were we so long?" she asked.

"It wasn't that. But I just remembered a dream I had last night. Such a strange dream, and I was afraid."

"No wonder you dreamed after all those dumplings. I dreamed, too, but now I don't remember what. Look. Descoux bought some wine for us, and I got a cauliflower."

On the way home Descoux excused himself from them a moment and crossed the street to speak to a small girl with a dark skin and black, straight hair who had been slouching along on the opposite pavement. She had looked no older than Lisette as she stood with head bent talking to Descoux. She seemed not to relish the encounter, to want to slip past him and escape, but she did not do so, she stood glancing up from under her black eyes and once or twice smiled and shook her head.

When Descoux returned to them, Halka asked him if he had found a new *chérie*, and he said:

"Her mother is a Martinique and does a trade in picture cards. I have ordered a couple of hundred from her. There's a business to be done with them in the small towns."

Lisette recalled the pictures Descoux' friend had shown her. She had hardly glimpsed them, but she had an impression of entrails, of horrible physical exposures such as might be depicted from a torture chamber. To her it belonged to all that Halka told her about the executioners.

Shortly after Halka and Lisette had gone out, Petrov had called round and found Dominic alone, at work in his corner on the couch. Petrov had brought a new pile of French periodicals with him. He was glad that the sisters were out, because there was something about which he wished to speak to Dominic in private.

"It is about the two girls," he began with his slow manner of getting around a subject. His face took on the heavy ugliness that Dominic had seen settle down on it when Petrov was given up to an intense concentration on what he had to say. His long nose seemed to grow longer and his eyelids to droop heavily over his oblique eyes.

Dominic made a place for him on the couch and offered him one of Halka's precious cigarettes to put him at his ease.

"I believe," he went on, "that you and I, and those like us who have been exposed to the cataclysm and been changed by it, can ask each other any questions, even the most intimate and singular questions, without offence."

"Yes," said Dominic, smiling at the ponderous movement of the spirit of Petrov that reminded him of the persistent, patient movement of some creature feeling its way along the floor of the sea with a slow waving of its tentacles.

"Yes. I believe so too."

"I heard from Frau Arnheim," Petrov went on, "that you share this room with the two girls. And what I came to ask you was if this is simply an arrangement forced on you by the room-shortage or whether it is an integral part of your way of living."

"Neither one nor the other," said Dominic. "It simply came about so. After my release I did not want to return to my room and be alone. While I was in the cellar in the Nietzschestrasse, I saw how good life could be if only we understood the secret of real communion—not just physical contact or even friendship, but fraternity; and especially fraternity with a woman."

"In fraternity with a woman? Yes. I understand that. I understand it with all my heart," went on Petrov. He was in that trance of intense concentration that came over him when he was carried away. His face seemed to lengthen and grow uglier with every word. "But my question, as you know, is not an idle one. Not just inspired by love of gossip, such as, I am afraid, our good Aunty is sometimes concerned with. I have a very urgent reason for asking you if you have this fraternity that you speak of with both or only one of the sisters?"

Dominic laughed. For a moment Petrov looked at him incomprehendingly and then his long, tranced face melted into laughter too. At that moment Dominic felt close to him as he had never yet felt, in spite of a certain deep respect he had for him.

"For some reason, that reminded me of my interrogation," Dominic said. "But the answer to your question is that I don't live with both of the girls, but only with one of them. Though even that is perhaps not strictly the right term for our relationship."

"Good," said Petrov. "Then, as far as you are concerned, there would be nothing against me having the hope of living with the other one, of having this fraternity with her as you so well put it, perhaps even of marrying her?"

"No," said Dominic. "There would be nothing against it. But you haven't yet asked which of the two it is."

"I was coming to that," said Petrov. "You see, I know them both; I have seen and studied them both a little at Frau Arnheim's, and I would be happy if I could have either of them. It is true that I know Lisette the best, and I am more at ease with her, but she is a little young. The elder Miss Mayersky I know less, but she is older, has suffered more and would perhaps be more likely to understand and consider my proposal. So you see it is for me all the same. These two girls are two rare and precious beings, and I am, in a sense, glad that it is not left to me to have to decide which of them to approach."

At that very moment the door opened and the two "precious beings" returned with Descoux. Lisette proudly showed Dominic the cauliflower and Descoux put the bottles of wine on the table.

"We will have a Christmas party after all," Lisette said. "And Monsieur Petrov must come to it, too." She looked at him and Petrov looked back at her. He was confused by the interruption of his conversation with Dominic at a very vital point. Now as he looked back at Lisette he tried to fathom by her bearing whether it was she that fate had chosen as the one to whom he could make his proposal. But he could not tell. He looked from her to Halka. Lisette was certainly very young, but he did not think that that would matter. He had no "designs" on her; it was not for that that he wanted to have her with him. That would come naturally as part of the companionship, but, if she wished, it could wait until later. The main thing for him was to have one of these girls with him at all hours of the day, in the fraternity of which Dominic had spoken and which he too saw as the fulfilment of his lonely existence. But Lisette was still looking at him, waiting for an answer to her invitation.

"When is the party?" he asked.

"Now. To-day. You don't think we could keep these things, that we could *store them up*, do you? We will have it to-day, won't we, Monsieur Descoux?"

"*Ah, oui. Bien sûr*," said Descoux. He would have agreed in the same way had she suggested having it next week. He had a happy art of accepting everything, of seeming glad if he himself did not have to come to a decision or make a plan. And this was a part of his great nonchalance that charmed them so much.

"What time to-day?" asked the punctilious Petrov.

"What time? Any time! As soon as possible," said Lisette.

"Now that you are here, you had better stay on," Halka told him. "We don't know. It might start any time. We would like to wait till evening, but it's so hard to wait when the stuff is there under our noses."

So Petrov stayed on and had lunch with them. Halka prepared a surprisingly good lunch with the cauliflower, cheese that came from no one knew where, and coffee.

Descoux went off, but promised to come back early in the afternoon.

"You should have seen him in the street with a little

Martinique girl," Lisette told Dominic. "He has his eye everywhere. He saw her on the other side of the crowded street, from far away, and slipped over so stealthily to her."

"Don't gossip, Lisette," said Halka. "That has nothing to do with you."

"I don't gossip," said Lisette, a little hurt.

She went and sat beside Petrov on the couch. She began to ask him about Aunty, whom neither she nor Halka had been to see for some time.

"Aunty is very worried," Petrov told her, "over the loss of some ring or other. She does not speak of it much, but I believe that it belonged to a friend for whom she was keeping it locked up in her jewel-box, and when she went to look for it the other day it was gone."

Lisette had gone pale as Petrov spoke of the ring. She looked anxiously at Dominic. Halka was busy in the kitchen, which she was allowed to use at certain hours.

Dominic thought that Halka had given Frau Arnheim some explanation about the ring at the time of his arrest. He had meant to tell her to do so, but probably in the stress of those days he had forgotten and left to herself the matter had not crossed her mind.

"Did nobody tell her?" Lisette asked him.

"Tell her what?" asked Petrov.

But Lisette had once made her confession. She had made it to Dominic and she could not make it all over again, especially to Petrov. She looked at Dominic appealingly, with that defensive look that seemed always to hover not far from her face.

There was a moment or two of awkward silence while Dominic made up his mind whether to tell Petrov the truth or not. In one way, he knew Petrov so little. It was true, Petrov had come to him with his singular question on the plea that all could now be said, all could now be asked in distinction to the far-off-days before the cataclysm when everyone tried to live with a protecting wall around him. But could Petrov carry his awareness of the new way of life— or, rather, of the new morality—to the point of accepting Lisette's theft from Frau Arnheim while the latter had been keeping her and looking after her? To Dominic this moral anarchy was natural enough. The old code of honour and the old law was gone, and he did not regret it. The old law had been based, not on love, but on social convenience. It had been part of the whole civilised structure that had largely broken down. Now there was a time without standards, an inner anarchy, and Lisette was a child of this time. Whether out of this anarchy a new morality would grow, a morality without falseness as he hoped, he did not know.

He looked at Petrov and said:

"Lisette stole the ring."

He could have said: "The ring belonged to me and Lisette took it with my knowledge." He could have made it into nothing at all. And so he would have, had not Petrov asked him the question and made the confession of an hour before. Now if he really wanted Lisette, he must first know her. It was not as if this theft had been committed by Lisette in the stress of great need, not as if it was a single, exceptional aberration of hers that would never be likely to be repeated. Dominic knew very well that she had the makings of a little thief, as many others of her age had in these ruined and hungry towns, and that if Petrov wanted her he had better take her with his eyes open to this and the other problems that went with her.

Petrov said nothing for a moment. He did not know what to make of Dominic's direct statement. If only he knew whether Lisette was his girl! He had no way of following the process in Dominic's mind that had made him tell the truth. On the contrary it seemed to him an indication that there was a great intimacy between Dominic and Lisette. The fact of the theft was a very secondary consideration, for he was so under the spell of the young girl that had he heard of twenty thefts it would not have in any way lessened his longing for her.

"Forgive me, forgive me," said Lisette suddenly, before he could speak, turning to him and gripping his long, bony hand in her little white claw.

"Ah, if only I had the right to forgive you, to forgive you for everything and for ever," said Petrov in his clumsy, groping way.

"You can forgive her or not, punish her or reward her, do what you like about her," said Dominic, laughing, "as far as I am concerned."

Petrov looked at him, understanding him slowly as was his way, and into his face, more ugly than ever at this moment, passed a look of exultation.

CHAPTER VII

AN EVENING BEFORE CHRISTMAS

THEY POSTPONED THE moment of opening the wine and beginning the "party" as long as they could, but in the end it was not really evening when Lisette took a bottle and gave it to Descoux to draw the cork. He had returned with some bread and meat out of which Halka had made sandwiches.

Dominic rejoiced at this little Christmas celebration. Again he felt the fullness of life was being given to him. Only a few weeks ago on that last evening in his dungeon, in darkness and misery, he had seen life taken from him and he had struggled to let it go, not to rebel. He had been ready to lose his life, and now it was being given back to him in full measure.

Petrov and Lisette remained sitting together on the couch. They were absorbed in each other as though in all these months they had never really seen each other. Dominic and Halka were also talking together and although Descoux was left alone in the one armchair he did not seem to mind. Halka suggested that he should go and fetch himself a companion, the little Martinique or another, but he only smiled and said: "*Ah, non. Je suis content.*"

Bottle after bottle of wine was opened. Dominic, Descoux and Petrov kept drinking, but the two girls drank little. It was long since Dominic had drunk more than a glass or two, and on his starved stomach the alcohol had a quick effect. It struck him once that he should cease drinking and go back to Halka, whom he had left sitting alone. But this old sensation, that he knew well, had a new charm, this being lifted above all the cares and anxieties of the last months and years, this spreading of wings to carry him far, far above the desolation, and he stayed on at the table with Descoux. Petrov had stopped drinking and was deep in conversation with Lisette.

Gradually a strange blankness settled down over Dominic and he was no longer conscious of the passing of time, of the continuity of events, but only of vivid and isolated pictures. Once he came to himself to find himself deep in some discussion with Descoux about the little Martinique. He seemed suddenly to understand exactly the attraction that Descoux found in this young girl. There was a moment when he himself was appalled at this understanding, but then, the next moment, he was absorbed and excited by this experience, by this power that seemed to be in him of sharing all things, of being all things.

He saw Descoux looking at him and smiling, and through the haze of drunkenness that was before his eyes he caught in the expression of Descoux amused and secret understanding. Then there was a later picture: of Halka's face close to him, regarding him. But later it was withdrawn from him. And then he was beside Lisette on the couch. He was close to her and his flesh and blood seemed to be burning. There was nothing left but this burning in a darkness haunted by the cool young bodies of Lisette and the Martinique. He turned, looking for Halka in a drunken instinct that only she could help him. But she was not where he had remembered her last, at the table.

It took him a moment or two to discover her. She was standing in the far corner. She had taken off her blouse and bound a scarf around her breasts and was in the middle of performing a dance.

Dominic watched her dancing with growing wonder. She was dancing a dance she had learnt in a cabaret where she had once worked. But he did not like it. He jumped up and, taking her bare arm, pulled her with him out of the room. In the passage she stood with her back to the door, smiling at him and still breathless.

"Wait here," he said to her, "while I fetch your blouse and coat and then let us go out for a few minutes into the street."

"Into the street? Why into the street? It is snowing," she said.

"Only for a few moments, before we go back into our room again. I saw suddenly that the room was full of devils."

"But they can't touch you. You are far above them," she said. "You know I had a dream last night and at the end of it you were kneeling beside me in the Cathedral, teaching me how to pray. And that's why I began to dance—and if you hadn't stopped me I would have danced the final part, what we used to call 'dancing the second degree of pornography.' I wanted to free myself from that dream and from that you who was beside me in it. Because I don't want to play the part of a penitent Magdalene; that is something nasty. I wanted to hurt you and to show you that I was not going to be 'saved' by your saintliness and innocence."

"Shall I tell you the truth?" he said to her. "It is just because I am capable of the greatest sins that I cling to what you call innocence. I could commit a great crime if circumstances were to push me far enough."

"What circumstances?" she asked.

"Oh, I cannot foresee the circumstances. If I could foresee them I would be armed against them. And yet that's not quite true. I can half foresee them. I know that just now, in our room, I was beginning to be caught into just one of these nightmares where all seem to conspire for one's destruction. Because, Halka, it is so terribly easy to fall into a great and destructive sin. I remember you saying with horror how terribly easy it was to fall into the hands of the executioners. And I will always think of those words. But this too is another horror that can overtake us with an unexpected ease."

"What was it that you saw just now in our room?" she asked.

"I saw that I was on the brim of a great calamity. I saw that it would only need another few moments, only that you should go dancing and I drink another glass or two of wine for the devils to have possessed me."

"Then what would you have done?" she asked curiously.

"I don't know. But at such moments the opportunity is always given to one, something insiduously destructive and evil. Not perhaps only one thing; because it is seldom that it is a question of committing one great and solitary sin. It is much more likely that one slips step by step into the hell that is always waiting."

"My God! How you speak! I never heard you speak like this. I thought you couldn't speak like this."

"Listen to me, Halka. I speak of what I know. What would have happened, that I do not know. I cannot prophesy exactly how it would have begun. Perhaps with Lisette. The devils had already shown me her. I saw her as I had never seen her before. They showed her body to me as part of the sweet fruit of creation that was given me to devour. But if I had resisted that temptation another would have been presented to me. Another equally destructive. And you would have gone on with your dancing, drunken or not, I don't know. Perhaps, as you say, out of some instinct of rebellion against me. It is all the same. We would have both destroyed and destroyed, all that we have, this new fraternity. There would have come the diabolic lust to destroy all that is most precious to one. For that is the final lust always lurking in the darkness within one! Or don't you know it? Is that something you are too innocent to know? Perhaps you would have come to me to reproach me for what I had done and I, by then cold and nauseated with myself and with the world, would not have been capable of the patience and humility to bow under your reproaches. Perhaps you would have hit me, have slapped me. And in the state I would then be, in that hell of remorse and hopelessness, I would not have remained passive and let you slap me. I would have seized any excuse to escape from the deathly coldness of reaction that had overtaken me. I would have held you by the hands, or by the hair, and have slapped you to teach you, as the devils would have whispered, to control yourself. And the lust of destruction would have caught fire in me as flame catches dead wood and I would have hit you and hit you. . . . One blow for your dancing, another for your having been

84

Descoux' *chérie*, and another for having been in the asylum, until each blow was aimed at your heart, at all that I would normally heal and shelter."

"But I would never have slapped you," she cried. "Why do you speak like that, as though you knew each step on the way to a murder? There were some with me in the asylum who knew such things, but you—you shouldn't know such things."

"Oh yes, little witch. I must know them. I must look into the very jaws of the pit within me and be saved by the mercy of God."

"I don't believe in the mercy of God," she said. "Perhaps I lived too long in places into which the mercy of God did not penetrate."

She put on her blouse and got into her overcoat and they went downstairs and out into the street. It had snowed again since the morning and the snow lay stamped hard and dry on the pavement as though it would never melt. The air was still and icy and it seemed that no mild breeze would ever blow out of the steel-grey sky. The winter had begun early and the town was stricken by its onslaught.

Yet the ruined streets were crowded with people hurrying hither and thither, as though desperately trying to make the last preparations for the long, icy months in front of them.

But Dominic was glad of the cold, bringing him back completely to himself. They turned up a street between blocks of modern and largely undamaged flats. Here many French families lived and it was quieter with fewer people in the street, in which the snow lay still soft and powdery. Halfway along it a tall figure in a French officer's overcoat was about to pass them when he stopped and held out his hand. Dominic recognised the fair face, the small blue eyes and the always tightly closed mouth of Captain Renier.

"How are you getting on?" he asked them. "Not yet tired of freedom?" he added to Dominic.

Dominic smiled and shook his hand.

"Will you come up with me for a cup of coffee?" Captain Renier asked them. "I live just here."

They turned with him and a couple of doors down the street followed him into his flat. It was an apartment very like the one in which Descoux lived, but on entering it Dominic at once sensed a subtle difference. Descoux' flat had always been overheated and in the air there had always been a lingering scent of cooking, of perfume and cigarettes.

In Captain Renier's small parlour there were many books, many periodicals and newspapers and in the kitchen they had a glimpse of an elderly woman in a white apron, and a white Pomeranian terrier came running out of the bedroom and threw itself in a series of springs against the legs of its master.

"Sit down and make yourselves comfortable while I go and wash off the dirt of the office," their host said. In a few moments he returned, even sprucer than ever. There was something in his face and in his movements that reminded Dominic of his Uncle Egan, or still more of a sister of Uncle Egan's, who held herself with a maidenly straightness, whose cheeks always shone as though freshly scrubbed and whose lips seemed to press with the same firmness one on the other.

"And how are you managing? How are you pulling through?" he asked them.

"Like everyone else in this miserable town," said Halka.

"Yes. It is hard. But it is not much better anywhere else," Captain Renier said. "Everywhere the same misery, physical and moral, for which the politicians have not yet found any solution."

Dominic was surprised at the openness with which the other spoke, and for a time he could not reconcile this man with the official who had interrogated him through all those long, successive days in the Nietzschestrasse.

"And it will never be found politically," said Dominic, emboldened by the friendliness and simplicity of the other. "It will never be found in any political system. Look what is happening; the night has closed over us."

"You may well call it a night. And that brings me to what I have to say to you here," said Captain Renier, fixing Dominic with his small blue eyes, at the corners of which were a network of tiny wrinkles.

Dominic felt that sinking of his heart that he knew from of old. It had happened when the policeman had appeared

86

at his door, when the French soldier had come into the empty kitchen and told him to take everything out of his pockets. Again he saw the steps down into the cellar descending before him. Halka put her hand over his.

Captain Renier saw either in Dominic's face or in the little gesture of Halka the effect of his words. He went on quickly: "Don't distrust me. Here in my flat you are perfectly safe; not a hair of your heads shall be touched." He smiled at them out of his small blue eyes.

"We can't help it any more," said Halka. "I can't help distrusting everyone in uniform—in any uniform, all officials and investigators. Not you and your uniform, but just all uniforms without exception."

"I know it. I know very well the fear that is everywhere to-day, that haunts both the guilty and the innocent," said the officer. "I see it on so many faces, in the very look that I am met with."

"And yet you don't know it as we know it," said Halka. "You live in the midst of it, but it doesn't enter into you. You are safe."

"To-day that is true. But it has not always been so, Mademoiselle. I know a great deal about fear, not only from the outside, but from the inside. I can say I have made a study of fear. I know, for instance, that three-quarters of the depravity that is everywhere is due to fear or the after-effects of fear."

"But to come back to what you were beginning to say about why you had asked us here, Captain," Dominic reminded him.

"It is not a question of 'coming back.' I have never strayed from it. I asked you here to try to free you from your fear."

"To undo with one hand what you do with the other," Halka said.

"There is going to be an end to fear," said Captain Renier, ignoring her interruption. His fair face with the small blue eyes had its own singular attraction for Dominic. It seemed to him to belong to an age that was past, to have an uprightness, almost a primness about it.

"I would have come to see you," he went on to Dominic,

"but I knew that it would have given you a shock if you had opened your door and found me standing at it."

He stroked the furry little dog curled up on his lap. Dominic had the impression of being back at home, long ago, in the drawing-room of his aunt.

"I don't see any end of all the fears," said Dominic. "They can only be forgotten for a time. You forget the fear of famine in the joy of a parcel coming and of having two days of feasting. Or you forget the fear of the dungeons and prisons by companionship and communion with someone in a room without bars, or in other ways. I know a fellow countryman of yours here, Captain, who forgets in the company of very young girls—the younger the better—his horror of having been kept for years behind bars."

"Yes. I know these things," said Captain Renier. "Fear has deep and strange effects. It is from fear that men must be freed, from all the fears."

"We can only free each other from fear; two people coming together and making a little world without fear," said Halka.

"That is to escape into an ivory tower," said Captain Renier, "and leave the world, or Europe, to perish."

He began to speak of Europe and of the "revolution." He sat with the Pomeranian on his knees. But it was hard for Dominic to forget his uniform, to forget that he was an officer of the French security police.

"Till now," he was saying, "states have ruled by fear; some by a real reign of terror and others by a moderate amount of fear. But always order has been kept by fear, either more or less."

He went on to speak of a movement that would do away with this rule based on fear. Dominic listened without at first taking very much interest in what the other was saying. He was only glad to sit there in the warm room and sip the hot coffee and come back from the depths of drunkenness in which he had been. But when Captain Renier spoke of the anarchists he began to listen. Not that he believed in the anarchists, but at least the talk was not developing into the old, political or social generalisations that he was so used to and so tired of.

"If you have heard of us," said the Captain, "it has no doubt been as a group of people out to destroy society— destructive, without any policy. That is because we are per- haps the one revolutionary movement of which the powers that be are really afraid."

"I am quite ready to believe, Captain," said Dominic, "that if a real change of heart and soul, a real inner revolution was to take place, it would be hushed up and kept quiet for as long as possible because the powers that be, all powers irrespective of their social and political colour, would know that they were threatened as they have never been threatened. But that is a dream, such an inner rebellion can never become a movement; it must always remain the prerogative of a few isolated and powerless people."

"Once it was a dream, as you say. Once it was the dream of a few isolated people and if the great calamity of the war and its aftermath had not overtaken us, it might have remained a dream. But people have gone through too much, they have been pushed too far. We French, Mr. Malone, have gone through too much agony. And now we have this new word of hope for the world, or at least for Europe, because the rest of the world is probably not yet ripe for it.

"Our activities are given as little publicity as possible, or else cleverly attributed to other movements," he went on.

"What are your activities?" asked Dominic. He was both sceptical and at the same time drawn to hear more.

"They are manifold," said Captain Renier. "But our main weapon is the strike. That is the one we shall use successfully when the time is ripe. There have been many great strikes inspired by us, although the papers were quick to give them another cause. The papers fear us, Mr. Malone, and the whole host of officials that wield the real power in all countries fear us as they fear no other movement. And the reason is very simple. All other movements, whether revolu- tionary or reactionary, would always have need of them, of one mass of officials or another. We alone could dispense with them."

Dominic experienced a curious sensation. Was it possible that at last the miracle had happened, that a *penchant de l'âme,* a pure and secret movement of soul, had manifested itself outwardly in power and had caused a strike? Even supposing that Captain Renier was exaggerating when he attributed a series of large strikes to his party, and that there had only been one strike attributable to it, this all the same was enough. For to Dominic, that the subtle, inarticulate longing of the heart for an equity that would consist in its being left alone, in not being asked to submit itself to this or that form of officialdom, even a so-called beneficent officialdom, had come out into the open, had inspired enough men so that they had done something, not only suffered in secret and isolation, but performed an action together—therein lay the miracle.

But he could not believe it. There was a catch somewhere.

"Very well. I am ready to believe in the possibility of the anarchists having a certain power, though even that astonishes me. But I cannot believe that they are inspired by that absolute liberalism and love of freedom. I can't believe in the miracle of a group of men staging in the streets of Paris, or in the streets of Lille or Bordeaux, anywhere, a parade or a strike or whatever it may be, inspired by that vision of a pure equity that has been dreamed of but that no one has ever dared to utter a word about in public."

"All the same, that is what has happened and will go on happening, whether you believe it or not. And it could have begun nowhere else but in France," said Captain Renier.

"But what about the Spanish anarchists and the Russia nihilists?" asked Dominic, trying to order and make sense of what he had heard.

"Oh, I am not likely to forget the Spanish anarchists in the Spanish civil war," Captain Renier said. "I was with the C.N.T. in Barcelona myself. But they did not yet know all that we know to-day, because they had not seen the fullness of the calamity."

"What is it you want?" asked Halka. She knew these political discussions between men, and even between men and women, and to her they had a bitter taste. There was in them none of the balm that she needed for her wounds.

"It is first what we don't want," said Captain Renier.

"We don't want uniforms, frontiers, documents, governments. And when we have done away with that order and got rid of the host of officials who are necessary to impose it, we shall begin with our anarchist society without officials."

Halka was listening, her white face, with its slightly pointed nose, open, receptive, as no other face, Dominic thought, was ever quite so open. She raised her arms and lifted back her hair from her cheeks and shoulders, in a gentle, familiar gesture that always touched Dominic. It reminded him of the soft movement of a child stretching itself at the end of a long day.

The big block of flats in which Captain Renier lived, although itself intact, looked out on to a sea of ruins. From the window of the little parlour they could see the winter sun sinking over the snowy waste.

Captain Renier told them about the movement which alone, he said, at this last hour, could save them.

"We must return to a state of unorganised society, because all organisation has the seed of destruction in it. We may organise for the protection of the weak, or for the establishment of justice or for whatever good cause it may be, but the very organisation that we set up is in itself a threat to the weak and to justice. There is no good saying, 'Disarm.' The question is a far deeper one. We do not merely say, 'Disarm.' We say, 'Disorganise.' Let men be, let them alone. Don't organise them into states, into classes, communities, don't put them in uniforms, don't put them behind desks in offices full of files, don't make them slaves of endless papers and documents. Go back voluntarily and with open eyes to the unorganised society in which man lived blindly a few thousand years ago, and in which some peoples still live. Go back to that humbly, with the bitter experience of the lost centuries, especially of the first half of this bloody century, engraved in our minds. And then we shall have taken out of our own hands the possibility of tormenting each other and destroying each other on a large scale. It is true that minor and private crimes will continue, but private crimes don't produce a state of terror. Perhaps it can sometimes go so far that a murderer can for a short time terrorise a district of a city or the whole of a small town. But there cannot be a nation-wide sense of fear that lasts for years, for generations. There cannot be mass fear.

"But what I say now is only a word—a word let drop so that you know that there are others with the same thoughts as yours," Captain Renier said. "Later you will meet someone whose words you will listen to with hope and astonishment. You will hear words of inspiration from the man who alone to-day has vision enough to save us and deliver us from our fear."

"And yet, you know, Captain," said Halka after a short pause, "I don't think you or this other can save me or deliver me from my fear, as you put it. There is only one who can do that."

"Who? Which one?" asked Captain Renier, still absorbed in his own thoughts of movements and "causes."

"This one, here," said Halka with a flash of her sweet, singular smile, looking at Dominic. "Only since I have been with him are the terrible dreams that I used to have beginning to leave me. I had them so long, even before I was sent to a concentration camp, though since then they became such a torment that I thought at times I would go mad. And perhaps I really was mad, perhaps the doctor who signed the certificate and sent me to the asylum was right."

"No. He was not right," said Dominic. He was deeply moved. Never before by so much as a word had she let him know that he had been of any comfort to her, that this fraternity of theirs that he had tried to create had in fact been more than an idea of his.

"For weeks now I have hardly had a single nightmare," she went on, "and last night I had a dream that was given me by you"—she was looking at Dominic—"a dream full of light and sweetness."

The Captain smiled. "Surely, Mademoiselle, in the arms of a man who loves you it would be strange if your dreams were not sweet. But as I said a few minutes ago, lovers' dreams are not, alas! enough to deliver you or the rest of us from the universal catastrophe."

"Oh no, Captain Renier," she answered. "I have lain in

too many arms and had too many lovers to think that they can save me. My dream has nothing to do with that. I have had enough of all that. I am not a young girl to have those illusions, as you must very well know. Because you know everything; you have records in that villa of yours about everyone."

"Yes. I know that when you came to visit Monsieur Malone while he was detained you were registered as the maid of one of our soldiers and were living with him."

"And I am sure you know other things about me, Captain," Halka went on; "but the real things are never put down in records and these you can't know. You can't know why these parables of yours about organisation and disorganisation are not what I can ever put my hope in. It is not they that can lift me out of my nightmare."

Captain Renier laughed. Halka's outburst had come so unexpectedly. It had been to Dominic that he had really addressed himself and had given very little thought to this girl. She had seemed to him a common enough type: one of these "displaced persons," passive victims of the war, who had never known a normal life, shelter, security. He had her record, as she supposed, and, except for the short interlude in the asylum which he was quite ready to regard as a miscarriage of medical probity, it was similar to the records of thousands of other young foreigners in the zone.

While she spoke he had regarded her out his small, blue eyes and had noticed that behind her pallor, thinness and general air of undernourishment, which were common enough these days, there was something else about her not so common.

"In your papers, it is stated," he said, "that you have scars on your body of the beatings you received while in a concentration camp during the war."

Halka did not answer.

"Is that true?" Dominic asked her.

Captain Renier regarded him curiously.

"Surely you must know if it is so or not," he said to him.

"I do not know," said Dominic.

Halka was still silent, and Captain Renier took a loaf, cut a slice from it and began to crumble it into a saucer. He did all with careful, precise movements. He took the jug of milk and poured some into the saucer and then put the saucer down on the carpet for the Pomeranian. All the time Halka watched him. The little white dog slid lazily from his lap and began to sniff the saucer of bread and milk indifferently.

"There are many people who would like to be your dog, Captain," said Halka.

"But I wouldn't find one among them to give me what Trosti does."

"What is that?"

"What is it?" Captain Renier repeated. "I suppose it is companionship."

"Is that then so hard to get?" she asked.

"Everything else can be got before that," said the other. "Have not you found it so?" he added to Dominic.

"Yes. Real fraternity—that is of all relationships the rarest and the most precious."

"Ah! I don't suppose that Trosti can give me that," said Captain Renier, his big, "old-fashioned" face suddenly melting into a smile for the first time during their visit. "But you saw how he greets me when I come back in the evenings, and his greeting never grows less. I can know that in this changing chaos *that* will not change and my coming will be always the same joy for him. And I don't like change; I don't like change and uncertainty."

As they took leave of him, he said to Dominic: "And now if there should be a ring at your door any time and you find me standing outside it you won't get a shock, will you? Because I think you know now why I am here, and that it is not only to strike terror into the hearts of others. There is still the rest of the mess to be cleaned up, but then there must be no more fear and no more suspicion. Let us make a start between us, Monsieur Malone."

Dominic felt the big, fair hand with its strong fingers whose back were covered with fine golden hair grip his in an honest grip. A part of him would have liked to have said the easy, expected thing. He saw the eyes of the other burning like little blue flames, full of fire. But somehow, somehow he hesitated, he could not quite kindle to the fire in the other, to the proffered fraternity. He said: "Oh no, Captain, I won't get a shock. You have reassured me."

But as he uttered them, the words seemed to fall flat; they were heavy and unresponsive.

When he was once more alone with Halka in the dusk of the snowy street he said to her: "What was the dream that you had last night, that you say you dreamt because of me? Why in all these weeks have you never uttered a word like that before? Why did you wait till we were with a stranger to hint at something that would have given me such joy if you had said it to me alone?"

She smiled at him and put her arm through his, trying to avoid stepping into the worst pools of slush with her broken shoes.

"So many questions. Where can I begin to answer them? But wait a little and they will be answered. They will all be answered, Dominic, if we live a little longer together as we have been living."

"That we shall surely do, Halka."

"Yes. If it is not boring for you. I think sometimes you must get fed up with it, sleeping on a couch, with two girls in the other bed. And never anything good to eat, never any surprise or excitement."

"Oh, the excitement is there all right," he told her. "It is only a new sort of excitement; and there is a great deal of surprise. I don't want the old sort of excitement any more; that is what I would find boring in the end. And as for the questions, let us leave them, as you say, for the present. Only one other thing I would like to know—something quite outward this time. Why didn't you answer Captain Renier when he asked you about the scars on your body?"

"Because I don't know yet whether I should tell him and have that set down as coming out of my own mouth; and then perhaps later be called as a witness to testify against my executioners. Should I not forgive them? Tell me; only you can tell me. Would you not wish me to forgive them?"

CHAPTER VIII

LISETTE

WINTER CAME TO THE ruined town. They had grown used to the ruins and hardly saw them any more. It was very cold in their room, as they had very little wood to heat it with, and after the first cold month their supply was exhausted.

There was hunger and cold and always the snow-covered ruins and the shops in which there was nothing to be bought.

"And quite close, just over the frontier in Switzerland, there are people who have everything," Lisette said. She had been hearing about Switzerland from Descoux, who sometimes made trips there.

"But for us there is only the wilderness," said Halka. "My God, to see one undamaged street, with bright lights and shop windows full of things to buy, and restaurants; to spend one evening in such a street, just once. That is something I have never been able to do in my life."

Sometimes Dominic got letters and even parcels of food from former friends. But when he did not return and when the novelty of sending food parcels to someone in Germany had worn off, they stopped writing. He did not mind. All that was unreal to him. It was only from his Uncle Egan that he wanted to hear.

He wrote to Dominic, and sometimes he sent him a parcel, and he never asked him why he did not come back. At most he said how fine it would be when one evening they were on the lake again, the two of them and perhaps Hand, with a bottle of whisky and the soft evening breeze ruffling the water, "just enough to make them bite," he wrote. But no questions, no reproaches.

"Ah, how sensitive he is, in his spirit," Dominic said. "And I never knew him. And if there hadn't been a war and if I hadn't gone through it I would never have known him."

"Many things we wouldn't have known," said Halka. "Much we know that the lucky ones don't know. And what

96

they know and have and are bored with, perhaps, like that lit street of plenty, I have never even seen. But now don't you know enough?" she went on. "Haven't you been through enough? What more is there to know?"

"What more?" he said. "There is still much more. I think I am only at the very beginning of this revelation. Do you know, I wouldn't exchange this icy little room with its bare cupboard for the whole rest of the world."

Not that he did not at times long for the world. There was a part of him that dreamt of Paris, London, Dublin and the blessed peace and security of the Irish countryside. Of evening on the lake at home with Uncle Egan and Hand—of wandering over the sand-dunes with a golf-club in his hand and the minute world of wild flowers, that at the time he had hardly seemed to notice and yet now saw in all their secret glory, at his feet.

But even the vision of the tiny, brilliant pansies and dark violets could not turn his heart homewards.

"The pearl is hidden here," he said. "And I have sold all else that I possessed in exchange for this room."

"Why do you always speak to me in parables?" Halka asked.

"Don't you like me to? How else can I say these things?"

"Oh yes. I like it. As I told Captain Renier I like your parables far better than his, far better than any of the others. Only sometimes I would like you to explain them. I would like you to tell me what this pearl really is."

"But when I say it, it diminishes it. It is you."

"Me? What have you from me? You have nothing from me except a burden."

"Perhaps. But the burden is sweet."

One morning Frau Arnheim arrived round in a state of great excitement. She had received notice that one of the famous "Bethlehem" food parcels from America, of which everyone spoke but very few had ever seen, had arrived for her and was to be called for at the office of the society.

"I came straight here for you to come with me. Such a joy we must share together," and she put her arm round Lisette's shoulder and laid her cheek to the girl's cheek.

Dominic was touched by the sight of this woman with her white hair and aristocratic bearing running round to them so simply, pouring her joy out to them, giving herself so spontaneously. But Lisette's shoulder seemed to stiffen; to Dominic, who was beginning to know her well, there was no answering joy in the face she turned to Frau Arnheim. It was Halka who put a thin arm around her and laughed and called her "Aunty."

The four of them went off together and fetched the parcel, and brought it back to Frau Arnheim's flat. Then there was the unpacking of it, the sensuous delight, putting on water for coffee, laying the table. This was her great moment; now she could call the hungry around her and give them to eat. She presided at the table and there was something patriarchal about her with her white hair, her dark, arched brows and her slightly hooked nose, smiling over them, smiling even while she ate, in the satisfaction of a mother, Dominic thought, who gathers her children around her and fills their out-stretched hands.

But when the last crumb was carefully picked from the plates and the last drop of coffee drunk she began to admonish them, speaking of something that had been for some time on her mind.

"The other day I met Frau Osterheim," she said, addressing herself to Halka, "who has a flat in the same house as you. You know, Halka, it is not that I listen to gossip, but I am an old woman compared to you and I have seen that one cannot do just what one likes and ignore one's neighbours—at least, not in a rather small town like this."

"What is it? What have we done to her?" Halka asked.

"You may not have done anything, Halka dear, but you've ignored her feelings and those of the other families who are your neighbours, by the three of you living together in one room."

Frau Arnheim spoke to Halka. She especially avoided addressing a word to Dominic because she was not sure of him. He was always so silent and so unexacting, not like the German men, who always asserted themselves. Yet it was just this quietness that she did not make out.

"My God, Aunty, why can't we live in one room? Can't we be a little family, too, and a happier one than most of the other families around us? Or isn't that allowed? Must we have a permit for that, too?"

"No, Halka, you don't understand me. You can live as you like, of course, and with whoever you like, but I think it would be in many ways better if Lisette was to have a room of her own. Or she could come back here to me. There is always a corner here for you, you know," she added to Lisette, laying her strong, capable hand on that of the young girl.

Lisette looked at Halka. Halka softly brushed back her hair from her shoulders with the half-weary little gesture of her hands so familiar to Dominic.

"What harm can come to Lisette through being with us?" she asked.

"Lisette is still a child," said Frau Arnheim.

"Not a child as you were once a child, Aunty; she has seen all there is to see of death and destruction. You forget, Aunty, that she went through the worst air-raids and saw the charred corpses lined out along the pavements afterwards. And we lived for days with the smell of them in our noses and in our hair."

"But the facts of death are one thing, and the facts of life another," said Frau Arnheim.

"Ah, Aunty," said Halka, "I can only tell you that in our room my little sister will never encounter anything half so shocking or revolting as the scenes that were forced on her many times during the war."

Frau Arnheim was not satisfied, but for the moment she let the subject drop. She had a pile of wood in the garden at the back of the house that she had collected from the street where the lime trees had just had many of their branches lopped off. She asked Dominic to help her cut them. She gave him an axe and they went out through the basement lumber-room into the garden.

Dominic began to chop the branches, wielding the axe with the rhythmic swing that came back to him from long ago. He felt a great energy; with his hunger gone and the axe swinging, he felt his blood begin to flow through him with a new warmth. And suddenly he felt that the air around him had lost its bitterness. He paused in his work and brushed back the hair from his face. In the earth beside him he saw the greenish-white buds of snowdrops, hanging like drops of milky sap on their stalks. He stood staring at them, very still, as though if he moved they might vanish. Then he called Halka. He wanted her to come without the others; he wanted to have this moment alone with her. And she came alone. They stood looking at this sign that the long winter in which they had endured so much was at an end.

"Why, it's mild!" she said. She turned her face to the pale sun shining in a clear, tender sky. "It's the breath of spring," she added. He felt it too and it was like a balm, like an ointment dripping on to him, on to his face and arms and hands.

Frau Arnheim came up, her white hair dishevelled, dragging branches, but doing all in her calm, majestic way. She had always such an imposing air, that Dominic was ever surprised to see her give way to simple, childlike glee as over the parcel, or intent on rolling a cigarette from a few crumbs of tobacco she had gathered together from somewhere.

He went on with his chopping, exulting in the work, in the strength that he felt coming back to him, in the mildness that had crept back into the air, in the snowdrops at his feet. Halka stacked the chopped wood in a clothes-basket and, when it was full, she and Lisette carried it up on to the balcony.

"Don't send me back here to her," Lisette said to her sister. "You won't do that, Halka?"

"No, of course not."

"I can go to Petrov if I have to go anywhere."

"Yes. You might go to Petrov. But I shall think what will be best for you," said Halka.

"And what about you?" her sister asked.

"I will stay where I am."

The two sisters stood together in the balm of the first breath of spring on the balcony, and in a few words all was said. They knew that a change was coming, but they were not sure what it would be. Halka was worried about Lisette's health. With the beginning of spring and the breath of new life in the air she began to turn over in her mind a way of saving Lisette. In the winter, there could be no going forth, no thought of much activity, but a huddling together in the one bed for warmth, a sitting together close to the stove on the days when they were lucky enough to have had wood to heat it.

Halka arranged the last few blocks of wood in the corner and then she straightened herself and kissed Lisette. And Lisette laid, for a moment, her head on her sister's shoulder. She knew that she must not cling to Halka, that that would spoil all. They had spoken of this, and she had once reproached Halka with having had the intention of letting her down and deserting her when she had, on the day of her release from the asylum, gone to the river with the idea of drowning herself. Or afterwards going to Descoux without bothering to let her, Lisette, know that she was back again. Halka had said:

"I bear you in my heart everywhere, into the water if I had gone down in it and into Descoux' bed in that hot little room. But you mustn't cling to me—let there be no clinging and demanding between us."

Dominic worked on with the axe until blisters formed at the base of his fingers. Then he went in and washed his hands and face in Frau Arnheim's tiny kitchen.

"You must stay for supper," she told him. "The two girls are peeling potatoes."

He thought it was a kind of supper that they had had. He had not expected another meal that day; at most a slice of bread each when they got home. But in the sitting-room, Halka and Lisette were crouching over a big dish of potatoes on the floor.

"Isn't it marvellous," Lisette said, "to be able to go on eating?"

After a little, Frau Arnheim sailed into the room, her hair again in order, her face powdered. She offered Dominic a cigarette from one of the packets of American cigarettes that the "Bethlehem" parcel had contained and took one herself. When she had something to smoke and a few supplies in the cupboard of her tiny kitchen she was happy. She settled herself on her chair by the stove and was soon launched on one of her favourite subjects of conversation, which was a tale about the "old days." About her relatives and their doings. To Dominic, who never listened very closely, it always seemed the same tale: the same names of brothers and sisters and titled cousins flowed past him.

This evening even Lisette, who could never stand these reminiscences, listened without impatience. She only exchanged a sly little glance of mockery with Dominic and her sister. It was as obvious to her as to them that, if it came to speaking of children, Frau Arnheim was the child. But now with another fine meal before them and the spring before them it was easy to be what Frau Arnheim expected of them, inexperienced and living in a dead world where nothing really happened any more, ready to drink in the rich adventures through which she, and those of her circle, had passed long ago.

Lisette sat appearing to listen, with her eyes fixed on Frau Arnheim. But she was thinking of very different things. She was turning in her mind the whole question of Petrov and her going to him. She thought she would get on with Petrov well enough, and that to live in his two attic rooms would be pleasant if it were only not for the business of sleeping with him. For he might say what he liked, she was not going to go to him and then hold herself back from him. She looked on the whole thing as a deal, like all the other deals, like the Black Market deals that were going on around her, and she would never dream of trying to get the better of it.

But she was filled with disgust at the thought of what she had to do. She had a disgust and fear of bodies, of all bodies except that of her sister. Whether it was the memory of the naked, burnt bodies that, stumbling through the pall of smoke with Halka, she had come on lying in a row on the pavement that still haunted her, she did not know. There was this picture, but it had grown fainter. There were other visions that were more sinister: the glimpse of the pictures the Frenchman had shown her and which had seemed to her the image of another massacre all over again. And then there had been the red weals under and across the breast of Halka when she had come back from the camp. Now they were faint scars, she didn't notice them any more, but at first they had given her the same sense of horror as the burnt, reeking flesh.

She did not want to take part in any act by which she would become one flesh with a man, as she had read in the Bible. Say what you liked, it was a kind of mixing of intestines, a kind of more or less painless massacre. It was like the air-raids all over again and the prison-camps.

But for this she must be ready. She must prepare herself for it if she was to go to Petrov, as she had made up her mind to do. Oh, she would do the thing properly; she would keep her side of the transaction without reckoning. She must not let him see what it cost her. Therefore she must get over her fear and disgust, she must accustom herself to this bloodless massacre.

Quickly—quickly and simply—she made her plans. She would prepare herself for the sacrifice; she would come to the sacrifice as a fitting and pleasing victim. And for her preparation she would go to Descoux. She would use Descoux to accustom her body to the ordeal.

She knew that the little Martinique had finally promised Descoux to accompany him for a week-end to Switzerland. Lately she had drifted in to a kind of intimacy with the girl and she had confided in Lisette. Descoux had the papers of his wife, including a *laissez-passer* to cross the frontier into Switzerland. He was going to take her with him on this pass. There was a photo of his wife, taken when she had been no more than twenty-two or -three, and with a slight re-arrangement of her hair the little Martinique could pass as this age. Especially as Descoux had said there was no very careful scrutiny.

If the dark little lizard of a girl could pass, so could she, Lisette. She was only a few months younger, and she was not dark-skinned. She knew very well, with her sly, instinctive knowledge, that Descoux would sooner take her than Paula.

Bad it would be, but it was demanded of her. Her "angel," as she thought of it, demanded it of her—her "angel" that had brought her through the wilderness of her childhood, as Dominic's angel had led him out of his blindness into a new life. She must come to Petrov a fitting and acceptable victim; she must deal with him to the height of her honour.

To-morrow she would speak to Descoux. Having made her plan, she felt a weight taken from her heart. Now she felt a strange freedom. She was, as it were, now worthy of the kiss Halka had given her on the balcony—the kiss, not of a mother, a protector, but of an equal, of a free spirit for a sister spirit, sealing the bond of a free fraternity.

Having come this far, she began to think of an excuse to leave the room and have a peep into Aunty's kitchen to see whether it was not possible to take one or two of the many tins that the parcel had contained and which no doubt Frau Arnheim had stored away in her cupboard. But as they took their leave, Frau Arnheim stuffed a couple of tins into Halka's handbag and Lisette was glad that she had been too busy with her "plans" to make a raid of the kitchen.

The spring flowed from heaven and anointed the earth, and Dominic and Halka went out together into the mild days and the first fragrant evenings. They discovered an old cemetery not far from where Frau Arnheim lived. Here there were long, neglected alleys flanked by huge sycamores and there was a wilderness of shrubs and bushes among which the grey, slanting tombstones leant, half hidden. An old chapel that had stood at the junction of the two main alleys had been hit by a bomb and largely demolished, so that nothing remained whole or upright except the strong, pale columns of the trees.

There were many birds there, a continual rustle in the bushes and in the thick ivy on the tombstones and walls. The song of birds was again filling the world and they heard it as they strolled and talked as a new sound in the background of their words. As the days got warmer, they could even sit on one of the crumbling wooden benches. Dominic hardly knew why he liked it there so much.

"Perhaps because it is a little like the evenings on the lake with Uncle Egan," he said. "How far one must go until one can come back to almost the same place, but bringing something added that one hadn't before," he went on.

"You have such great faith. You believe. But I'm never sure. We come back to the same place, in our lives, as you say, but aren't we always poorer and poorer? You only see what is added, Dominic, and you close your eyes to what has been taken away."

"It may seem so," he said. "It may seem to us that we always get poorer in one sense and lose more and more. We lose everything; we go down into a kind of death as must have happened to you that night when Descoux met you by the river. But afterwards, if we survive, there is a resurrection. Then we live in a new way; we are 'risen.' That is the miracle."

"I only believe in one miracle—the miracle of pain," she said. "Because it *is* a miracle that the heart can bear what it is given to bear. And when it can't bear it any more, it is a miracle, too, to have a way to escape. That was what I was thinking of that evening when Descoux spoke to me. I was dreaming of a state in which I would feel no more fear or pain or humiliation. All would be lifted from me. And I didn't think much more than that. It was such a miraculous thought that I hardly bothered to look beyond it. I was really happy at that moment. I was going into darkness that was without pain and humiliation, without men, and there would be no returning, nothing."

"You didn't believe in the resurrection?"

She shook her head. "There is no resurrection. In the whole world, there is only pain, there are only victims and executioners, and if you don't fall into the hands of one lot of executioners you will fall into those of another. It's all the same. It's not even necessary to fall into the hands of men. There's disease and accidents, famine and cold. That is the great reality. And in between there are all the make-believes, the kissing and coupling and gorging and cinema-going. And that is all. Look where you like, go down into the depths, into the dungeons and the asylums, or soar up to the heights of idyllic love (because I have been there, too;

when I was as old as Lisette, I had six months of such a love),
go where you like, you won't see any sign of a resurrection.
You'll see the sign of the Cross, the sign of the Crucifixion
as you have taught me to see it. And that is already something,
that is a great wonder. But more you won't see, because there
isn't more."

Never had he heard her speak so much, pouring out her
heart, pouring out all her doubt and unfaith, all her despair.
Because he knew it was a despair for her that she could not
believe in a great, universal equity in which those who
wept would laugh and the hungry would be filled with good
things. For others it might be a matter of indifference. They
might console themselves with believing in the possibility
of an earthly equity. But for her there was no such escape.

"How sound they sleep here under their tombstones," she
went on, "and don't torment each other any more. For among
them there are no more executioners, and no more fear or
dreams. Only we living, we lost little band, wander about
over the face of the earth full of hatred and fear, and a few
try to have what you call 'faith.' But only the fear is true,
and hatred and faith are dreams. Dreams of horror or happy
dreams. Ah, how small we are, this little band of the living!
When one sits here and thinks of all the hosts and hosts of
the dead! Then we who happen to be alive are so few, and
we should at least be able to love each other and comfort
each other before we are separated for ever. But we don't.
Only here and there, by a miracle, does someone discover
what it is to have fraternity with some other being. As we
have it, as you have given it to me."

"All the noise we make, all the shouting and the weeping,
how little it is in the face of their great silence," he said.

"If they could hear, how vain it would all seem to them,
the cries of children and the chatter of old women! I don't
think they would envy even the couples who come here," she
went on. "Nothing would they envy, and nothing of all this
could touch them down there in their darkness but fraternity.
Ah, Dominic, if they had ears to hear, wouldn't they at last
be moved when they overheard me say to you out of the
depths of my fear: 'My comrade, my brother!' Aren't those

the only words that are not meaningless on the brink of the grave?"

She laid her hand on his knee and bowed her head. The pillars of the trees stood up in the silence that the songs of the birds could not break. A blackbird perched on the top of a hollytree and sang, but the stillness in the long alleys between the sycamores was not stirred.

"Don't fear, Halka. No, they are not meaningless, those words. Have faith in them. Don't you feel already that the wounds are beginning to heal?"

She nodded. The blackbird was singing. The air was mild—mild with a softness that touched her heart.

CHAPTER IX

LOVE ONE ANOTHER

Dominic received a long letter from his Uncle Egan. It was full of the spring in Ireland. Although Uncle Egan wrote the simplest sentences without any trace of trying to be poetic, the letter breathed the breath of the sea air bright above the sand-hills on the spring mornings and the evening air, dim and hushed, over the lake. He wrote of playing golf and of fishing.

His Uncle Egan had gone on living that life that Dominic had once lived, too, and now could hardly imagine any more. Through all the years of the cataclysm that for those in the midst of it had seemed to draw down the whole world into the abyss, Uncle Egan had gone on sleeping in his big bed that was like a ship anchored, with its green sail of a coverlet, in the placid pool of the big room. He had taken his bath and come down to the breakfast of porridge and eggs cooked by his housekeeper. When for Dominic and Halka and all the others the noonday had been dark with smoke clouds and the nights bright with fire, a pillar of cloud by day and a pillar of fire by night, Uncle Egan had strolled over the sand-hills with his golf-clubs, slept in his quiet bed, gone fishing on the lake.

When there had been here a little soup poured out of buckets into tin mugs, pushed in through the holes in prison doors, or a slice of dry bread eaten in the corner of some half-demolished, icy station, or when there had been nothing at all, when fear and waiting had been their daily bread, there had been the dark mahogany table laid as usual in the big, secluded dining-room.

Dominic read Halka the letter. Halfway through, she stopped him.

"That reminds me of a dream I had last night, of how we came to the gates of peace. I tried to see through them, but I could not."

When he had finished reading the letter, he said: "We could go there if we were to get married. Then I could take you with me."

"Oh no, no," she said. "The gates of peace will never open for me. Besides, I can get on on this side of them. It is far more Lisette."

"Lisette? But won't she go and live with Petrov?"

"He can't save her. He has only a cold little attic, too, and not much more to eat than we have," Halka said.

The gates of peace. The peculiar expression that she had used stuck in his mind. Where were they? In Ireland? In the realisation of the ideas of Captain Renier? Or here where they were, here in this room?

"But it is you I would like to marry," he said.

"Marriage?" she repeated. "But marriage is merely an arrangement, a registration like all the other forms of registration. And it is better that we are not registered in the same name yet."

"Why not yet?" he asked.

"That I can only tell you later," she said. "There is something that I still have to think over. But you remember that day in the old graveyard; that was more than a registration, that was the recognition of our fraternity. And one day I will ask from you a great gift in the name of this fraternity of ours."

108

He was silent. He half knew what it was that she would ask. And he still had not the strength to accede. But the time was not come; she too perhaps felt this, knew that all must ripen, that they must come even closer in their communion, and then it would be given.

It was another beautiful day of spring. They were on Frau Arnheim's balcony, where they sometimes came to sit in the early sun of spring and revel in the first breath of the coming warmth. He took her hand: "We will not worry now. One day, but not yet," he said.

From the balcony there was a view over the gardens of the other villas on the outskirts of the town. It was beautiful there in the evenings of early summer, and Dominic liked to sit there with her and watch the flight of the birds. Out there in the mild, deep pool of air beyond the balcony, the swallows circled, sweeping, darting through the heaven above the trees. Then there were other birds, whose names he did not know, with their different flight, another wing-beat; smaller birds, undulating, dipping and rising, weaving the air to their own pattern. And below the bird heaven was the heaven of the trees, another realm in which space had another substance, mixed with the green, luminous tissue of the leaf masses. Here there was another flow of time, almost beyond his power to observe, the long, still flow of the time of trees.

"Here on this balcony is one dimension of time," he thought, "and out there another, or many others. And in the dungeon there was another and in Ireland again a different one. And the dead," he thought, remembering their conversation in the graveyard, "pass into their own time dimensions."

But that she did not believe in, she had no faith in this yet. She had felt only the time of the dungeons, the stagnant, unbearable weight of the time of the captives and the time of the asylums.

That evening, when they got back to their room, there was a scribbled note from Lisette on the table, telling Halka that she had gone away for a few days and was taking with her Dominic's leather suitcase.

"She has gone to Petrov," Dominic said.

"But then why take the suitcase?" said Halka. "She

doesn't need a suitcase to spend a week-end with Petrov in his room."

"They have probably gone into the mountains."

"Even so, there was no need of a suitcase. And besides, if it was Petrov that she was going to, she would have told me. She knew that I was quite ready for her to go to him."

"With whom else would she go?" Dominic asked.

"With Descoux."

"Why with Descoux? He would only take her for the one reason, and Lisette has a horror of that."

"I don't know. Even I hardly know her."

"But she wouldn't just go with him out of viciousness."

"Viciousness? What is that? It is easy to give names to everything, but that has not much to do with understanding them."

Dominic was silent. He was ashamed of his words. He who should always be so gentle in all ways to her, so far from being a judge, of her and hers.

"It must have been because of you that she went off like that, without saying anything," Halka said.

"But would you have let her go with Descoux?" Dominic asked her.

"Of course. I am not her keeper. To be a keeper is the beginning of the whole horror. Haven't we had enough of keepers?"

Dominic was silent. Although her words startled him, he would not argue with her. That was never the way with her. Besides, he could not really judge whether she might not be right.

"If she had gone to Basel, I could have given her some Swiss francs that I still have from Descoux," Halka went on. She was lying on her bed. He was conscious of her body, of the small fountains of her breasts and of the deep well of her belly under the veil of her summer dress.

But he dare not touch her; he must not lay hands on her. He must leave her alone to recover from all the violence that had been done to her. He went and sat on his couch and pretended to read. He heard her undressing and getting into bed.

"Whoever shall offend one of these little ones . . ." And he knew that these were the words of life to which he must bow. She was in truth "one of these little ones." To the world, that was foolishness, but this room was not the world. He had taken her from the world.

"What are you reading?" she asked him.

He told her. He was reading one of the few English books that he had managed to save through air-raids and flights, and which he had already read several times.

"Do I interrupt you by talking?" she asked him.

"No. Not if you want to."

"I want to ask you something. It is what we were speaking of this afternoon. I thought I wouldn't have to ask you yet, because it is a very great gift, and I wanted to wait until we had had more time together."

"Ask me and I will give it to you," he said. He had suddenly the strength, though he did not know where it came from.

"Will you marry Lisette and take her to Ireland? If she stays on here in these conditions much longer, it is all up with her. She coughs and gets thinner and thinner."

"She doesn't love me," said Dominic. "She loves only you. I don't know if she would marry me."

"Ah, why talk about love? And, anyhow, it is you she believes in. You are what I used to be for her."

"You don't know what you ask, Halka. Even for the sake of our fraternity. Let me think now, and I will answer you in the morning."

"It would have been better if I had asked you before. It would have been easier for you, too, before she had gone off like this with Descoux. But I had not the courage then."

"That makes no difference," Dominic said. "None at all. And what do you mean by courage?"

Halka said nothing.

"What do you mean by courage?" he asked her again.

"My love was not perfect enough to ask all for her and nothing for myself," said Halka.

"Listen, Halka! I cannot answer you now. I must think. I will tell you in the morning."

"Leave it. I see, too, that it is too late. It is my fault that I didn't speak to you before this happened."

"That would have made no difference to me," Dominic repeated. "As I do not love her, it is indifferent to me whether I marry her as a virgin or after she comes back from Descoux. Don't you see that has nothing to do with it? If I marry her, it is not for her sake, but for yours. But let us leave it now, little witch. I must have time to think in my own way. In the morning I will tell you."

Dominic turned out the light and lay on his couch. At first he felt only anger against Halka. What right had she to ask him this? He felt a hatred of her because of the enormity of her request. At the same time, the desire for her never left him a moment. If she could make such an unheard of demand on him, what was it if he went over to her and took her? That would be as nothing compared to what she was ready to ask of him. Yet this "nothing" was what he wanted above all things. If he could have her now let all else go, let all go to pieces in a world that was crumbling in its own rottenness.

If she had asked of him a very great gift, it was because in the strange simplicity of her heart it was thus she understood the union between them that she had found no words to distinguish but the hackneyed ones of "brother," of "comrade." It was only that in her great innocence she had taken him at his word, when he had spoken of their "fraternity." He knew very well that she, in her turn, would shrink from nothing that he might ask her. If he was to ask her to go back down to the river and throw herself into it and could convince her that he would in some way be helped by her doing so, she would do it without a word and without reproach. Even more, for his sake, she would, if he asked her, solely because he asked her, feign madness and submit herself to being taken back to the asylum and to what was for her the horror of all horrors—the electro-shock. He might have liked to hide these things from himself, but he could not. He had spoken the fatal word "fraternity," and she had accepted it without measure, as she did everything.

When he heard by her breathing that she slept, he got up and went over and stood by her bed. In sleep she seemed

112

so withdrawn from him; even her body was withdrawn. He wondered through what gates of peace she was passing in her dreams, these dreams that she told him had replaced her nightmares since he had been with her. And he did not dare to wake her, to bring her back into the night with its fears and passions. She lay with her pale face exposed to him, in the trance of sleep. Her lips were slightly parted. He stood beside her tense with the struggle that went on in him. Then he returned to his couch.

In the morning she went out as usual for their small ration of skimmed milk and to buy bread. In the queue at the bakers she saw the little Martinique girl and went up to her and asked her if she knew anything about where Descoux was.

The olive-skinned, slatternly girl looked at her with a sly timidity.

"Oh yes. I know where he is. I know very well."

"Where?" Halka asked.

The girl looked at the fresh loaf of yellow bread in Halka's shopping net.

"What will you give me if I tell you? I know where he is and where your sister is, too."

"What do you want? Some bread?"

The girl nodded quickly; her black eyes never met Halka's. They were always looking somewhere else with an intent stare. Halka broke the loaf and gave one half to the girl.

"Monsieur Descoux wanted to take me at first, like he did the other time. But your sister came and said she would go with him, so this time he took her instead because she was new and it was more fun with her. I did not like it, because he had promised me and we had a little disagreement, your sister and I, and she slapped me."

"Where are they gone? To Basel?" Halka asked.

"Yes. And I bet he has taken her to the Hôtel Helvetia, where he took me. Do you know the Hôtel Helvetia in Basel, miss?" The girl had begun to munch the dry bread. Halka shook her head.

"How will he get her across the frontier?" she asked.

"On his wife's papers, of course. The same as with me.

There is a photo of his wife on her pass taken years ago and, anyhow, they don't look so closely at it, you know. When I went, I wore a dress of Madame Descoux' that she had left here and did my hair in the French way with a bow so that I could have easily passed for twenty."

"How old are you?" Halka asked.

"You should see the Helvetia Hôtel in Basel," she went on, without answering Halka's question, beginning to get over her initial timidity. "It is so big and there is not a pane of glass out of any of the windows, not as much as a tiny crack in any of the walls. Every day they put clean towels in our room—imagine that, miss. And the grub we had! I couldn't tell you all that we got through. Monsieur Descoux didn't eat so much, but what I ate you wouldn't believe."

"Oh yes, I would. I know what *I'd* eat if I was taken to your Hôtel Helvetia," Halka said. She felt a sympathy for this child whom Lisette had slapped.

At their meagre breakfast, Halka told Dominic about her meeting with the little Martinique.

"What was wrong of Lisette was to slap her," she said.

"That worries you more than her going off with Descoux," Dominic said.

"Yes. Because that is the sin of violence and I know where that leads. But about the other thing, what is there to worry? Only perhaps that for you it would have been easier to make the sacrifice that I ask of you, if Lisette had not gone off. Because in this way you are still very conventional."

"I will try to be meek and humble," Dominic said with a certain annoyance. "You are right. To marry Lisette, even if I don't love her, is in one sense a great good for me. In one sense, and perhaps the true sense, it is a happiness I don't deserve." He spoke without irony. His aversion was suddenly gone. "To be alive at all, in the midst of so much death, to be healthy and to be free, and then to be asked to take a young and good girl into my care, to marry her, that is not something to complain of. I know that, little witch. What right have I to demand more, or something different? And I won't do so, Halka; on the contrary, I will hurry to accomplish what you ask of me. Now that we know where she is, I will go after her. I will go first to Captain Renier and ask for a *laissez-passer*, and if I get that, and they have not returned, I will go to Basel and bring Lisette back with me."

"How strangely you speak! As if you were rushing to your bride! Ah, you don't know how you touch me!"

"And shall I never touch you in the other way, physically?" he wondered.

He took her hands and clasped them. He would not say more. All the love in his heart for her, fraternal and unfraternal, must not be poured out now. He must not lay hands on her. All must be expended and expressed, not in the body, but in doing what he had to do for her.

This impulse that was so strange and new to him, grew strong in him so that he could do all without reluctance, even with a kind of new joy that he hardly recognised as joy. It was something totally unexpected and unknown, this compassionate love, this passion. When he had first spoken to her of it, he had only half believed in it. But now he was overcome by it, as in the past he had been carried away by the other passion with its demands and its self-seeking.

He went to the Nietzschestrasse, to the office of Captain Renier. It was an ordeal to walk up the path to the door of the villa past the cellar window with its iron bars. And inside the villa, he had to wait in the empty kitchen while the policeman took up his name.

"So you have actually ventured into the lion's den?" said Captain Renier when Dominic entered his office.

Dominic explained the reason of his visit. He said nothing about Lisette, but asked for a *laissez-passer* for Basel in order to make some purchases with the few thousand francs that he happened to have. Captain Renier made no difficulty about recommending him for the necessary papers, which he would have to call for the following day at the office where they were given out. Meanwhile, Dominic would have to get a Swiss *visa* at the Swiss Consulate.

In spite of the helpfulness of the other, Dominic foresaw a certain amount of the hateful running around, of going from office to office before he would have all in order for the journey. But he felt no reluctance. There was even a peculiar sweetness in the thought of the trudging round and of the long waits for Halka's sake. And gradually the journey and its object was no longer repugnant to him.

"I thought when you began to speak of a *laissez-passer* you were going to ask for one in order to return home to your own country," Captain Renier said.

"Not yet, Captain. I don't want to go back yet."

"No? In spite of the fact that there you would certainly have everything that you haven't got here? Can this trip to Basel really content you, when you know that you could get right out?"

"If he only knew the real object of this trip to Basel," Dominic thought. And at the same time he had the feeling that he did know, that he knew everything. Captain Renier looked at him out of his small blue eyes and knew everything about him, he felt, down to the last detail.

"Though, as a matter of fact, when you have the *laissez-passer* there is nothing to stop you going right through to Paris and taking a plane to Ireland," Captain Renier went on, "if you should change your mind."

"Yes. But I won't change my mind."

"I don't want to appear to be meddling in your private life," said the Captain, "but since that time of your interrogation I have felt an interest in your case. I sometimes wonder, Monsieur Malone, what you find in the two girls with whom you share a room. You would find so many better women in your own country."

"I wouldn't find anyone there who needed me as they do," said Dominic.

"Yes. They are the victims of the last war. I might even ſ one of the victims of our society. And, of course, there is a great attraction in playing the part of saviour to these lost sheep. But whether it is possible to do much for them, I don't know. You will forgive me for speaking to you frankly, but that is my method, learnt, no doubt, from my work. When there is something really vital to discuss, then I believe in complete straightforwardness. Mostly, of course, there is

116

nothing vital to say and then one can allow oneself the luxury of civil phrases."

"To me you can certainly say what you like, Captain. I will listen to you without offence, but I don't suppose I shall agree with you."

"Agreement or disagreement is unimportant, as long as we understand each other. And I believe that I do understand you, at least up to a point. I know very well what an attraction for someone like you one of these lost sheep in the shape of a woman may have. You will dream of bringing her back to a life of happiness and normality. But it is very hard to succeed. I know what I'm talking about. So many of these people pass through my hands, young men and women of various nationalities, all these riff-raff that are hanging around Central Europe, homeless and mostly workless, the girls living on men, drifting from one to the other, and the men living on various 'dealings,' on various forms of Black-Marketeering."

"And you want to warn me that Halka Mayersky is one of these?" Dominic asked.

"Her record points to it. But one of the most unfortunate, that is certain. One who has suffered more than most," said Captain Renier. "But if you are determined to remain here with us, well and good. In that case I suggest that while you are in Basel, you call on a very old friend of mine and one of the leading spirits in the movement of which I spoke to you that evening at my flat."

"An anarchist?"

"Yes." Captain Renier wrote out a name and address on a slip of paper. "Because if you are determined to remain here you will find your only refuge in such a doctrine as ours, the only doctrine that is based on true brotherhood."

"But brotherhood cannot be a doctrine," said Dominic. "Brotherhood must be a passion, must be something born in the heart."

"Go and see Papa Varreau, as we call him. It is a great opportunity. You will meet one of the few men living who is capable of saving Europe. After you have seen him much will be clear to you."

"I will go and see him," Dominic said. "If only out of curiosity. I am curious to see someone whom you say could save Europe. There have been so many who thought they could save the world and who would not have known how to save one fellow creature."

"And come and see me when you get back; if you do get back, that is. If you don't decide to take that plane in Paris," said Captain Renier.

"You must have a good idea of how people are likely to behave, Captain," said Dominic. "You must know whether I shall come back or not."

The Captain's small blue eyes twinkled. "You will come back. And come and see me when you do. Not here; at my flat in the evening."

In the afternoon Dominic took Halka to the old graveyard. He loved the still, greenish light in the long, overgrown alleys of sycamores with their smooth, peeling barks and the grey, half-hidden tombstones along the edges of the wild lawns. Never was she so close to him as here and never had she been so close as on this evening. "Whoever seeks to save his life shall lose it and whoever is ready to lose it shall save it." And life was all that was precious. Now when he was prepared to lose her their union was growing and blossoming.

"Does this remind you of your graveyard at home near the lake? Is that why you like it so much?" she asked him.

"A little, perhaps."

"And had you a woman with whom you used to walk there too? You have told me so much of the lake and the sand-hills and of your Uncle Egan, but nothing about the women you knew then. Wasn't there one whom you took on the lake and strolled with among the tombstones?"

"No. Not one. They would have been very bored, and so would I then. We had no time for strolling or for rowing on the lake. We were always going somewhere or doing something. It was only with Uncle Egan that I sometimes could savour the gentle flow of those days in quiet. Or when I was alone. But even then I always had to take a golf-club with me or a fishing-rod; there had always to be the pretence of doing something, of playing some game."

They sat on a bench by the ruined chapel at the meeting of the four main alleys.

"And if I had taken a woman for a walk down by the lake I would have had to flirt with her. If I hadn't she would have been bored and disappointed and I too; I would have felt that I was missing something, not enjoying life to its full. So I would have kissed her and would have persuaded myself that that was exciting and 'an adventure.' But all the time the little watchful beast within me would not have been taken in. It would have watched unmoved."

"What little beast is that?" she asked with a smile at his words.

"I don't know what it is. The heart, the spirit perhaps, witch."

"Look. There is our blackbird," she said.

On the topmost stone of the ruined chapel a blackbird perched and sang, like a small black tongue of flame that had descended out of heaven.

"Let us come here often," she went on. "Let us come and stroll and sit here often in the evenings, you and I, before you go."

"Even when I am married to Lisette?" he asked.

Halka was silent. He knew he should not have said that.

"The three of us will come," he added.

"Yes."

She was looking up at the blackbird. It was the first time he had ever seen tears in her eyes.

CHAPTER X

EXCURSION TO BASEL

Halka wanted to make him a little packet for the journey with the last of her bread and a scrap of cheese that she had got hold of from he did not know where. But he pointed out that once over the frontier he could buy quantities of food. He was not himself quite clear what was unrationed in Switzerland, but he had heard enough to feel confident that once let loose in Basel with plenty of francs he would not be long before he had managed to have a good meal.

The journey was far pleasanter than he had expected. He was not conscious of any of the depression that he had foreseen. But that was how it always was. What he looked forward to, sometimes for days before, usually was disappointing and flat, and what he expected with misgiving often turned out to have hidden in its very shadow a little blossom.

The train was crowded as usual. The carriage was full of Germans with their inevitable rucksacks travelling to intermediate stations. To Dominic Germans were still largely a mystery, although he had lived for years among them. They lacked any art of living. Not only now after their defeat, but they had always lacked it. They moved through life heavily, carefully, with the inexhaustible patience of beasts of burden plodding over stony paths. And this carefulness, with all the saving and scraping that it involved, was unpleasant to him. The heavy deliberation of their souls weighed on him when he came close to them. And yet there they were with a strange power in them that he couldn't deny. The women especially had a power in them. The men were like little internal-combustion machines, grinding away, grinding away, and if you didn't look out, Dominic felt, you would be caught by them and ground out too.

It was a warm May morning. At home, he thought, Uncle Egan may well be starting off with his packet of ham sandwiches and flask of whisky for a morning's fishing on the lake. All would be done with a certain ceremony. Hand, the gravedigger, would have the rods and the flies. There would be a drink together at the hotel bar on the way, there would be a delay by the shore of the lake while the "condition" of the water was studied and the direction of the breeze.

Suddenly Dominic saw that between himself starting out on his singular mission to Basel and his Uncle Egan preparing for a morning on the lake there was an unexpected similarity. Because it was not what was done that betrayed the *penchant* of soul, but the inner gesture that accompanied it. Uncle Egan made out of fishing an act full of a kind of tenderness and peace. And Dominic saw that that was a great art. He himself had never achieved it. He had never in those days been able to fill any of his actions with that serenity, with that peculiar air of doing something that added to peace on earth. But now, taking this journey, he felt, for almost the first time in his life, how Uncle Egan must have felt on almost every fine morning. He saw that the question was not what he did or did not do, not "Thou shalt" or "Thou shalt not," but that what was done should be done in peace and serenity and what was left undone should be left in the same way.

"If I could sit in this train and go on to Paris with the ease and serenity of soul that I have now, then I would be right to go," he reflected. "But as I know I should lose it if I did, then there can be no good in my going."

That was very simple. Like all the important truths that he had managed to grasp, it was completely simple and admitted of no arguments.

At Basel, he walked out into the station square with a sense of at last stepping into the outside world. He seemed to feel the difference in the very air, in the way the people walked along the street, in the aspect of the houses. Behind these windows women were cooking food that was at least real food, men were reading the papers at tables from which the breakfast things had been cleared away, reading the sport news, the murders. There was a touch of the prodigality of life in the very air, of town life in its manifold vulgarities and luxuries, while in the town he had come from the air was empty and the very windows seemed to shine sombrely in the walls of the houses.

There were several hotels on the other side of the square. None were very imposing by his former standards, but now to see hotels, undamaged and open, inviting one to enter, was a shock. On the largest of them, at the door of which stood a porter in uniform, he read the name: Hôtel Helvetia.

He did not enter it immediately. He had not expected to find it so soon and he wanted a little time to think what he would say in explanation of his appearance. Although he was only going on the guess of the little Martinique, he felt certain that he would find Lisette and Descoux there. He walked slowly down the street, looking at the shops, at the passers-by, sensing the newness of this world, of this teeming life. For life teemed here as he had forgotten it teemed whenever it got the least chance. He was used to living in a place where the bounds were too narrow, where the movement of living was still cramped and deadened.

By the time he had reached the hotel again, he had not thought of what he would say. But he turned in through the revolving doors without further hesitation. He had no fear of doing the wrong thing or of not finding the right words. He felt like the blackbird they had watched a couple of evenings before perched on the top of the ruin; he had only to open his mouth and the song he had to sing would come out of it. He went up to the reception desk and asked for Monsieur Descoux. The clerk looked at the numbered board at the back of the desk on which the room-keys hung and told Dominic that Monsieur and Madame Descoux were still in their room.

Dominic went up in the lift and stepped out on to a carpeted corridor along which a waiter was carrying a breakfast tray. It was as if he was seeing such things for the first time, so strangely they struck him. He found the door he was seeking and knocked on it. He heard Descoux' voice in answer and went in.

Descoux was sitting in his uniform at a table in the centre of the room with the parts of a Meccano set spread in front of him. Lisette, in a brand new pink morning gown, was pouring water from an electric kettle into a coffee pot. The room smelt of coffee and eau-de-Cologne.

Descoux smiled at Dominic with his engaging nonchalance, but his swarthy face went a tinge darker and his black eyes shifted quickly away. Lisette looked up at Dominic, defensive and secretive, with the kettle in one hand.

"Why have you come? Did Halka send you?" she asked.

"No. I came on my own. Halka sent her devoted love. She told me specially to say to you, 'her devoted love.' "

He shook hands with Descoux. Lisette said nothing. She went on pouring the water into the coffee pot, her small face secret and brilliant as he had never seen it. He did not know

122

what he had expected of her, but not this. He had been prepared to see her disillusioned and ashamed or even exhausted, with shadows under her eyes, or perhaps even defiant, brazen. But not to find her secret, brilliant and with a strange dignity. That was something extraordinary and, as it seemed to him, out of place, so that in the first few minutes, as he talked with Descoux, he kept watching her to see if his first impression had not been a false one. But no, there she was in her new morning gown, making the coffee, doing all with a kind of gentle coolness, with really a new little dignity of movement that shocked him because it did not fit in with his ideas.

In the train he had thought of his Uncle Egan and had discovered that in the way he lived, in the manner of his doing things, was it only going fishing, lay the secret of his wisdom. And further he had seen that in starting on this journey he himself, almost for the first time, had managed to do something not to the strident time-rhythm of the world, but to a tender and serene movement of his heart. This was so far well and good. He had been ready to admit that it was possible to go fishing "for the glory of God," as the prayers of his childhood put it; and this journey of his too was "for the glory of God"; but that at the end of it he should be faced with a Lisette who also in her own way had this air of adding to the glory of God and the peace of the world by her escapade was a shock. Though he should have known by now that the "glory of God" was added to in mysterious, unexpected ways and not by the efforts of the professional doers-of-good.

Descoux soon regained his air of insouciance. *L'oiseau sauvage* that for a moment had feared being caught in some sort of trap, as Lisette put it later, became quickly himself again when he saw that Dominic had not come to make a lot of fuss and trouble. He turned back to his Meccano and left Dominic and Lisette to talk together in English and drink the coffee that she had made. He himself refused a cup.

"*Ah, non.* I've had enough. We've drunk several cups of coffee already this morning," he explained to Dominic.

"I drink it all day," said Lisette, "with plenty of sugar."

"And what else do you do?"

"I eat. I eat quantities of meat and cakes and conserves, of all the things we never get. But why did you come here?" she asked him.

"Why did *you* come? Isn't that the first question?" he answered.

"I came to prepare myself for Petrov. So that I could go to him as an acceptable sacrifice."

"Where did you hear that expression?" he asked.

"Oh, I found it in the English Missal you gave me. I wanted to be pleasing to him and to get over my fear of sex."

"And have you got over it?" He was astonished, but he immediately accepted what she said. He saw that it was true.

"I'm getting used to it. At first it was a little massacre. It was like Halka's electro-shock. And I was never safe from it. It could happen at any odd moment, in the middle of the day or the middle of the night. But I stuck it out. I drank plenty of strong coffee and I said to myself: 'It doesn't last longer than the air-raids used to and it's not dangerous. And when you get it over, you will be a pleasing companion for Petrov.' "

"Do you love Petrov?"

"Oh no."

"Then why make such a sacrifice for him?"

"Because I am going to him. I must go to someone sooner or later. I can't stay always with you and Halka. And whoever I go to, I must do my best for," she said.

She was sitting in a deep chair on one side of a small table, with Dominic on the other. Her small face was pale, but it was a brilliant pallor as though within her was burning a hidden lamp.

"And now why did *you* come?" she asked.

"I came to visit an anarchist, a friend of Captain Renier's."

She looked at him with a small, puzzled frown.

"No. That isn't true," he said. "I came to see you."

"To see me? But you see me always, all the days, and the weeks."

"I came to ask you to marry me."

"To marry you?" she repeated. "But not on your own.

Was it your angel that put that into your head, the angel that appeared to you on the lake and sent you to Germany?"

"Perhaps."

"That is a peculiar angel of yours, eh?"

"Peculiar or not, I must follow it."

"Yes. But why don't you marry Halka?"

"She won't marry me," he said.

"Do you think your angel really wants me to be your bride?"

"Not only my bride, but my wife."

"Let me first be your bride—that is as much as I can bear—and then we shall see," she said.

"As much as you can bear of what?"

"I don't know. Of everything together. Of joy and of hope and of fear."

He leant across the table and took her thin hand and kissed it. "We won't kiss each other," he said. "You've had enough of that."

A little later the three of them went out into the town together, first to a shop where Descoux bought all the Paris papers, then to a little restaurant for lunch which Descoux had discovered on one of his previous visits and where Lisette was already known for her appetite.

To be sitting here at the small white-clothed table in the heart of the fabulous town which he had first glimpsed that morning from the train like a miracle on the fringe of desolation dilated his heart, his being, with a fleeting pleasure. The three of them chattered together, and Descoux did the ordering in his careless way, seeming to agree to all the suggestions of the waiter, saying "*Ah, oui*" and "*Bien sûr*," but always, when it came to it, getting his own way. And Dominic was ready to make the best of being here with them, with Lisette and even with Descoux. It did not matter to him what their relationship was or would be. He said to Descoux easily and without embarrassment:

"Do you know what? Lisette and I are going to get married."

Even Descoux' nonchalance was for a moment in danger of vanishing.

"Married?" he repeated, looking up from his *crème de*

something-or-other soup. "*Ah, oui?*" however, he added in his customary tone of finding everything quite *comme il faut*, natural. "Then accept my very best felicitations."

The three of them raised their glasses filled with the wine that Descoux had actually carefully selected without seeming to.

"When was it agreed on? Just now in my room?" Descoux asked. Dominic noticed that he now said "my" room, not "our" room, with his quick, easy way of adjusting himself to every situation.

"Yes. Just now," Dominic said. "While you were absorbed in your Meccano."

"I bought it for my kids, *pour mes gosses*," said Descoux. "They will be coming to me for the summer holidays."

"And your wife too?" asked Lisette.

"Oh, yes. Lucille will come with them."

"How easy-going she must be to let you have her papers so that you can take trips with other girls," Lisette said.

"Why should she mind? She has a friend of her own."

After lunch they went to the cinema and saw a French film that had in it something of the easy French insouciance and grace. And Dominic was relieved after the heavy deliberation of most German films that he always felt as an insult to one's very nerves, to the quick subtlety of the nervous receptiveness.

In the darkness of the cinema he took Lisette's hand. He did it simply, without thought. Not because he thought she might expect it. Even though they were going to be married, he knew that she expected nothing. And perhaps just because of that he felt a peculiar desire to be to her as any man would be who was in love with a girl. And although he was not in love with her and although it might be all the same to her, he felt urged by a kind of humility. He would act like all the others, he would be as a young man engaged to her would be, doing all that he would do.

"I am happy, happy," Lisette whispered, close to his ear.

When they emerged again into the sunny, teeming street, Descoux took leave of them. He said he would go to a café and read his papers and then return to the hotel, where he would meet them for dinner.

"And I'll book you a room," he said to Dominic. "Or would you like to go to another hotel with Lisette?"

"Oh no. I like it there."

"*A tout à l'heure.*"

Dominic and Lisette strolled through the busy streets, sometimes going into shops and making a few small purchases just for the pleasure of it. They moved through the glamour of the great world seething around them as two people from the dead might have.

"In a sense, we are from the dead," Dominic said.

"I am from the dead," said Lisette. "But you are from above."

"From above?"

She nodded. "You were sent here by your angel. I would know it even if you hadn't told me it yourself."

"That is not what I meant," he said, laughing.

She laughed too. It did not matter. All was so surprisingly easy after all, so simple, he had no need to contradict or explain.

He stopped a taxi and got into it with her, directing the driver to the address of the friend of Captain Renier's. It had suddenly entered his head to visit this man and to take Lisette with him. In the taxi, in spite of what he had said earlier in the hotel, he kissed her. He felt her tremble, but he did not know whether with fear or happiness.

"If there's enough of Halka's money over when I've paid the hotel, I'll buy you a ring," he said.

"Oh no. I don't need a ring. Better we bring back some food."

"We'll bring back food too, but I don't think we'll be allowed to take much across the frontier."

The taxi stopped at a huge building near the river which seemed to be not yet quite finished. It appeared to be intended as a huge surgical clinic. The hall smelled of plaster and fresh cement, and Dominic was already a little chilled by the place as he went to the porter's cubicle and enquired for Dr. Varreau.

The porter rose and stretched and said: "I don't know whether the Herr Doktor is about or not, I'm sure. Better come with me and you can have a look for yourself."

They followed him down several long, newly plastered corridors. When they came to a staircase, the porter gave them some directions and mentioned a door with certain initials on it that they would find on the third floor. They climbed the stairs. They met no one. The whole building lay vast and empty around them. They stopped at the top of the third flight, uncertain which of several corridors to take. There was complete silence. The long, newly-glazed windows let into the well of the staircase appeared to give out on to an interior court. Lisette leant against one of the smooth white walls, getting her breath after the exertion of the climb.

"My God, how weak you are!" Dominic exclaimed. He suddenly noticed the thinness of her legs and arms as though he saw them for the first time.

"Oh, it's nothing. I'm just out of breath."

"You've starved for too long," he said.

"I've starved all my life. I see that since I've been here. I don't think I ever knew before what eating really was," she said, gradually getting her breath again.

In the end they came to a door beyond which was the sound of voices. Dominic knocked and opened it timidly. There was a group of men and a couple of women sitting around on chairs and tables in the midst of some general discussion. When Dominic enquired for Dr. Varreau an old man got up from a chair around which the others appeared to be roughly grouped and, a way being made for him, came over to Dominic and Lisette. He shook hands with them and, with a word to the group he had left, led them into a corner of the bare room, where they sat down on three of the same hard chairs on which the others were sitting.

"I am glad you have come to me," said the old man, after glancing at the note of introduction that Dominic had brought him from Captain Renier. "I am particularly glad, because you have come from the place where the misery is at its greatest."

Dominic made some reply. He was waiting, not yet sure, a little damped by the cheerlessness of the room, by the vastness of the building and perhaps even by something in the long face of the old man. A strange face always disturbed him. It was something that he had to accept, to get used to. It was so easy to dislike another face, to find in it the signs of avarice, stupidity or vanity. It was so easy to despise other faces in one's heart. Dominic searched the other's features for some sign, but he found none.

"Papa Varreau! Papa Varreau!" cried one of the women, a girl of twenty or so with glasses. "May I interrupt you a moment to settle a very important question in an argument between Gregory and myself?"

The old man looked round and held up his hand, old and blue-veined.

"No, not now, Suzanne," he said. "You must settle it among yourselves. And how do you find it to be in a peaceful country again after so many years? And you, my poor child," he went on to Lisette, "I dare say you can't even remember what it was like to live a normal life?"

Lisette shook her head. She was sitting very straight on her hard chair, close to Dominic, and she wished she could take refuge altogether behind him. She did not like this place; it was far too like many rooms back in Germany. It had none of the glamour of the restaurant, the hotel or the taxi.

"But don't lose courage," the old man continued. "You are young and you will see what many have longed to see and have not seen: the end of governments, of frontiers, of armies and police forces and the proclamation of the brotherhood and unity of man."

Dr. Varreau spoke of movements, of strikes, of signs in the air. He spoke of the things that Captain Renier had spoken of, but with more passion and power. There was real power in this old man, Dominic thought. He understood very well why there were many glances from the other group towards him. Without him, around whom to gather, their discussion, whatever it was, was missing fire.

It was not only that he mentioned with familiarity the names of world figures, not that he told of something that

Lenin had once said to him while he was an exile here in this very town, or that he spoke of an evening with Gandhi. None of this would have impressed Dominic, but rather the reverse, had he not been aware of the working of the same power, like a dark magic, like a spell, that, he thought, must be the secret that these others whom he spoke of had carried within them too. He was not sure wherein the magic power lay, but only that as the old man spoke he forgot the cheerless room, the vast, unfinished building, he forgot even that he was here in the fabulous town of Basel and was absorbed in the vision that the old prophet conjured up. For he was a prophet, as the others were prophets, and as those of old had been prophets.

The power was there and yet it was not enough. Dominic knew while the old man was speaking, weaving his spell, that this power and this vision could not stand against the power of darkness and the vision of chaos. It was all no good, no good. No prophet of a brotherhood of man, no matter what spell he could cast, no organisation, no words, no promises of a new era of peace on earth were any use in the face of the night that had descended. All this was part of the old temptation. To try to establish peace and equity on earth through organising, calculating, planning. And even the anarchist's plan to do away with all organising and all plans was a plan just the same, a plan based on certain calculations, and these calculations would prove in the end inadequate, powerless against the great power of darkness.

"When you speak to us, I recognise the power in your words," said Dominic to the old man, "and I know it is the true power of the prophet. But it will take more than a prophet to save us. There is no good any more in having a plan, even a great and good plan, as I believe yours to be. Because no plan can touch the depths of scepticism and unfaith that the victims have in their hearts."

"How then can they be touched?" asked the old man, looking curiously, a little taken aback by the unaccustomed contradiction.

"Not by any promise, not even by the promise of peace on earth. Only by something that is neither promise nor plan."

"What is that?" asked the other. Strangers came here from many countries and pulled up their chairs around him and let themselves sink into the spell of his power, but this man seemed to believe that he had a power of his own. But Dr. Varreau was not only old; he had a certain ripeness in his years and patience. He listened and waited, albeit a little sceptically.

"Your vision won't be realised by any plan. Not by trying to grasp it, but by losing ourselves for it, when we cast our bread on the waters," said Dominic. "If I love my brother or sister for the sake of ultimate peace and fraternity on earth, then it is really for my own sake and the love is already corrupt in its root. It is the old tale of the Devil offering Christ the kingdoms of the earth. But the peace and fraternity that Christ had to reveal could not be imposed like that, as reforms and revolutions are imposed."

"And what was this marvel that Christ had to reveal? Has Christ helped matters in the end?" asked the old man. "Would things be worse now without Him? Can you honestly say that?"

"Yes. I can and do believe it. Not that the desolation would be worse, that there would be even more ruins, more hunger, more misery on earth, but that there would not be any possibility of understanding these things. And that would be the ultimate horror—if Christ had not suffered these things and foreseen them, then it would be the end. But He was the one prophet who did not promise peace on earth, but destruction and desolation, from the razing of Jerusalem to the end of the world. And He was the one prophet who has been right. And if that had been all, He would still have been a very great prophet. But it was not all, it was only in fact the beginning. He did not preach any revolution or any counter-measures. He said: these things must be, and remember that I have told you. But above all: 'Love one another as I have loved you.' That is, through all these things, even through passion and death. And that is our fraternity, and the only true fraternity."

"Yes, all that is very well, very fine," said the other with his patient smile, "but what would come of this fraternity of yours without hope, without the slightest guarantee of any dawn?"

"I don't know what will come of it," said Dominic. "I don't even care what will come of it, if only I can begin to feel it and to live by it. Then let come what may." He was free of the old man's spell and was in another one more powerful, even if darker, more obscure. He had spoken words out of this other spell in the power of which he had been with Halka these last weeks and especially that evening in the churchyard, and in which he had come here to Basel and asked Lisette to marry him. As he said to Dr. Varreau, he did not know where it would lead him or what might come of it. He could do no more than follow it. The words he had spoken on the spur of the moment had surprised himself, for never before had he come to so nearly formulating what lay behind the impulse that had kept him in Germany and now kept him with Halka. And perhaps he had said too much, more than had yet really taken shape for him and ripened in him. But he did not care. He had spoken as much for the sake of Lisette as for that of the old man, to try to reveal to her what he could not have revealed at any time when they were alone.

When they were out in the street again they walked along by the broad dark flow of the river, gleaming and mysterious in the calm power of its movement through the town.

"Did Christ really prophesy all the ruins and hunger?" Lisette asked him.

"Yes."

"And what was the other thing that he said? That we should love each other?"

"Yes. But not with the old sort of love; with His new compassionate love."

"And what else?" she asked with the curiosity of a child.

"Isn't that enough, Lisette, for the present?"

She wrinkled up her small face: "I suppose so. But I like when you tell of these things; it is almost as good as when you tell of the lake and fishing with Uncle Egan. Couldn't you tell me more to-night? I needn't sleep with Descoux to-night, need I? Anyhow, I think he will have found another girl."

"You will have a room of your own."

"Then you can come when I'm in bed and tell me one of these stories, *nicht*? Like in the old days of Aunty's."

They went to a book-shop and bought a copy of the New Testament in English and he promised to read something from it to her that evening.

CHAPTER XI

INSIDE AND OUTSIDE THE TAVERN

WHEN THEY GOT BACK to the hotel, they found, just as Lisette had foreseen, that Descoux had picked up a girl and was sitting with her waiting for them in the lounge. He had bought some new periodicals—French police magazines— but they lay on the table and he was deep in conversation with his companion. He enjoyed having a woman again with whom he could talk about the one subject that was a continual source of interest and wonder to him. He had hoped to have aroused some interest in Lisette by explaining to her some of the mysteries of "love," but she had remained suspicious and detached. She had only livened up when he had discussed with her the choice of restaurants and the food that they would order.

After he had introduced them to his companion, there was the question of what they should do next. Since the arrival of Dominic, Lisette had begun to look on all these hours as precious; she had got into the holiday spirit which Descoux, in his insouciant way, had had from the start.

"First I'm going up to make some coffee," Lisette announced, "and who likes can come too."

"By the way, I booked you a room; it's number ninety, next to mine," Descoux told Dominic.

Dominic saw that he took it for granted that Lisette would move into it too. He left it at that. It would draw too much attention to them to now take a separate room for her, which, while travelling on the papers of Madame Descoux, it was better to avoid.

Dominic went up with Lisette and she brought her few things, which were no more than a pair of stockings, a towel and a piece of soap, the electric kettle and her tin of coffee, from which nothing would part her. There were two beds in the room and Dominic allotted one to her.

"What a pity that Halka isn't here!" Lisette exclaimed.

Dominic was silent. With Halka here, he knew that he would not have had the strength to go through with his engagement to Lisette.

Here, with the plentiful good food, the wine, the general air of teeming life, it would have been very hard to keep his relationship to Halka on its former plane.

"Halka has never had a life like this, even for a few days," Lisette said.

"What happened to your parents?" Dominic asked. "Were you not with them before the war?"

Halka had never told him anything at all about her early years.

"I hardly remember them. The first thing that I can remember clearly is our time in Lodz, after our mother died. I was seven or eight and Halka fourteen or fifteen. We had a big room, bigger than this one, with two big, bare windows. I remember the windows, they were so big and bare, and the light that came through them does not seem like the same light as now, when I look back. It must have been a very poor place in which we lived, but of course I didn't know that. For me it was a lovely room and one corner was my special delight. In it there was a little shrine with a tiny red lamp burning and a picture of St. Thérèse de Lisieux."

She made the coffee and they each lay on their bed with the small table between and drank the strong coffee with plenty of sugar. The very sound of traffic that came in a low hum from the street seemed a different sound to the noise of the Marheim streets. Here, below their window, flowed a different stream. Outside in the street and here in the room there was ease and security and the air was filled with the scent of the blossom of luxury.

"For me the picture of St. Thérèse was a picture of Halka," Lisette went on. "I don't know how I got it into my head, but when I tended the little red lamp it was out of devotion to Halka, in honour of her really, that I did it. There was a prayer to St. Thérèse written on a card with a lovely wreath of roses painted around the edge, and one of the sentences in it went: 'O little saint who has suffered so much, I offer you my heart and all my devoted love.' I often said those words, but I always meant them for Halka as well. That's why she gave you that message for me: 'Give her my devoted love.' She wanted to remind me of those days that we have never spoken of since. I never dared to speak to Halka of what I remember of that time. I often think of it, but I never speak of it."

"Why did she want to remind you of it specially now?" Dominic asked.

"That's what I'm going to tell you," said Lisette. She lay in her old dress and her new silk stockings, that Descoux had bought her, on the silk coverlet and sipped the coffee. She suddenly looked tired. Dominic felt tired too. They were not used to all this going about, to a day full of events, to the tempo of peace.

"There was a public-house on the corner of the street where we lived. I remember it because of the lights at night and the singing and the smell of drink and warm air that came out of it into the icy street on winter evenings. There were always horses and wagons and sleighs outside, and Halka went there and watched the horses for a few pennies while the peasants were inside drinking their vodka.

"Sometimes I went with her but I was very afraid of the horses. They were to me such huge, fierce horses, perhaps because of only seeing them in the dark with the light from inside the tavern falling on their big, shiny flanks and the whites of their eyes. How the whites of their eyes used to gleam! But in the end I got a little used to them. I was always a bit scared of them; they were like great dark monsters and they filled the whole night for me with their great flanks and

135

white gleaming eyes, but I used sometimes to stay alone and watch them. Halka left me with them and went home. But she came back before the tavern closed.

"I never knew why she went and left me and I never dared to ask her. She was my Thérèse, my guardian angel, and I could not question her comings and goings.

"And, do you know," Lisette went on, "it is only now, after all these years, that I know that she went back to our room with one or other of the peasants. She always walked off alone because, I suppose, she was too young to risk being seen walking down the street with one of them. But I remember the whispering that went on between her and the owners of the horses. Only now it has dawned on me. Because only now I have grasped that that's what's behind three-quarters of all that goes on."

Dominic was silent.

"At the first moment of grasping it, it was a shock," Lisette went on. "So that was my little Thérèse, I said to myself! But very soon I saw that there was nothing to mind, but, on the contrary, only another reason for loving her. Because she had to do that so that we should not starve or be taken away to an orphanage. The old woman who let us have the room pretended to the authorities that she looked after us, and so we were left alone. But in return for her protection she charged Halka a big rent, and I suppose she must have known how Halka got the money to pay her. Oh no," Lisette concluded, "there is nothing but greater love for her in me when I think of it. And when Halka sent me that message through you it was as if she had said to me: 'See, little Lisette, I went through that massacre that time long ago for your sake, so that we could live, and never hold it against me, because to live is so hard and we have only each other.' It is something like that that she meant. Let us drink more coffee, Dominic."

He drank more coffee in order to keep awake. He did not want to lose any of these precious hours in sleep.

"Living is so hard," Dominic repeated, "and there is only the one secret of how to make it easier."

Although it was getting late, Dominic did not want to move. These moments with dusk falling in the street outside and they talking—talking with the coffee-pot on the small table between the beds—were full of such peace that he could not interrupt them. He knew, anyhow, that Descoux would not wait long for them. He would have his own idea of what was keeping them and would go off and eat with his girl.

"Are you hungry?" he asked Lisette.

"Oh yes. I've an appetite like a wolf, but let's not go yet. We won't be too late to eat later, will we?"

He reassured her, and they stayed on, talking and talking as though they were a long-separated couple who had just come together again and had endless things to tell each other.

"I think in the midst of the misery and insecurity one never does really speak and open one's heart," Dominic said. "One learns a kind of secretiveness. You seemed to be always to be so secretive, and perhaps I seemed to be so too."

"Yes," she said. "There I was sly and secretive. All my life I had to be secretive. But not you; you were different, as in all ways you are different. You come from another world."

"Though in one way it was not so very different," said Dominic. "It was only that you were outside the tavern, out in the street with the horses, and I was inside. I used to come up to the city from the country, and those were the best moments of the whole outing, the first drink or two in the bright little tavern with the whole exciting night still in front of me with its appointments and rendezvous.

"There was one pub in London, in a steep, narrow street leading up from the Adelphi to the Strand. As soon as I arrived from Ireland on the evening train and had left my suitcase in a room in a hotel, I would ring up a couple of friends to announce my arrival and then make straight for this tavern to begin a week's carousal.

"When a man from the country came out of that tavern into the dark street where you were watching the horses and, with two companions, jumped into one of the sleighs, it might have been me. And if when I came out of the pub in the Adelphi there had been a barefoot little urchin in the street, it was you," he said. "But I did not see you. I passed you by in the blindness and isolation in which I moved. I saw and loved no one. I was isolated from all my fellow creatures, from my two companions as much as from anyone else. I drank and caroused with them and I shared with them my last penny, but all the same I did not know what it was to once grasp their hands in a true impulse of fraternity.

"Oh yes, Lisette, I would have come out and seen you waiting with the horses and dropped a handful of coins into your little paw and passed you by. And if I had been already in bed with my girl and had heard you crying in the street, if I had heard a child crying in the street in the middle of the night, would I have got up and come down to see what was wrong, to try to comfort it? I don't know. I think, in my isolation, I might have remained where I was and you could have gone on crying. I would have said: 'It is not my business. Someone else, some woman, is bound to hear it and go down.' Or else: 'As sure as I get up and put on my coat, the crying will stop; the brat will clear off, or its mother will find it.'

"But nobody found you, nobody comforted you," he went on.

"Now you are here," Lisette said. "Now you have come and it is good." She stretched her hand across the narrow space between the beds and he took it for a moment in his.

They roused themselves reluctantly and switched on the light and washed their faces and hands in the basin whose gleaming taps, from one of which hot water gushed, fascinated Lisette. Of all the varied signs of being in the midst of peace and plenty that she saw in these days, that was the one that struck her most. This shining tap at a turn of which hot water flowed at any hour of the day or night!

Descoux had left a message at the desk telling them to which restaurant he had gone.

"He's all right. He has a new girl and the new evening papers," Lisette said. "Let's not look for him. We can find somewhere for ourselves, can't we?"

Dominic agreed and they walked through the streets looking for somewhere to eat. When they did not find a place at once, Lisette became nervous.

"We'd better ask someone. It's getting late and everything good will be gone."

138

He reassured her. "We're in a place where the good things don't go," he said. "The good things are always there for those who have the money to buy them."

She was then assailed with another fear: that they had not enough money. He reassured her once more.

"What a fussy little fool you must think me," she said. "But I can't believe in it all so easily."

"Oh, you'd believe in it very soon if you were here long enough," he said. "There would even be the danger that you'd begin to take it all for granted, and there'd be no joy in it any more."

They found a restaurant and went in and sat down at a small table and a waiter immediately slipped up to them and presented them each with a menu sufficiently long to still all Lisette's fears.

"And you," she said after they had ordered a dinner that seemed calculated to satisfy even their endless hunger, "wouldn't you take it for granted too? Wouldn't you soon get as you were before?"

"No. I'm not afraid of that. I was brought so low, I was weighed down to such a point that something in me broke. That power of taking anything good for granted was destroyed in me. Never again, by the grace of God, will I be able to say to myself: 'It is quite natural to be sitting here with Lisette at a table with flowers on it, eating fish and meat and *crème caramel*.' Because on the fringe of the small glow of light on the knives and forks and dishes there will ever be the shadows from which stone steps lead down into cellars and cold dungeons where there is nothing and time stands almost still."

"But would food like this always taste as marvellous if we went on eating it every day?" she asked.

"Oh no, of course not. That is certainly a joy that would lose its intensity."

"I think I would never get tired of it," she said. "But Descoux, he must always have new things. He is only happy when he has a new girl, and then quite soon he is bored with her."

She talked through the meal, pouring out all the strange

and manifold impression of their crowded days, of Descoux, of Monsieur Varreau, of food, films, the hotel. He listened to her and regarded her across the small, laden table.

After dinner, Lisette was quite ready to go on somewhere else, but he thought that for one day—even though it was their only day, for to-morrow they must leave—she had had enough excitement.

At the hotel desk they gave her the key of Descoux' room and she left it in his door.

She had not forgotten Dominic's promise to read to her, and she reminded him of it when she was in bed. He sat on the edge of her bed and opened the New Testament that he had bought that afternoon. He turned over a few leaves and came on the telling of the washing of Christ's feet by Mary Magdalene, and began to read it to Lisette:

" 'And one of the Pharisees desired him that he would eat with him. And he went into the Pharisee's house and sat down to meat. And, behold, a woman in the city, which was a sinner, when she knew that Jesus sat at meat in the Pharisee's house, brought an alabaster box of ointment, and stood at his feet behind him, weeping, and began to wash his feet with tears, and did wipe them with the hairs of her head, and kissed his feet and anointed them with the ointment.' "

In the morning, there was the saying goodbye to Basel, to the world of freedom and peace, and the prospect of returning to the desolation of Marheim. But Dominic felt no regret, only impatience to be back and to see Halka again. These twenty-four hours of freedom had not given him what sometimes a short hour, such as those in the old graveyard, with her could give him.

They changed at Weil, just inside the German frontier, and from there there was a slow journey in an incredibly grimy compartment with broken and boarded-up windows. On their left were orchards sloping down to the Rhine and beyond it the flat, wooded plain of Alsace. And among the fruit trees and along the banks of the broad stream were the big, broken slabs of concrete of the blown-up redoubts.

Dominic thought of the words of the old Swiss anarchist about the coming of a millennium without frontiers, without governments. And although at the time he had discountenanced much of what Monsieur Varreau had said, he knew that unless the insanity of frontiers and fortifications disappeared a cataclysm would overtake the world on an even greater scale than the one through which they had come. Only he did not believe that this could be prevented by preaching against these evils, by holding meetings or calling strikes. There was no short-cut to bringing about peace between men. All short-cuts were temptations, were the refusal to begin at the very beginning. One must act as though the world had to start completely afresh. One had to start from the very beginning, from the heart, from each room and cellar and hovel where two or three were gathered together.

"We are three gathered together," he thought. "Halka and Lisette and I." And he knew how difficult it was to make a beginning.

There was no good in preaching campaigns to do away with armies and governments. All that was negative. First there must begin to blossom this flower of peace and compassionate love between men, and if it should ever establish itself in the hearts of enough people then these things would fall away of themselves.

"But of course that will never happen," a voice in him answered. "Look at those around you. See the faces of these in the carriage. Is it possible that such a state of beatitude should ever enter into them?"

This did not disturb him. It might well be that true peace would never descend on the earth. He thought of the New Testament and of the passage he had read to Lisette.

Christ had worked in a very small way. From a worldly standard, He had done all in a hole-and-corner manner. He had moved among a handful of people in one small corner of Asia Minor and had not appeared to bother about or even to have been greatly conscious of the rest of the world. In this sense, He had cut a very small figure compared to the great revolutionaries and conquerors.

But, thinking of Christ, he was troubled. The name had become a stumbling-block. If he was to mention it to Descoux, for example, it would be received with suspicion or scepticism.

Those who professed to honour it had turned it into a name that had lost almost all its power, that had become a banner, a slogan like all the other slogans. The prerogative of a party, a pious sect.

The very name of Christ would be suspect to Descoux. It would be for him a stone of stumbling. The name of Christ would suggest to him a kind of super-Gandhi, a Being whose main concern had been preaching and fasting, condemning the sins of the flesh and all else that made one forget the drabness and hardship of life.

Only for someone like Lisette who had never heard a sermon in her life, had never had one hour of religious instruction, for whom the name of Christ was an oath rather than anything else, or which conjured up for her at most some dark and potent spirit, was there the possibility of an open mind. She would listen to the New Testament with the same unspoilt curiosity with which she listened when he told her about his Uncle Egan. She was open and receptive, critical and yet without any *a priori* prejudices.

If the story seemed to her good and true, if it seemed real to her in the way she had learnt reality, then Dominic's own faith in the power of Christ would be strengthened. Because for all the others Christ was dead; He had been destroyed by the moralists and the priests and the professional doers-of-good. Only if He had the power to make Lisette or Halka His disciples, as it was written He had made Mary Magdalene, would it be a step forward out of chaos.

CHAPTER XII

AT HIGH NOON

As MIDSUMMER APPROACHED it grew hot in the town under the dark, pine-clad hills that hung around it on three sides like a heavy curtain. Dominic had made the application and filled up the forms that were necessary before he could marry Lisette, and meanwhile, in the hot, sultry noons, he and the two girls used to go to a swimming-pool on the outskirts of the town. Halka had contrived to fashion for them strange-looking but serviceable bathing-suits, knitting and stitching for several days with odds and ends of wool and material. She always astonished Dominic by the way she could do things. With her air of not doing anything, she always got the necessary things done promptly and well—their meagre meals cooked, the dishes washed, their clothes patched and mended, the room kept in some sort of order. Their German landlady, on the contrary, with her continual busyness, her endless sweeping, dusting and polishing, her hours over the gas in the kitchen, never seemed to them to really get anything done. The dishes that she prepared, the cakes that she baked, were always tasteless when Lisette came back with a slice hidden in her pocket from one of her raids into the kitchen.

When they bought their tickets and the door closed after them in the wall that surrounded the meadow and the pool they passed out of the dust of the town, out of the ruins into a place of sun and grass and water. It was true that the grass was thin, worn by many sun-baked bodies, and the water smelt of chloride, but all this was nothing to Halka and Lisette. Sometimes when Dominic remembered the wide, deserted strand at home with the tide far out on a summer morning, when he felt again the warm, ribbed sand under his feet and the faint, salty breeze wafted from the far, pale horizon, his heart was heavy. But he knew that should he be there again alone with Lisette he would see and feel none of it, all his powers of seeing and feeling would be turned back here to this drab little meadow and the narrow confines of this pool.

Lying there on the grey blanket in the hot sun beside the two girls, he knew that he was where he wanted to be. And he knew that to realise that one is where one wants to be with the whole heart is a rare and precious kind of peace, only given to those who have been in many alien places, lost and alone.

They often met Petrov in the meadow. He had found a

girl soon after Lisette, on her return from Basel, had asked him to let her take back her promise. Dominic had also spoken to him, and Petrov had accepted the situation in his quiet way. And shortly afterwards he had appeared with a Frenchwoman, a young widow. She was fat and had a large nose and small, sparkling eyes and she chattered incessantly. But, to celebrate her union with Petrov, she asked Dominic, Halka and Lisette to dinner at her flat and heaped their plates with huge portions from the dishes that she had spent the whole afternoon preparing. She flowed over with good-heartedness and with good spirits. She enjoyed every moment of life; there would be with her no hours of silence, depression or dullness. She was like a sparkling brook flowing along in the height of a sunny day.

"But Marianne has suffered too," Petrov told them. "She too was in prison during the occupation when the Germans were looking for her husband."

"Oh yes, they shut me up for six months," she said. "But we made our own life there too. We were six girls in the cell and twenty or thirty in the *atelier* where we worked. But I lost all my surplus flesh. I had nothing left on me that you could take hold of! Come, you are not drinking." She poured more wine into Dominic's glass. "*Carrousel*, Monsieur Malone!"

When they met her at the swimming pool, she had always fruit and cigarettes with her to offer them. Her stomach rippled in folds of golden flesh above the lower part of her bright, two-piece bathing costume. She mothered Petrov, looking after him, and she seemed to deliver him from his moods of depression.

"Living with Marianne is a continual excitement," Petrov told them. They were sun-bathing in the meadow, while Marianne was in the pool. She was a great swimmer and could dive in all manners of arcs and, in spite of her size, slipped into the water with scarcely a splash. "Formerly I was always waiting for the postman to ring or for it to be time to go and get the papers or to have lunch. But now the days go by and I never give a thought to whether the postman has been or not, and I often don't even go for the papers at all."

"It's a good thing you didn't take me," said Lisette. "I would never have amused you like that."

"No. With you it would have been quite different. But in the kingdom of marriage, like the Kingdom of Heaven, there are many mansions."

"Are you going to marry her?"

"Yes. But not here. She has a flat in Paris, and as soon as it has been done up we shall go there."

When Petrov and his Marianne had gone, Lisette asked Dominic: "Aren't you envious of him? Would not you like to have found her so that all would be made smooth and easy?"

"Such a woman is always a temptation," Dominic said. "To give myself up to a woman like that and not to have to care any more about anything, oh yes, that's a temptation all right. It's the temptation to try to enter into the Kingdom of Heaven through the broad and easy gate."

"It's a broad gate all right," said Lisette.

"And it wouldn't work," Dominic went on. "Many men dream of motherly young women, rich and plump, a goddess of plenty, who would turn life for them into a bed of roses. And, of course, I have had this dream too. The fact is I think I must have had almost all the dreams at one time or another."

"What sort of dreams?" asked Lisette.

"Waking dreams. The dreams of childhood and then the dreams of youth. The first that I can remember is a wood near our house. This wood was the first heaven that I discovered on earth, the first holy place. In the middle of the wood there was a thicket of rhododendrons, and in the centre of this thicket I made a small clearing, sawing away the branches and digging out the roots until I had a secret room, a kind of inner holy of holies. There I spent whole days."

"What did you do?"

"I was happy. I felt the stillness of the air, and the dark, dull green of the rhododendron leaves glowed for me and the little eddy of gnats circled for me."

It was getting so hot that they rose and went over to the

pool where Marianne was disporting herself in the greenish water like a small whale. Halka and Lisette were not much good at swimming, but they descended into the water while Dominic sat on the tiled edge of the pool with Petrov.

They began to talk about Marianne and the flat in Paris. Petrov talked of their plans of getting away. As he talked, Dominic had the feeling that this was quite a different Petrov to the one who used to sit by the stove at Frau Arnheim's and speak of the new French literature, of the night that had descended on Europe and of the words of light that a few poets and prophets had brought back with them from the prison-camps. A different Petrov too, to the one who had come and enquired of Dominic which of the two sisters was free for him to propose to.

"Marianne has a villa in Algiers," he was saying, "and after we have been in Paris a bit, we shall go there. Paris is not far enough. I want to get away to somewhere where I can work in peace, beyond the shadow."

"When you wanted to marry Lisette, you didn't think like that," Dominic said.

Petrov did not answer immediately. The tranced ugliness came over his long face, a sign that he was struggling with his thoughts, clumsily and heavily trying to get them in sufficient order to express them.

"That was my last effort to go through with all this," he said. "If Lisette had come to me, I would have gone on hungering and freezing and waiting for news from home which never comes. With Lisette beside me, I would have accepted having no country, no home, no future, and have gone on clinging to my faith that out of this darkness a new dawn would come. But when Lisette told me that she was not going to come to me after all, it was like a sign to me. Perhaps it gave me the excuse for which I had been half waiting. At any rate, it was enough. I knew Marianne already slightly, and the very next day I went to her flat and had one of her dinners, and late that night it was all arranged between us."

Dominic was watching the bathers. He watched the bodies of the women. They were strange beasts prowling around the pool with the double bands of the bathing dresses bound around them, veiling them. They were the living mystery, as long ago the wood had been, the veiled wood with its stream and the secret grove of rhododendrons. The brown glow of their flesh was like the dull green glow of the flesh of the rhododendrons, tender and fecund. They were the inner sanctuary of the earth, the pale, fecund groves of the holy of holies. Their faces might reflect all the trivial daily passions and calculations, but their bodies moved glowing with their ancient and savage secret. For savage were the groves of their bodies; not a garden grove like the rhododendrons had been.

Petrov was talking about the villa in Algiers with its court and fountain and shadowy cloisters that were cool even on the hottest days.

"There I will work," he said. "I am not going there to live in idleness and luxury. Because, you know, I can't do anything here. In winter I get as near as possible to whatever stove is available, which is usually Frau Arnheim's, and in summer I wander round, picking up whatever I can get, making minor transactions on the Black Market, queuing up for permits to get my shoes mended and then looking for cigarettes to give the cobbler so that he will do the work within a reasonable time. And in the midst of all these distractions it is impossible to ponder and concentrate."

Yet Dominic knew that there was somewhere an error in all this plausible reasoning. And he knew that in his heart of hearts Petrov suspected the presence of this error too. It was the old question of trying too hard to save one's life.

Marianne was teaching the other two girls the art of swimming. Lisette, following her instructions, was swimming with long strokes, burying her face in the water and bringing it out again to take deep breaths. But when she reached the far end of the pool and climbed out, she was panting and shivering. She came and sat down beside Dominic.

"How was that? Wasn't I good?" she said between her shallow, quick breaths.

"You shouldn't exert yourself like that. You can't do that on what we eat."

When Dominic was dressed, he waited as usual for the other two outside the entrance. But to-day they were longer.

That's because Lisette got her hair wet, he thought, and it must be dried and brushed. At last they came. But they did not come lightly as usual, running down the few steps in their faded summer dresses, as though glad of the flutter of the light dresses around their legs again. They came slowly down the steps and Lisette's eyes were large and scared as she looked at him. She came up to him and laid her hand on his arm and he felt how cold it still was.

"What is it?" he asked.

"Come," said Lisette. "It is nothing. Let's go home."

On the way Halka told him that as they had been dressing and Lisette had bent down to put on her shoes she had begun to cough and a gush of blood had poured from her mouth.

As Dominic listened the hot noon seemed to turn chill. His heart shed a chill over him—a chill that was stronger than the heat shed by the sun in the clear blue sky.

Back in their room, Lisette went to bed. She undressed and put on the costly, silk nightdress that Descoux had bought her in Basel.

"Make some coffee," she asked Halka. "I am so cold."

There was still some of the coffee they had brought with them, but apart from that and a loaf of maize bread they had nothing.

"I will go to Auntie," Dominic said.

"Or to Marianne," suggested Halka. "She is nearer."

But Dominic preferred to go to Frau Arnheim. Marianne might have everything that they needed, but she was a stranger, and he shrank from having to explain to her their plight. Frau Arnheim, for all her limitations, was in this way nearer to them. There was much that she could never grasp, but this she would grasp at once; to all pain and misfortune she was quickly responsive.

And so it was. Without fuss or questions, she took all into her hands. She sat down and wrote a note to her own doctor for Dominic. Had he gone to a strange doctor, he would have had to have waited for hours with others in the waiting-room, and even then it would have been doubtful how soon he could have persuaded a doctor to come to Lisette. Overworked and inured to widespread illness and disease, the doctors were not inclined to run round to the bedsides of those for whom they could do nothing except prescribe nourishment that was not to be got.

While Dominic went to the doctor, Frau Arnheim said she would buy what she could in the way of meat, milk and butter and then go to Lisette.

Although there was the usual crowd in the doctor's waiting-room, he came out of his consulting-room at once when he had read the note that Dominic brought him. He was one of these thick, heavy Germans, with thinning, pale hair and pale eyes like celluloid and a grey skin, that Dominic knew so well.

"You are Irish, eh? And your fiancée has had a hæmor-rhage," he said, glancing again at the note in his hand. Dominic saw that Frau Arnheim had put all in the light she judged best calculated to impress the doctor. Funny, he thought, that, without knowing it, she has hit on the fact.

"I will come and have a look at the young lady, but my advice to you is to take her out of here as quickly as possible."

When Dominic returned with the doctor, Frau Arnheim was already there with her purchases and Halka was preparing some soup. The doctor, with his slow and ponderous move-ments, took out his stethoscope and bending over Lisette, over her child-like torso, began to sound her back and breast.

Afterwards Dominic went out with him into the corridor and Halka came from the kitchen. The doctor stood there and spoke the words that Dominic tried to listen to carefully, exactly. But all took place in that unreal state, in that vacuum that obtained in the offices and rooms of officials. He heard the words and the sentences: "Left lung, right lung, contu-sion . . ."

He was conscious of Halka beside him, a bowl in her hand, half-turned to him, waiting for him to speak, not bothering with the doctor. For to her, in a certain sense, the doctor was just another of the "executioners," or if not an "executioner," their herald. Dominic knew that in him alone she placed what hope and trust she still had.

"If I take her away, can she be saved?" he asked.

"It is possible, but it must be quickly. It is not only the question of combating the state of extreme under-nourishment, but also the mental change of atmosphere."

After the doctor had gone, Dominic and Halka left Frau Arnheim with Lisette and went into the kitchen, which was empty at this hour of the day when their landlady was out on her endless search of the shops.

"What is always so hard is the swiftness, the terrible swiftness with which the hand of destruction reaches out and touches one. It reaches into the middle of a quiet afternoon or into the middle of a quiet, silent night, like when they came and took me to the prison camp. And an hour before or a minute before one knows nothing, all is as usual, one is even a little happy, as we were in the swimming-pool; there is not the slightest foreboding and then, softly, in a second, the blow falls."

"They promised they would give me the final papers that we need to-morrow," Dominic said.

"My God! How long it takes!"

"To-morrow they will come and in a day or two we will be married, and then as soon as we get the permit from the French we will go."

"What pain there is on your face as you say that."

"Ah, my little witch, show me the scar on your breast that Captain Renier spoke of. Only show me that wound, let me touch it and then I will have faith and strength to do all for your sake, even to the leaving of you."

She loosened her blouse from the band of her skirt and pulled it high. He saw across her breasts three thin white lines, whiter than the blue-white of her flesh. He put out his hand and traced his finger along them in a kind of trance. From one breast to the other he followed the white scars, not really consciously knowing what he meant by so doing, but in his trance knowing and marvelling.

They went back into the room and Halka brought the soup she had made for Lisette with the bones Frau Arnheim had brought with her. Since the first horror with which the bright flow of blood had filled her, Lisette had regained some of her calm. As soon as Dominic came into the room, her eyes fixed on him. Like her sister, it was in him that she put her trust.

"What did the doctor say?" she asked.

"That I must take you away. We can be married in a few days and then we will leave Germany."

"And what about Halka?"

"She will come later."

He went and sat on her bed. In her eyes there was a look of anguish, as though there was nothing on which they could rest and repose. They kept searching his face to find there some security. She felt as if nothing was left of which she could be sure. All was slipping away; the whole world had receded a little from her, as though it was being shifted from under her feet.

Frau Arnheim was talking to her, asking her about the trip to Basel, of which she had heard something from Halka. She herself had often been in Switzerland in the days before the war and liked to talk about it. She liked in general to talk about the old days and to boast a little of her family and her house, her rich friends and her travels. She could not bring herself to accept the present destitution and she had no future to look forward to. So she dwelt on the glories of the past.

She scarcely noticed Lisette's reluctance to speak of her own few days in Switzerland, the one trip she had ever really had in her life. Of the time alone there with Descoux she could not have spoken without shocking Frau Arnheim, and of the second part of her time there after Dominic's arrival she would not speak.

Frau Arnheim sat on, drinking cup after cup of the coffee that Halka had made for Lisette. Dominic wished she would go and leave them to themselves, but he knew that as long as there was a drop of coffee left in the pot, she would not move. She could never be "happy-go-lucky" as the Irish, or insouciant as the French; she must never miss whatever there was to be got, never forgo an opportunity of profiting. And at times Dominic hated this care and calculation. Frau Arnheim was not mean; she was one of the most generous souls he had ever met, but that did not prevent her from profiting whenever the opportunity arose with a kind of childish glee.

At last she saw the very last dregs of the coffee pot had been drained away and the last cigarette butts opened and re-rolled and smoked, and she got up with her stately air and kissed Lisette on the cheek, and Dominic accompanied her to the door of the flat.

"But, my dear Dominic," she said to him, "you can't marry that poor child. Even in order to get her out of here, you can't do that. To begin with, you don't love her."

"Should she then be let die because I don't have that accidental and transient feeling about her that came to be known by the word 'love'?"

"You can't marry her and tie yourself to her, all the same," Frau Arnheim went on. "Even if you don't like the word 'love,' that doesn't hide the fact that between you and Lisette there is nothing."

But he said no more. There was no use in speaking to her about what he was doing, because it was something that she could never grasp. She had been through the night, she had lost her husband, she had lost many possessions and had starved, but all the same she had not been touched or changed by it. And he knew that there were many, many who had not been touched or changed, who still clung to the old life-order, to the old mode and the old pretences.

The next days were given up to the endless running round that was necessary to hasten the machinery that was turning out the piece of paper covered with rubber stamps that would permit of the marriage. Dominic had also to write to his Embassy in Paris for the agreement of his own Government. He recalled the words of Monsieur Varreau denouncing all governments and officialdom, and felt more sympathy for him and his movement than ever, though his sense of realism told him that they would never achieve their aims.

Then there was the application to be made for their exit *visa* and another that she could receive the small amount of increased butter and meat rations that were given to those suffering from advanced tuberculosis. There was the going from office to office, the waiting in passages, the interviews with petty officials who were trying to compensate for the emptiness of their lives by getting satisfaction out of their power over the applicants standing before their desks.

"Soon you will be free of all this, and of the ruins," Halka said as she and Dominic sat in the corridor outside an office in the Town Hall from where Dominic was to receive the marriage permit.

"And I will long only for ruins; whenever I see a broken wall it will seem beautiful for me because you dwell among them."

Lisette had several visitors. Besides Frau Arnheim, Petrov came, and Descoux, and once the little Martinique, Paula.

The girl sat on a chair by the bed in her slatternly blouse and skirt and a pair of old tennis-shoes. Her dark head was bent and she only glanced up at Lisette now and then with a quick flicker of her black eyes.

"It is good of you to come," said Lisette. She was glad that she had on her smart new nightdress. In the presence of Paula, she wanted to shine, she had still a kind of sly coquetry.

"You have forgiven me for that slap I gave you?" she asked.

"That is all right. And you, did you have a fine time in Basel? Did you stay at the Hôtel Helvetia?"

"Yes. It was very fine. All was marvellous," Lisette said.

"Do you know what I thought, when I heard you were sick?" went on Paula. "I thought that fellow Descoux had made you a baby."

"No. It is my lungs."

"That is bad. A baby would have been not so bad. It is all the same, to have a baby or not. I told him: 'You can make me a baby as much as you like. I don't care,' " said Paula. "What a pretty night-dress," she went on. "Did you get that there?"

"Would you like it? I will give it to you," said Lisette.

The black eyes of the little Martinique shone. But with an effort she shook her head.

Lisette looked at Dominic, who was sitting in his corner on the couch reading. She had offered the nightdress to Paula for his sake, to please him. When he was in the room she felt a certain repose, but when he was not there, she was mostly fearful and lost. She wanted him to approve of her, to be a fitting bride for him. She waited for him to look up from his book. Then she would take off the nightdress and give it to Paula. But his eyes must be on her; he was to look at her with approval and then she would have the strength.

But he did not look up. He had heard their conversation, but he pretended not to have done so.

At times a great longing for solitude came over him. He longed to be far from everyone, from all his fellow beings. He thought of the lake at home and of how on summer or autumn evenings it was the loneliest place on earth, full of a dark, still solitude under the mountains. He felt that only there, rowing alone, out of sight and sound of men, would he be at rest and free. Here there was no solitude; it was a land without solitude—even in its wildest mountains there was always a sense of being observed. There were mountain railways, skiing huts and hostels and cables and God knew what. These people had no sense for loneliness, they could not bear it. They did everything in groups and crowds. Without being capable of solitude, there could be no true communion. They were the poles which balanced and gave power to each other.

It had been on the lake that the angel of the Lord had spoken to him. In the silence and darkness of the lake and in the solitary evening breeze that blew from the gap between the hills down over the dark face of the water.

He knew that ultimately he did not and would never really long for the shelter and ease of his Uncle Egan's house, with its well-stocked larders, its big turf fires in winter, its bathroom with the gleaming porcelain, shining taps and foamy, sweet-smelling soap. Of all that he had no final need. But of the breath of solitude that blew in from the sea and filled his room, of that he had need. He remembered some words of Halka when she had told him of that evening when she had meant to drown herself. The solitude of death had drawn her because in it she would be at last freed from mankind. Ah! he too knew that nausea of mankind; sometimes it overcame him completely. And then it seemed to him that all human activity was either cruel or vulgar. Men were either tormenting each other or else sprawling over each other. Either shooting and imprisoning or coupling and breeding. A mixture of cruelty and vulgarity. Only death was pure—a pure, perfect act, the act of dying.

CHAPTER XIII

THE COLOURED BALL

LISETTE'S NEXT VISIT was from Petrov. He came without Marianne, but he brought some delicacies that she had sent.

He sat rather helplessly by Lisette, who had got up and was lying on the couch, not at ease, not seeming to have anything to say. It was Lisette, in the end, who broached the subject of Marianne as if she knew that this was what was lying heavy on his heart.

"Yes, to you, Lisette, I have much to explain. Not to anyone else do I owe an explanation, because my coming and going, my faith or unfaith, is my own affair. But when I asked you to come to me, Lisette, I spoke to you as I had never spoken to anyone else. But now you will ask: 'Is it possible that I was deceived?' No, Lisette, I did not deceive you then. That was the day of my life when I was farthest from any deception. That day and the next days I lived in a state of simple joy at the prospect of you coming to me. But then subtly and sinisterly a shadow clouded over my joy. The old pessimism and lack of faith took hold of me. I began to think how it would be when you came to me. I saw only hunger and cold and no prospects, no future for us, nothing but the night without a dawn.

"I had no more strength and no more faith. I had a clear vision of the world and man as they are. I saw that the night that had fallen over us showed no sign of breaking, but was growing deeper.

"For a long time I had tried to believe in the regeneration of mankind. I tried to believe that after all the horrors through which they had been, men's eyes would have been opened and that they would have begun to turn back from all their vain gods. And, do you know," he went on, turning to Dominic and making of him, too, a listener to his passionate denunciation, "all the slightest signs that men had turned from their savagery and vanity I treasured up and brooded over. I don't mean only in the realm of art, not only the poems and articles I found in the French magazines and used to bring to you to read. I knew that that was merely the work of a handful and was only understood by a handful. But sometimes I thought I found signs that among humanity in general there was the beginning of a regeneration. If I read the opinion of an English dramatist that since the war the audiences in England appreciated plays of greater intelligence than they had previously, I rejoiced and cut out the paragraph and kept it.

"I lived with the faith that Europe was emerging from the darkness that had fallen on her with a new vision. The Prodigal Son returning to his father after his time of misery and starvation. Or I remembered how the Children of Israel had returned to God after He had sent them afflictions and chastised them. I went on clinging to this faith as long as I could.

"When I came here to you, Lisette, and asked you to come to me, I still believed that we were not lost, that we would find our way back to peace and sanity. I was still convinced that if we struggled through the immediate future of privation we would see the lifting of the night.

"But it was shortly after that that I began to see what a great illusion I had been living on. I began to realise that there would be no regeneration, but on the contrary, that the blindness and the barbarity were increasing. All that I had formerly been shutting my eyes to became overwhelmingly clear to me. When I read of conferences, of speeches by statesmen, of the various organisations, parties and groups and their aims, I was shown all the mediocrity, the bad faith, the incredible smallness of the hearts of the men in whose power is our future. Like a diabolic vision, it appeared before me, a monster filling the whole night, with its ape's head and its huge wings of steel and, clasped to its breast, the casket containing its new inventions of torture and destruction.

"That is the vision of the Beast whose reign is beginning," Petrov went on. He was speaking with that trance-like look on his long, ugly face. He sat beside the couch on which Lisette lay with her small, pale face turned to him, listening, a little puzzled, glancing sometimes at Dominic as though in him was the truth about all this which later he would reveal to her.

"We are only a handful," Petrov continued, "you and I and a few others here and there. A handful in the midst of a blind multitude who follow after the Beast. And it is the greatest illusion to imagine that they are going to turn back, that they are capable of being converted and led into the paths of peace and justice and sanity.

"I saw that there was no good living and acting as though this night would lift and the dawn break, as though there was any hope. I couldn't come to you any more, Lisette, and say: 'Let us be together in privation and hardship and in faith.' Because there was no more faith in me. I no longer believed in being patient, in struggling and in trusting in the power and wisdom of God. For there is no God, in our sense of a beneficent Spirit under the shadow of whose wings those who believe in Him can shelter. There would have been no shelter for us, Lisette. There is only the Beast. We live in a world delivered up to the Beast of mediocrity armed with the weapons of destruction, and the only thing to do is to come to terms with it."

"And have you come to terms with it?" Dominic asked.

"Yes. I have simply given up believing, being patient, waiting. I am getting out of here as quickly as I can. In Marianne I have someone from whom I can get what is still left to be got, and with her I shall retire into an ivory tower beyond the borders of Europe. I have been a fool long enough, with my dreams of a humanity that learnt through suffering and chastisement, that gradually let its feet be turned into the paths of peace! *Ach*, what illusion on illusion!

157

Nowhere is there the slightest indication on which to base such fancies! There is chaos and there is the Beast set up in the midst of chaos. That is no fancy; it is clear for all to see!"

"To me it isn't all so clear," said Lisette. "Some of what you have been talking about is not clear at all. But I understood it when you said you were tired of patience and waiting. And that is wrong. It is just when we can't bear the waiting and patience any longer that we must wait on. You know I can't speak like you. I haven't the right way; the words don't come to me like to you. But I know that it is the time after the waiting has become hopeless that is the right time; then, if ever, something will happen. It is always so, always. I will tell about the first time that I got to know that.

"It was when Halka and I were living alone in the room that the old woman let to us in Lodz. The time I told you about, before," she said to Dominic.

She began to tell them of a fair on some waste land behind factories on the outskirts of the town and of how she had been drawn to this little centre of life, of colour and excitement.

Sometimes she went with Halka and sometimes alone, and on the last evening before the fair's departure she had stood before the stall where there was a big wheel that turned and stopped, turned and stopped, and at each stopping of the wheel numbers were called out by the big, elegantly dressed stall-owner, and those who held the corresponding tickets won toys and trinkets that were displayed on shelves at the back of the stall.

As Lisette spoke, lying on the couch, glad of the little company gathered round her, Dominic had a picture of that far-off evening. He saw the raggle-taggle crowd around the stall with the spinning wooden wheel, the factory hands and their girls, the peasants and the children. And amongst them, pushed well up to the front, the thin little girl in her ragged frock and wispy hair. She stood there, her dark, burning eyes on the big, coloured ball in the centre of the shelf at the back of the stall. She was rooted there, longing with her obstinate, hopeless longing. She had no money to buy a single ticket in the lottery, but nothing could have budged her from her

158

post. She saw toy after toy, trinket after trinket being won and taken from the shelf. She saw the spinning wheel, the colours mixing in a rainbow whirl and then separating again into a ring of bright spokes as the magic wheel slowed down and stopped.

Far away over the rim of the flat land between two factories the red sun was sinking. It was long after her time to be home. But she could not go without the ball. She was tired with standing, with being pushed and jostled. But her longing worked in her like a drug, keeping her there in a kind of trance. She had no hope, but only longing. But the hopelessness did not disturb or distract her. She prayed the one prayer that she knew, the prayer underneath the picture of St. Thérèse of Lisieux in the corner of their room. She did not know who this Thérèse was or what she had done, and when she visualised her as a living being it was as Halka. But that was unimportant. The words of the prayer were a formula in which her tense willing and longing found secret utterance. She stood there, rooted, obstinate, scowling, and the sun went down and evening fell over the strip of littered, waste land. But time was nothing to her, had no more power over her.

The other day in Basel, when Descoux had taken her on the first evening to that small, expensive restaurant and had ordered duck, the waiter had told him that there would be a delay of a quarter of an hour before that particular dish could be served. "A quarter of an hour," she had thought, in astonishment. "Are there really people who demur at waiting a quarter of an hour for something that they want?" and she could not grasp it, thinking of the hours and hours she had stood there, tired and hungry, before the little stall. And that had only been the beginning of her waiting. Later there had been the endless waiting in air-raid shelters, in queues, in railway stations, in all sorts of cold and ruined places. And someone thought it worth mentioning a quarter of an hour!

But this first time of waiting had been different to all the others. There she had stood and her body had been tense with her willing.

The big, elegant stall-owner had begun a speech about the valuable prizes that would now be offered. Tickets for every number would be distributed so that at each turn of the wheel a prize must be won. But all this went over her head and had nothing to do with her. Her burning eyes rested on his big, florid face as he spoke, but without comprehension. There was nothing for her to comprehend except the hopelessness of her long vigil, but that was something that was beyond her. There was no need to try to follow what he said. There was only the standing there, first on one foot, and then on another, pushing back her hair when it was brushed into her eyes by the jackets and sleeves of those crowding up to hear what was being said.

Perhaps the fixity of her gaze or her abiding presence had finally caught the eye of the stall-owner. In any case, when, for the final turn of the wheel, he distributed some free tickets that had remained unsold he gave one to her. She took it automatically and clenched it in her grubby little fist. She was far too shy to open her mouth to thank him. Besides, she was far beyond thanks or of thinking of manners and politeness.

She stood on her aching legs, resting one by standing on the other, and the wheel whirled. There was once more the calling out of the winning numbers and everyone looking at the tickets that they held. She looked at hers too, but only for a moment, then her eyes were drawn back to the beautiful big ball that the stall-owner had just reached up for and was taking from the shelf.

"Here, you," said a man beside her. "Here—you have it —number twenty-eight!" He took the ticket from her and waved it and the stall-owner smiled, his big face smiled at her, and he handed her the ball.

She took it and clasped it with both hands to her breast and, with her head down, ducked her way out of the crowd. She saw nothing, nothing any more. She turned instinctively towards home, but she saw nothing of the fair around her, of the path, of the ugly, gaunt factories. There was a sweet darkness around her, and she was in the darkness alone with the ball pressed to her heart, burning her, burning into her as though it had been the great red sun that had lately set.

Gradually, the illness of Lisette became, as do all things, part of the rhythm of living. Not that she was always lying down. She was up for a time every day and went out and sat in the sun on a bench by the river.

When Dominic was not running round, making applications, he wrote his poetry. Since the summer had come, he had begun at long last to get back to his work. There had been the long break of the war years in which he had done little and then, after the war, there had been a time of waiting—waiting for things to improve, for hunger to be stilled, for conditions to get better. But they had not improved and he had learnt that his work was work that would not wait to be done. He learnt that it must be done in any corner, hungry or not hungry, that it was a prayer, that it was a transcending of the time and not something to be postponed until the time altered.

But then there had been many common difficulties. Even the difficulties of paper and ink and pen-nibs. At last he had made a start, but very soon the winter had come and it had been too cold to hold a pen or pencil in his fingers.

So now he was beginning all over again. In the mornings he sat in his corner and worked. It was not easy to make his poetry say what poetry must now say. It must speak the words that were an answer to the words of mediocrity on everyone's lips. Its song must be the old song and yet a new one, one that would have more power in it than the timid evasions of the priests and statesmen.

Only to those who had passed through the depths of the night and come back again would the words be given. He dared only count himself as the last and the least of this company.

His poetry must be holy. There can be no speaking of what is holy except in words that are holy. That is why the sermons that he sometimes heard in the Cathedral were meaningless. The priests spoke of God, but their words were the words of those submerged in the world. He had often thought to himself: Substitute for the words "God" or "Jesus Christ" in their sermons, the words "Fatherland" or "social justice" or even "a successful trading year," and you might be listening to a politician or a company director at a board meeting.

Not that the words of poetry were long or difficult words. They were the most simple words. But they could not be found except by those who were free, even if only momentarily, from the drag of the world. In the fierce, low whispers of some of the couples along the river in the evenings there was more holiness, as Dominic saw it, than in the sermons. Substitute for their "thou" God, and what they whispered would make a better sermon than the Cathedral sermons, having at least a vital breath of poetry, tenderness and passion.

Much of the time he could not write because there was so much running round to be done. But at last all was accomplished, the final permit came and the wedding could take place.

It was a hot, sunny morning as Dominic, Halka and Lisette walked down the street along the river to the undamaged red-brick church where the ceremony was to take place.

The river was nearly dry, its bed full of stones, and over it loomed the bluish-green mass of the poplars. The trees and the river and the dark, pine-clad hills pressing down above the ruined walls of the town were all strange and oppressive to him. The very stones in the river-bed were not the stones of his homeland. They were dead stones.

He took Lisette's arm and they walked very slowly. She was soon out of breath and they sat down on one of the benches above the dry river-bed. There were many people sprawled along the dusty banks of the river, the men without shirts and the women in their petticoats. A few had bathing-dresses. Children paddled in the shallow pools.

During the last week, Lisette had improved a little, but on the previous evening she had had another hæmorrhage, induced perhaps by the excitement of the approach of the wedding morn. But now that the day had actually arrived, it was not the ceremony itself that formed its centre, but the meal that they would have afterwards. The three of them were very hungry, for even Lisette had not lost her appetite, and it was of this they spoke, of what Marianne would be

162

likely to bring with her. She had promised to provide some things for the wedding feast and Descoux was also coming and would bring the wine. Frau Arnheim, too, would certainly have something for them saved out of her own meagre supplies.

They sat in a transept of the big, ugly church and a priest said the nuptial mass at a side altar.

There was another couple to be married before them, a girl in a white dress and the bridegroom nervous and tense by her side, kneeling before the priest, who stood above them with his back to the altar.

Dominic watched. He had never really attended a wedding before. If he had seen one, it had been without really seeing, without any attempt at comprehending. Now he was aware that here, after all, was something moving, momentous.

One walked in here, into the cool, big church out of the hot busy street, full of traffic, full of the business of common day, the offices, the queues, the military cars, the cinemas. And here there was marriage; two people in the dim church come to be bound together, to be made "one flesh." Ah, how moving it was! Let one say what one liked, it was moving. If it had been Halka with whom he was going to kneel there and hear the strange words said over them, if it had been her in a white dress, singled out and set apart for him, if they had been going to stand there together and she given to him in this mystery, he would have given the whole world for that moment.

But it was not so; what was happening was something different. Their turn came and he led Lisette up to the altar. As he knelt there and heard the words of the priest and the intermittent sound of the traffic when someone entered or left the church, he glanced at Lisette and saw her little figure tense, her dark eyes burning, and he knew that it was thus she had stood before the stall at the fair.

He thought: "Petrov is not right. His diabolic vision is not the only one. His vision of the Beast with the ape's head and the wings of steel and the newest machine of annihilation clasped to its hairy breast is not the final vision. If I believed it was, I should not be here. I should have long ago gone

163

back home, to the well-spread table and the gleaming taps, to the lake and the sand-hills. For then it would be a matter of 'let him save himself who can.' Although in the end there would be no real salvation, no final escape."

The priest went on, with the book held in front of his nose, quickly reading the marriage ceremony.

"But what, after all, if Petrov is right?" Dominic thought. "Is there not the possibility that he is right?" But he saw that there must be that possibility; there must be the vision of chaos. Side by side within him must be the vision of chaos and the other vision, his "angel."

Afterwards, with the other couple and Halka, they went into the sacristy and there was the signing of their names in a book and the passing of some notes to the priest. And then began the hot, dusty walk back to their room, which took a long time because Lisette had to rest on the way.

The wedding breakfast was a great success. The guests had not been to the church. They had understood that because of the special circumstances of the marriage and because of the condition of Lisette the quieter the ceremony the better. So they had not minded when Dominic had suggested they all meet after in the room that he shared with the girls.

Descoux came with his leather brief-case bulging with wine-bottles, which he put quietly into a corner without a word, as was his way. Most of the eatables were brought by Marianne. She had so much to say in her rapid French that Halka thought she would never remember to unpack the basket so that she could begin to lay the table. Frau Arnheim came sailing into the room with a peculiar expression of reserve on her big white face. Her appearance with her white hair and her stiffly held back produced at first a slight shock, especially on the two French people, Marianne and Descoux. She seemed to them quite out of place in such an informal gathering and her arrival even damped the flow of Marianne's chatter and she began to produce the magic packages from her bag.

Lisette arranged herself on the couch, to which the table,

164

spread with a new white cloth, was drawn up. She kept her hand, on which was the wedding ring, as far as possible out of sight, under the blanket that Dominic had drawn over her. She did not yet want it to be exposed to the eyes of all.

Petrov sat at one end of the table, his long, ugly face intent on the cup of coffee which he was slowly stirring. Halfway through the meal Frau Arnheim had completely unbent. Under the influence of the coffee and cigarettes, without which she could hardly live, her big face relaxed and her eyes under their arched, aristocratic brows softened. After she had smoked each cigarette, she opened her handbag and dropped in the butt. Later she even began to collect the other butts, pouncing on the long, red-stained ones left by Marianne as special prizes.

She did not approve of the marriage. To begin with, she considered that Lisette was far too young to get married and in any case she thought that it was a quixotic act on the part of Dominic, which he would later deeply regret. In her heart of hearts she had no use for any of these foreigners, neither for the French nor for the people from the east of Europe. They were not reliable, clean, hard-working as were the Germans. All the same, she had to admit that when they gave a party, then it was a party. There was none of the sipping and nipping that went on at most German parties, none of the half-filled glasses of wine that had to be formally raised before being drunk from. Even in the old days she had never really liked these gatherings of her fellow countrymen. And now, in spite of her disapproval, she could not help enjoying herself. Her strands of white hair that had been carefully combed up on to the top of her head began to break away as she leaned over towards Dominic and with a hand on his shoulder said: *"Uns geht es gut, nicht?"* "Things are looking up for us, aren't they?"

"Yes, Auntie." Dominic spoke to her as he would to a child. For him she was a child. Her whole outlook, her beliefs, were those of an old-fashioned child.

Descoux was talking in French to Halka about venereal disease.

"The terror-by-night," she was saying. "Once it was bombs. Now it is that. Aren't you afraid of it? Aren't you sometimes afraid of it in the night when you're with one of your girls?"

"Oh, no. I can always tell. There were the sirens to warn when the bombs were coming and there is something that warns me of this. I can tell by their faces and their eyes." He smiled his wolfish smile.

He did not drink much wine and he did not smoke at all. He had brought his monthly ration of cigarettes as a wedding-present for Dominic, and for Lisette he had a set of six dinner-plates that Halka thought she had remembered seeing in his flat.

"You pinched them, didn't you?" she asked him.

"*Mais non*. My wife bought them when she was here. There was a distribution of dinner-sets. I thought they would come in handy when you set up your *ménage* in Ireland."

"But I am not going to Ireland," said Halka.

"No? I thought you were going with them."

These words brought back to Dominic the darkness of the way that lay before him. His eyes met Halka's across the table. She raised her arms and loosened back her hair from her shoulders in the familiar little gesture. When she did that, he wanted to grip her, to crush her. But that was no good to her. That was the love she did not want. And in his heart he did not want it either. He wanted to have her beside him. Her presence that was like a vindication of the out-of-joint time. With her he was at peace—not with the old precarious peace based on a sheltered existence such as Frau Arnheim loved to recall, but peace in the face of chaos. This, he knew, was the true love, that was patient, that was long-suffering, not puffed up, that did not seek itself. No, it did not seek itself; it was ready to lose itself, to lose her, to cast itself on the waters. But he was overcome by fear when he thought of it, and he did not try to listen to the long story that "Aunty" was telling him of her rich relations and of their former grandeur.

Lisette was silent. She lay on the couch with the coffee cup balanced on her thighs and watched the others. But her eyes were mostly on Dominic. And when he looked at her from time to time and smiled, she was happy. She knew that she had never before been so happy in her life.

CHAPTER XIV

THE WEDDING NIGHT

By EVENING, WHEN THE guests were gone, the accustomed quiet descended on the room. Halka did the clearing away and the cleaning up and Lisette went back to her bed. She had a fear of being left alone and could not bear it when Dominic began to help Halka, but asked him to come and sit beside her. It was hard to sink back into being alone after all the excitement of the day.

Halka found a bottle that was still half full of wine.

"Go and take your glass and sit by your wife," she said.

He went and sat by Lisette and drank the remains of the red wine. He remembered long ago sometimes feeling that this was the best moment of a party, when all were gone and, alone with the one or two who remained, to light a cigarette or drink the dregs of the wine in relaxation and an intensified intimacy.

Dominic sat talking to Lisette and drinking the wine. She was struggling against the exhaustion, trying to listen to him and to answer him, not to be left alone. And also there was something else in her mind, something on which her will was set, the one thing that she wanted above all else. But she did not know how to begin to speak about it.

This was her bridal night and she did not want to be alone in it. She wanted to lie in his arms. But she was so tired she could not long keep awake and her bridal night was going over and never again would there be another for her. She stretched out her arm from the bed and laid her hand on his. He saw in her dark eyes that were bright with fever the look of appeal. The thought of undressing and getting into the bed and taking her in his arms was horrible to him. His blood was in the orbit of Halka, she drew the tide of his blood with the moon-like, luminary power of her body, of the cool, magic flesh of her breasts and the dark, luminous pull of her belly.

The bed in which Lisette lay with her dark eyes fixed on him was before him and he must not shrink from it. He thought of the women with whom he had got into bed out of no more than the lust of the moment. Now for once let his flesh be submitted, let it be to-night not the old flesh but the new, the flesh that had suffered hunger and cold and incarceration and that had learnt a new tenderness. He thought of Blake's poem, "William Bond":

> *The fairies that fled from William Bond*
> *Danced around her shining head!*
> *They danced over the pillow white*
> *And the angels of Providence left the bed.*
>
> *I thought Love lived in the hot sunshine,*
> *But oh! he lives in the moony light!*
> *I thought to find Love in the heat of day,*
> *But sweet Love is the comforter of night.*
>
> *Seek Love in the Pity of other's woe,*
> *In the gentle relief of another's care,*
> *In the darkness of night and the winter's snow,*
> *With the naked and outcast—seek Love there.*

He got into bed with Lisette without letting her see that it was not where he was drawn with his blood, that on the contrary his flesh seemed to close up, as sea-plants close up when the tide recedes and they are left on the dry rock. He got in with Lisette and Halka took his place on the couch. He put his arms round Lisette and laid her head on his shoulder. Her thin, hot body was repugnant to him in the old way of the flesh. But in another sense he was, he felt, unworthy of this contact with her pure and suffering flesh. For, in spite of the excursion to Basel, she was untouched, her small breasts had never blossomed under the hand of a lover, but had only laid themselves bare, given themselves up in fear and trembling. Her body had only known cold and hunger and pain. He felt it in his arms, the heavy, hot burden of it that could not stir a single drop of his blood in the old way, but which, he knew, redeemed him and purified him. He felt her bony back slippy with sweat under his hand as he embraced her and her belly like a hot stone, and he buried his face in the damp, stifling flesh of her breast.

"This must be dull for you," she said, "compared to those other nights with other girls."

"It isn't dull, little Lisette. It isn't what I used to imagine was 'love,' that's all." He repeated as much of the poem of Blake to her as he could remember. She asked him to repeat it a second time. For some reason it fascinated her, but in the middle of the second repetition he heard from her breathing that she was already asleep.

For a long time he lay without moving his arms from around her. He could hear Halka awake and tossing on the couch. Gradually he felt a profound serenity touch him. From the bed which was beside the window he could see the moon tranquilly shining over the ruins. And from the moon or from the whole vast, tranquil heavens, it was as if a hand was stretched out touching him, absolving him and anointing him with strength and tranquillity.

On the same night, Petrov and Marianne were sitting on the balcony of their flat on the outskirts of the town. There was a small table beside their chairs on which Marianne had placed a dark-red shaded lamp and her sewing things. Petrov had brought out a pile of French literary periodicals and had been reading them. But he could not read them any more. It was painful to him reading the verses of these young French poets, many of whom had died or disappeared in the prisons or concentration camps in which they had been incarcerated.

He had been re-reading a poem by Benjamin Fondane, who had been in the Auschwitz camp until September, 1944, and of whom, as was stated in a note, nothing more had been heard.

Know, then, that I had a face like yours.
A mouth which prayed, as yours.
If a speck of dust, or a dream, entered the eye,
This eye wept a little salt. And when
A thorn pierced my flesh
It dripped a blood as red as yours!

Certainly, just as you, I was cruel, I had
A thirst for tenderness, for power,
For gold, for pleasure, and for grief . . .
Yes I have been a man like other men,
Nourished on bread, on dreams, on despair. Oh yes,
I have loved, I have wept, I have hated, I have suffered,
I have bought flowers and I have not always
Paid my debts.

And yet, no!
I was not a man like you . . .
You have not strayed from city to city
Tracked by the police,
You have not known disasters at dawn,
The cattle-trucks
And the bitter sigh of humiliation
Accused of an offence you did not commit,
The crime of existing,
Changing name and face
So as not to bear a name that they have derided,
A face which has served everyone
To spit upon!

Now Petrov sat without reading, his long face turned from the light. The calm face of the night with the moon high above the hills of the Black Forest seemed to him no more than a mockery and a cruel illusion. There could be no peace on earth, only chaos and blindness and torment.

Once he had believed that all those who had suffered and died were martyrs from whose wounds and blood the seed of a new wisdom and love would be nourished. And this faith had touched him inwardly with life. As long as he had had it,

170

he had been happy living in his unheated room on his meagre fare, or going out alone into the surrounding country, catching trout under the boulders in the mountain streams with his bare hands. The simplest things had given him joy because of the seed of strength within him—a seed, a little sprout, of the tree of new life that had been sown on earth with so much pain and watered with so much blood. He had wandered about the ruined streets, nearly always alone, so that his long, sombre face had become vaguely familiar to many, and he had never felt lonely or at a loss. Even going to the cinema alone, to a tedious film, had not bored him because of the secret faith within him, that all this was merely a time of waiting, that many, many others shared his secret too and were also waiting for a sign.

As he had confided to Dominic, he had caught at each straw. He had kept clippings from papers that seemed to prove that men were really touched, as he was touched, by a new sense of the kingdom of heaven being at hand. All the announcements of the meetings and lectures of many different sects that were suddenly springing up again seemed to him of great significance. He attended lectures by the Witnesses of Jehovah, by the Latter-Day Saints, by Theosophists, and in the evenings from his attic window when he watched the sun sink in a glowing red coal over the hills of France he sank into a kind of trance of hope and expectation. He often stood there long after the sun had set, gazing into the tranquil waves of green and amber. Beneath these waves there seemed to him to stir a ripple or to pass a shadow. And when night came and the depths were translucent there was still this presence, the unfolding out of the heavens to earth of a great lambent bush of which sun and moon and stars were the foliage.

It was after one of these evening trances that he had gone first to Dominic, and then to Lisette, and asked her to come to him. Then he had felt the need of a companion to share with him this secret, with whom he would wait in hardship and patience for what was to come. He wanted a woman who had suffered, who had been tempered and made patient, and together they would read the poems of these young

French writers and walk in the hills and watch the sunsets and the night heavens and even go to the cinema. Because when you had that faith in you it did not matter much what you did. All had a new significance.

Then quite suddenly he had ceased to believe. He had been drawn down and engulfed in the empty darkness. Although he would never have admitted it to anyone, it had begun by an unlucky accident. He had had some small piece of business to transact with Descoux, whom he knew slightly, and had gone round one evening to his flat. The door had been opened to him by Paula, to whom Descoux had given the keys to do a bit of tidying up while he was away in Basel with Lisette. And Paula, still smarting from the slap that Lisette had given her, and from disappointment at being robbed at the last moment of the trip, had poured out the story to him.

He had understood nothing of this betrayal of him by Lisette, as it had appeared to him. And in his shy solitariness he had never dared to mention it to her or to ask her. Her announcement of her engagement to Dominic had not mattered to him. It had been the first shock of her secretly going off like that with Descoux of all people! That was the beginning of the sense of chaos that overtook him. And then, as though to complete his downfall, many smaller incidents occurred, many small signs were given him that made him convinced that his faith had been an illusion.

He had been lonely. Nobody was so lonely as he. He had gone on so long discounting all the outward life around him, refusing to accept all the signs of materialism and blind self-seeking, that now when he was brought face to face with it he did not know where to turn.

He had turned to Marianne. He could not bear his miserable attic any more, the continual hollow in his stomach, the worn, frayed clothes that he was forced to wear day after day. Before, all this had been very little to him. As long as he had lived in the glow of a vision of a mysteriously ordered world, where all had its hidden reason and purpose, where whosoever sowed in tears would reap in joy and where no sparrow fell to the earth "without the Father," then all

172

could be borne. Then there was a secret patience strengthening him.

But now when he was face to face with another vision of the world, in which all was betrayed for a few good meals and a pair of silk stockings, where not only a sparrow but a few million men could perish, many of them in torment, without there being the slightest sign of any paternal spirit in the whole empty cosmos, every evidence of the misery in which he lived was horrible to him.

Marianne appeared at the critical moment, overflowing with chatter reeled out in the plausible French accents which seemed to give to everything she said a comforting knowingness. It fascinated him. She was a little fountain of good sense with her ripples of pale flesh, her dark, bird-like eyes, her full face, flowing with good nature, bubbling over with a sensuous glow of well-being. She was in the world, in the very midst of it, and she glowed with it. She was a mixture of all its cynicism and superstition. She believed in no one and yet in everything. When Petrov spoke to her of Dominic and his fraternal relationship to the two girls she had made a little explosive sound of good-humoured scepticism. She had been leaning over the well-laden table, putting down a dish of something or other, and he remembered the little snort of amusement and then the plausible flow of good French common sense that she had overwhelmed him with. That had been a surprise but he had ended by believing her, by submitting himself to her great, good-humoured, worldly wisdom.

What had surprised him, too, was her habit of making the sign of the Cross over a new loaf of bread before she cut it, although she never put her big nose inside a church. But this, too, in the end he found charming. She really charmed him, charming his nerves and his senses.

To-night as they sat together on the balcony he had re-read for the first time since he had been with her some of the French literary periodicals that had formerly meant so much to him. But now the words of these poets who had returned from the valley of the shadow of death, or who had disappeared in it, like Fondane, seemed to him deceptive. There was a peculiar kind of half-bitter relief in putting the little pile of magazines and the two or three slim volumes aside and of turning to Marianne. The world that she could give him was glowing, plausible, full of sensuousness.

When she saw he had finished reading, she got up and went into the flat. After a few minutes she came out with a tray on which there was a bottle of champagne and a plate of meat sandwiches. She had put on a flowery, pink kimono, and as she began to undo the wire from the cork she told him a story about an incident that she had observed that morning in the *économat* when she had been buying the things for the wedding breakfast. There was nothing in the story itself, but the rippling flow of words was a bright stream washing away the silence and the dark night beyond the balcony.

The shaded lamp-light fell on her pale bosom which was nestling in the folds of the kimono.

"That's not the best champagne that they gave me," she said. "I said to the girl: 'Where's the Cordon Bleu that came in last week?' And she was taken aback, because they were keeping it quiet; it was being reserved for a few of the senior officers and their families. 'If Madame will be so good as to wait a few minutes until I serve these customers, I will see if there are any bottles still in our cellar,' she said."

The long and short of it was she had got one bottle of the special champagne and two of lesser quality and the Cordon Bleu had been among the wine she had brought to the wedding breakfast. But with Marianne there was never a long and a short of it. There was only her flow of French that coloured all in a warm glow. One might be bored with her chatter, but it was never dull chatter. The words might be drab, and what she describes might be a very small, everyday affair, but all was lit by her own warmth and the very sentences rippled with a sensuous pleasure in all that she did: in the getting the better of sales-girls, in giving the right answer to the host of "*Petits fonctionnaires*" who controlled the lives of the French families here, in telling of her late husband.

Petrov liked this warm flow of French; the very sound of it, even when he did not listen closely, with its intonation that made all sound so plausible, more plausible than anything ever really was, fascinated him. And he liked her plumpness, her pale flesh that had the oily, healthy glisten of a chestnut just out of the burr in the parts where she did not powder it. To go to bed with her was to be smothered in a warm, plausible wave of sensuality. He did not know how she managed to put something plausible in her very act of loving, but it seemed to him she did. To make love to her was not to go down into depths of ecstasy and torment that it had been to him with the few women he had slept with. There was no darkness, no being on the edge of the unknown. She had a way of making love with the same sensuous dexterity with which she cooked.

With her he was protected from all his former brooding, his long half-trances. He was really very content with her. Far more content than he would have been with Lisette. Why go on thinking of Lisette? Because, perhaps, he had been reading these poems, this poem by Fondane. Or was it that Lisette's wedding had induced him to bring out these books and periodicals again? There was some connection between them. Life with Lisette would have been a life of much reading. He would have read these things with her and have discovered other poets and perhaps have tried to write himself.

Marianne had got up and had taken the tray with the empty plate and glasses from the table. She was leaning over him, and the pale swell of her bosom was close to him, between him and the night, between him and the great tranquil moon over the forest. He got up and switched out the lamp and they went into their bedroom.

In the same night, Lisette's bridal night, Descoux was sitting in the small kitchen of his three-roomed, requisitioned flat with a litter of illustrated crime-sheets on the table in front of him. He had sent Paula to take a bath. She had left the door of the bathroom open and he could hear her in the water, but at the moment he was more interested in poring over the pictures and stories of crime. His lean, bronzed face with its dark muzzle reflected the bright gleam of the bulb above the table under its enamel reflector.

There was a ring at the door. He got up and went into the tiny hall. He pulled the door of the bathroom to and opened the door of the flat. An officer, whom he recognised as Captain Renier, stood there with a gendarme. He led them into the parlour.

"Descoux?" Captain Renier asked. When Descoux assented, Renier asked to have a look at his papers and Descoux took them from his pocket and handed them to the other. All the reddish bronze had ebbed from his face. He stood there and looked very like *un oiseau sauvage* which had one foot in a trap.

"Are these all?" asked Captain Renier after he had glanced through them.

"*Oui, mon Capitaine.*"

"Search him," said Renier to the gendarme. But at the same moment, Descoux brought another paper, the identity card and *laissez-passer* of his wife, from an inside pocket and laid them on the table. He said nothing.

Captain Renier glanced at them and said: "Where is your wife?"

"In France."

"And twice within the last few weeks you have travelled to Switzerland with women who passed the frontier on your wife's papers," said Captain Renier.

Descoux said nothing. *Bon Dieu!* What a life! How he loathed this fellow with his small blue eyes and his pressed-together lips. No doubt an Alsatian. To go where one wanted with whom one wanted, that was no crime. But now they were making criminals out of everyone, making crimes out of everything.

Renier left the gendarme with Descoux and looked into the bedroom and then into the kitchen. His lips seemed to press together even more tightly as he took in the air of slatterliness that lay over the tiny flat. For such things he had an eye like a woman's. He took in at a glance the illustrated papers, the unswept floor, the dusty reflector. He peered into the small bedroom; he opened a drawer in the small, marble-topped table beside the unmade bed and glanced with the same prim displeasure at the untidy contents, at a bottle of aspirins, some articles of women's hygiene and old letters. His white Pomeranian followed him on his tour of the small flat, sniffing into all its corners.

Captain Renier returned to the tiny parlour and said to Descoux:

"Who is in the bathroom? A girl?"

"The maid."

"Go and tell her to give the place a thorough clean-up and to bring round the keys to me to-morrow morning."

Descoux knocked at the door of the bathroom and went in. There was the sound of water gurgling out of the bath. When Descoux did not immediately return, Captain Renier with a slight jerk of his head indicated to the gendarme to go and get him. He himself had a peculiar distaste of going into the bathroom. The whole subtle air of moral degradation that he found in the flat affected him unpleasantly; ever since he had entered it, he had been aware of traces of Descoux's women and of the life he led with them here. He had not gone into the bathroom because of what he expected to see there—the naked or half-clothed body of some street-girl. Captain Renier shrank from contact with the sensual, from that noxious breath of impurity that lay over the town and indeed, it sometimes seemed to him, over the whole of that world of which he had knowledge.

But at the call from the gendarme he followed him into the small bathroom. The little Martinique was standing just as she had jumped out of the bath-tub, making no attempt to veil her dark body, on which glistened drops of water. The small window above the lavatory basin was open on to the black sky. Descoux had vanished.

"Cover yourself, can't you?" said Renier to the girl.

CHAPTER XV

BY THE RIVER

As DOMINIC LAY WITH the sleeping Lisette in his arms there was the triple ring at the door of the flat that indicated a visitor for him or the girls. Halka, who had been long lying awake, got up and opened it and, without a word, Descoux slipped in.

"What's wrong?" she whispered. "Are they after you?"

"*Pas grand'chose* (Oh, it's no great matter)," said Descoux. "I'd like to stay here a bit if I don't disturb you."

Halka saw the fear in his dark eyes and knew it: the fear of falling into the hands of men. She did not ask him what he had done, because she knew that whatever he had done he was always one of the hunted, as she was, and had never been one of the hunters. And that was enough for her, beyond that she could not look.

"As long as I remember, since I was a child," she said, "that has always been my nightmare: that they would come for me. It doesn't matter who 'they' were; I have always lived in a time when one lot of men were hunting and tracking down others. Dominic says it hasn't always been like that and that a time will come again when it won't be any more. But for me, I think, it will always be so."

"There are free countries where one can live as one likes and be left alone," said Descoux. "It used to be like that in France, and it is like that in America, and probably in Monsieur Malone's country too."

"Oh no," said Dominic, who had been listening. "We have the same chase, the same hue and cry too. The respectable, the 'good' Catholics and most of the priests form a moral band, and woe to any helpless being who is delivered into their hands; a peasant girl who gets a baby or a doctor or lawyer in some small town who is touched by the breath of scandal, as they call it!"

Descoux looked upon it all as a matter of luck. If he had

luck he would remain free to enjoy his life in his own way, to do an occasional "deal," to change his girls, to drink wine and go to the cinema and read the papers. And if not, they would shut him up between four narrow walls where he could do none of these things, where there was the foretaste of death. He had no special feeling of animosity against Captain Renier or the others. They were acting according to their natures. Nor had he any sense of horror towards the criminals whose deeds he read of in the illustrated police journals. They, too, were acting according to their natures and, in some sense, it was easier for him to understand how they had become like that than to understand the mentality of men like Captain Renier. But he seldom got so far as to explore this mystery of the nature of men.

The nature of women, that concerned him more. That was something that he could feel and experience. It had been quite a different thing to go to Basel with Lisette to what it had been with the little Paula; or to live with his wife had been to live in another world from the world that one would enter with a woman like Halka. But these were all feelings that he could not, and did not want to, express. Or even to hear expressed.

As he sat there, he made his plans. He would take the early train to France. He would have to risk there being a watch for him at the station. The French were quite incalculable. Captain Renier, of course, was not pure French, but Alsatian, and might be more thorough in his methods.

"I'd have more chance if I had a civilian suit or at least a pair of trousers," he said to Halka.

That was his way. He would not ask for anything direct, because he did not believe in the goodness of his fellow men. He expected nothing for nothing. But when he was in a tight corner, like now, he went so far as to hint at his need and then, if nothing came of it, well and good; neither he nor they would be embarrassed.

She knew his ways well. Had he had the opportunity of stealing a suit of Dominic's, he would not have hesitated a moment. She knew that and did not resent it.

"Dominic will give you a pair of trousers," she said.

"Yes; and you can have a jacket too," Dominic told him.

He spoke low so as not to rouse Lisette. He was still lying with her in his arms. His legs and arms were damp from the sweat of her flesh. But he did not wish to move away from her. He had no more revulsion from her, but on the contrary felt the burden of her in his arms and pressed this burden to him with joy and humility.

"Yes; take the jacket too," he repeated when Descoux was going to refuse it. That was easy for him. Perhaps because he had only two suits it was easy for him to give one. When he had had six it might not have been so easy.

Halka took the suit out of the cupboard and gave it to Descoux. He changed into it from his uniform.

Lisette began to cough in her sleep. She went on coughing and, half-awake, with Dominic's arms still around her, a stream of blood flowed out of her mouth on to the pillow. Halka brought a basin of water and bathed her face. For a bit she lay back on the pillows, with her eyes closed. There was that self-willed look on her face that reminded Halka of how she had looked as a child. But what was her determination against the executioners? You fell into the hands of men or you fell into the hand of God, and in both cases you were persecuted and tormented. There was no escaping the *bourreaux*. There was the chief executioner, God, and men who were made in His image.

When Lisette opened her eyes they rested on Descoux, and for a moment she looked at him with fear. She seemed to be back in the Hôtel Helvetia alone with him in the room where she had submitted herself to the ordeal of physical love. For a moment the old horror returned to her and mingled with the horror of death. But then she felt Dominic beside her and turned her eyes to him and rested in his arms.

"Why are you here?" she asked Descoux, still regarding him with a shadow of doubt in her dark eyes.

"Me? I came to say goodbye. I am going to France."

She nodded. When she looked at him longer and heard him speak, he was again the *oiseau sauvage*, insecure and ever on the defensive, even as she was.

180

"Who are you going with this time?" she asked him.

"I'm going alone."

She said no more for a time. She leant back in the circle of Dominic's arm. She felt the touch of death on her flesh and she shrank from it as she had from Descoux' touches during the first long night in Basel.

"I'll come with you to the station," said Halka to Descoux. "I can keep a look-out for you and tell you if the way is clear and I can buy the ticket while you wait in the background."

It was soon time for them to go and Descoux stood by the bed in Dominic's suit in which he looked more of a ruffian than he had in his own, well-fitting uniform. He held out his hand to Dominic and then he took Lisette's hot hand in his, and an unexpectedly tender smile lit up his dark, unshaved muzzle.

"*Bonne chance*, little one," he said.

She kept his hand a moment when he would have withdrawn it. Ah, how glad she suddenly was that she had given him some hours of happiness! Not till this moment had she felt like that.

"Goodbye, Robert," she said, calling him by his first name, which she had never done, not even during those two days and nights. "And find yourself a nice girl. Find plenty of pretty girls!"

When Halka and Descoux went into the street the town was dark and silent. But it was not the darkness and silence of repose. In the very shadows of the ruined walls there lurked disquiet, uneasiness.

"Do you ever think what a vast graveyard these ruins are?" Halka said.

"*Ah oui, bien sûr*," said Descoux, from which she saw that he never did.

Not that for her it was the dead who haunted the town. It was the living they had to fear. As they walked towards the station, keeping to the back streets, they both felt that they were hunted.

At night Halka thought of the bones of the dead that lay under the ruins; then it was that this other town, the town of overturned stones where the dead dwelt was more real to her than the houses.

There were certain points that they knew were critical. One was when they had to cross the bridge over the river. They came out of the darkness of a side street on to the comparative brightness of the bridge. The brightly painted direction posts for the French military gleamed with their mysterious signs and initials and these, too, seemed to them part of the whole widespread net that had been spread to catch them.

They passed over the bridge under the street lamps, exposed, trying to walk with the easy, purposeful stride of those who are secure.

"Where will you go?" she asked.

"To Lille."

"Will you be safe there? Why not to Paris?" she asked.

"Paris is too big. But Lille, there is everything there and I have a comrade with whom I can stay."

The thought crossed her mind that it was not really to Lille that he intended to go. He would not tell her where he was going because it was better to trust no one. They might come round and question her, and it was better that she should not know.

But that he was not going to Paris, she believed. He was not the sort to settle down in a big city; he needed the sordid intimacy of a smaller place to feel at home.

"My comrade has a *bistro*," he went on, "and I can help in it until I look around. But I'll miss Marheim."

Halka glanced at him. She was surprised at his words. For him it was a lot to say that he would miss anything or anyone. But she saw it was true. He had in his own way had a fine time here, with his own flat and his four ration-cards (for he had managed to keep those of his wife and children as well).

The station was a flood of light and Descoux remained outside in the shadows while Halka went in and bought a ticket for Strasbourg. Then she strolled over to the barrier and had a look along the platform. It was empty except for three or four Germans with the inevitable rucksacks on their backs. She went back to him in the street and they waited there in the shadow of the ruined station buildings until the train from Basel was due.

There was a couple of gendarmes, thick-set in their khaki uniforms and black caps, strolling up and down the platform. *"Canaille!"* exclaimed Descoux.

It was much for him to say. She had never before heard him give vent to so much feeling. But she, too, felt a poignant nausea at the sight of these midnight, uniformed prowlers. It did not matter what uniforms they wore—to her all uniforms were the livery of the *bourreaux*.

They waited in the shadows until the two gendarmes had passed the barrier and gone on down the platform, and then they came out and passed through the barrier—she had bought herself a platform ticket—and Descoux climbed quickly into the nearest carriage. He had only time to glance back from the corridor above her for a moment and smile his wolfish smile, and then he disappeared.

She stood for a moment on the platform. The gendarmes turned and came back, but before they got to where she was they were accosted by a heavily built man in a light grey suit carrying a large leather suitcase and a fishing-rod.

She overheard his halting French and she was about to turn and leave the platform when she heard the name of the street in which she lived. She had a moment of intense fear when she turned again to the train with an instinct to get on to it, to hide in it, to get anywhere out of the bright platform lights, out of the sight of the gendarmes and the other man. But then she remembered he had certainly got off the train; he had not been on the platform before, and she was reassured. At that moment the train began to move. For a moment she had a glimpse of Descoux' dark, lean face at one of the windows looking down at her with a peculiar sadness that she had never seen on it before; she saw his thin lips move, but she could not catch what he said above the intermittent hiss of escaping steam from the locomotive. She stared up at him, moved as she had never been by him before, heavy at heart for him, and then he was gone and there was a tap on her shoulder and she was looking into the broad face of one of the gendarmes.

She did not shrink back; she did not give a sign. When it came so far, then she could show nothing.

"*Oui, Monsieur*," she answered almost nonchalantly to his question as to whether she spoke French.

"This foreign gentleman is looking for an address. Perhaps you could help him, mademoiselle."

"*Naturellement.*"

She turned to the traveller.

"Where do you want to go?"

He had a piece of paper in his hand and he glanced down at it and slowly mispronounced the name of her own street and the number of her own house.

"Come with me and I'll show you. I'm going in that direction."

"Can we get a taxi?" he asked in very bad French.

The two gendarmes grinned and in spite of the heaviness of her heart for the loss of Descoux that she had never expected to feel, she had to laugh.

"Where do you come from?" she asked.

"I? I have just come from Switzerland." He wanted to say something more, to explain something further, but the words failed him and he made a comic little gesture of hopelessness with his hand.

"Come with me," she said to him in English, leading him out through the barrier. He followed her, without noticing that she had spoken to him in his own language, glad to have found a guide in this desolate place where the station lights shone on to a heap of rubble and beyond was a sinister blackness and silence.

Once away from the gendarmes she took his large suitcase and fishing-rod and went with him to the left-luggage office, and then they started to walk together through the silent streets.

"You are Dominic's Uncle Egan?" she asked him.

"You know Dominic?" he said, stopping in surprise and turning to her.

"Yes. We live in the same house. He is married to my

184

sister." She did not say "the same room" because she grasped that this man came from a world that was not their world and she did not want to say anything that might make difficulties for Dominic. He would know best how to deal with the situation. It had been the fishing-rod and the enquiry for a taxi that had made her cautious.

When Uncle Egan got over his astonishment, he began to ask her questions about Dominic which she tried to answer with the same caution. He asked her too about Lisette.

"You will see her yourself in a few minutes," she said.

"Yes. I will see her. But 1 won't be able to make anything out of her, you know. I am not at all a good judge of people. It takes me a long time to get to know them. That is why I wanted to hear what you really thought, whether she is suited to Dominic and if you believe the marriage will be a happy one."

Since Halka had appeared like a guardian angel out of the ruins of the strange place in which he had landed and taken him under her wings and spoken to him in English he felt a certain trust towards her.

"My sister is very ill," Halka told him.

He and his fishing-rod and his happy marriages, she thought! She took his arm because he kept stumbling over the pot-holes in the dark street.

"I didn't know she was so ill. In fact, Dominic has written very seldom of late. That's partly why I decided to come over and see for myself what was going on. His letters, when he wrote any, were not at all clear. At first I had the idea that he had fallen into the hands of some designing woman who wouldn't let him go. That's why I asked you about your sister. You must understand I know nothing. I don't even know her name or how old she is. Of course she is older than you?"

"No. She is younger."

"Younger? Really? And do they love each other very much?"

"Ah," she thought, "where does he come from? What must this place be like where they talk like this with such assurance about love and happy marriages?"

"Listen," she said to him. "You don't yet know the sort of place into which you have landed. Nothing is quite the same here as with you, at least not among us refugees and foreigners. Marriage is mostly an arrangement to make things easier with papers, with getting out or with getting a room or extra rations or something like that. If a foreigner marries a German girl, or a stateless refugee girl, it is usually to give her his nationality."

"I see," said Uncle Egan. "And you mean that with Dominic and your sister it was some such arrangement?"

"Yes."

They reached the house and climbed the unlit staircase, Halka holding her companion tightly by the arm and guiding his steps. When they entered the room, they found Dominic sitting on the couch, reading by a shaded lamp while Lisette had again fallen asleep.

When Dominic looked up and saw his Uncle Egan standing inside the door it was as though he was suddenly faced with his own double. Not that in the past he had been so aware of the ties of the blood, of any great similarity between himself and Uncle Egan. But now he felt it, he felt the warm familiar contact of his own blood in the other; as he took his hand it was the first time in all these years that he had been in the presence of his own flesh and blood.

At first they exchanged only a few words, made a few polite, mutual enquiries while Halka began to make tea on the electric cooker. Then Uncle Egan went over and stood at the bed looking down at Lisette. The pale, childish face, almost as white as the pillow, with the bluish closed eyelids and the long dark lashes, seemed to him to have some special significance. This was Dominic's wife. And whatever Halka might have tried to explain to him, this was something that moved him. He looked down at Lisette and his keen grey eyes under his thick grey eyebrows regarded her with that old, half-puzzled look that Dominic remembered.

Was this girl not just another of these women whom Dominic had sometimes brought home and who had filled him, Uncle Egan, with a sense of distrust? He had never known what attraction these women had had for Dominic.

"Well, I hope you and she will be very happy," he said, and this time it was Dominic who winced at the word. "When you mentioned her in your letters you said nothing of her illness. But now I suppose there is nothing to stop the three of us returning home together."

Dominic did not say that the woman whom he had mentioned in his letters had not been Lisette, but Halka. He was not going to begin to explain all these things to his Uncle Egan.

The next days he spent a lot of time with his uncle. It was very strange, this companionship, this being with some-one who in so many ways was himself, but a self that he had been long, long ago and now came back to meet him with a disturbing contact.

There was this secret bond between them, the bond of blood. Now he knew what the bond was between Halka and Lisette. It was the deep subtle blood-bond that gave two people the same movements, the same rhythm; that went down to the marrow of their bones and out to the ends of their hair and the tips of their finger nails.

They walked through the alien streets together or sat in Uncle Egan's room that he had managed to get in one of the French-requisitioned hotels, on the strength of the papers he had brought with him. Dominic began to understand the Parable of the Prodigal Son. Not that he saw himself in the rôle of the son returning home. He had not returned home, but his uncle had come to him—that did not matter; but the bond between father and son on which the parable was based and from which it drew its meaning, the mystery of blood, that was what was now revealed to him.

He had been deeply touched by the arrival of his uncle. Before when he had read the parable, the passage in which is described how the father saw his son "while he was still a great way off" and went out to meet him had always stirred him, but not fully; there had been a lack of full understanding.

Now he knew what it was. Not his father, it is true, but an uncle who had always taken the place of his father, had come out to him "while he was still a great way off." And, of course, it had been far more complicated than in the parable. Parables always simplified everything; that was part of their power. The son would not have been alone; he would almost certainly have had a woman with him, just as the father was not alone, but had had an elder son.

Uncle Egan accepted the complications. They did not speak about them. They spoke about Ireland, about the lake, the fishing, golf, about Hand, the grave-digger, and some of the other cronies of Uncle Egan. Dominic heard about the small events that had happened in all these years and all was brought back to him, that other life, so sheltered and slow and intense. He remembered how it had often bored him, when he had been in the midst of it. And Uncle Egan had often bored him. But all that had been before Dominic had known what it was to hunger after the very pig-swill in a strange land.

"There have been some great days on the lake and we've had some good games on the links, and many a pleasant night we've spent drinking and playing cards. But it's never been the same thing to me since you left, Dominic. I never took the same pleasure in any of the things that I did in the old days."

"Yet I was often a very poor sort of companion, Uncle Egan."

"You needed a woman, a good woman, and now, thank God, it seems that you have found one."

"I needed more than that. I needed a war and hunger and cold and imprisonment. I needed all these things before my eyes were opened enough to see a good woman, as you call it, should I meet one."

But this was something that Uncle Egan did not respond to. The bond between them was an inarticulate one. There was something obstinate, limited, in Uncle Egan that prevented him from grasping what had happened to Dominic, nor indeed really grasping the effect of the great cataclysm from which he in Ireland had been spared. He had a peculiar shrinking from a discussion that might involve them in horrors and the description of sufferings. He had come here

188

with some excellent papers, signed by a French general, with his fishing-rod, with a dinner jacket in his suitcase, and he could never, Dominic saw, be one of them, never really accept the sort of people that were around him, Halka or Lisette or Descoux or Petrov. At the most he might understand Frau Arnheim with her simple goodness, because she, too, could not grasp that all the walls, protective, shutting out the night and chaos, had fallen.

Sometimes when the four of them were together, he, Uncle Egan and the two girls, Dominic caught a look of obstinacy in the faded grey eyes set in their network of minute wrinkles. In spite of all his humility, there was this obstinacy, this instinct against accepting what would have undermined all the tacit principles on which his own way of life was based.

In order to enjoy a good game of golf and come back to a glass or two of sherry in a well-appointed club-house, one must tacitly believe in the sacredness of property, in the sacredness of marriage, in the security of society, in the police force, in the established system of education. Dominic might once more play golf and even enjoy it, but it would always be with his tongue in his cheek, always with an amused wonder at there really being such things as golf links left in the world.

But Uncle Egan meant to cling to golf links and dinner jackets and a belief in the police. He had a kind of humble obstinacy. He looked up to Dominic. For him Dominic was very clever, knew many things that he would never know. But all the same he would stick to his own humble faith in golf and bacon and eggs for breakfast and church on Sunday mornings. These things gave life its flavour, and he did not want it to have another flavour; and so he stuck to his belief with the obstinate humility of the early Christians sticking to theirs, or so Dominic thought. In the past it had often really maddened him. But now he did not mind. It was even pathetic because his faith was being proved vain. Ten years ago it was still a tenable faith of sorts; now it was so no longer. Dominic loved him. There was this deep, wordless bond of blood between them. Dominic looked into Uncle Egan's weather-tanned, lined face with its grey eyes and he knew him. This was a strange, moving knowledge, this knowledge of another being through the bond of blood.

When he walked through the streets with him, there was a flow between them that was a communion of flesh and blood in the midst of this alien place. Dominic looked at the clothes that Uncle Egan wore and they were not strange clothes as all other people's were, but they might have been his. And he rejoiced at this new intimacy that was not like any other, not like that with Halka, but which was that of father and son.

"When can we go home together, the three of us?" Uncle Egan asked. He had a great longing to be home again with Dominic in security, in his own world. But he would not be too importunate; he would never try to force his will on Dominic. Only there was always the fear that Dominic might refuse to come.

"As soon as I can get the *laissez-passer* for Lisette," said Dominic.

Yet Uncle Egan could feel the heaviness of heart with which Dominic spoke. He knew that there was something keeping him here, that stopped him taking any joy in the prospect of returning to Ireland, but he did not know what it was. Nor would he ask. That would be too intrusive, that would be to spoil the tacit, restful trust that they had in one another. Never in the old days had Uncle Egan made the slightest criticism of Dominic's goings on, of his *affaires*, his running here and there, his restlessness and moodiness. Nor would he now say anything that might seem to be an interference in something which he could not grasp.

"They cannot delay the permits very long now that I am married to her," Dominic said; "and if they do we shall just have to go without."

"Could you do that? Is it possible?" asked Uncle Egan.

"If we travel with you we should have a good chance of getting through. If we wait much longer it will be too late. Lisette spits blood every day."

That evening Dominic went for a walk with Halka along the river and on under the railway bridge towards the outskirts of the town. It had been here that she had come that evening some months ago on the day of her release from the asylum.

"And it was just here that Descoux spoke to me," she said. "When I saw him off the other night at the station," she went on, "I don't know what came over me. But, do you know, if he had asked me at the last minute, I would have gone with him."

"You'd have gone with him? Where?" asked Dominic.

"To Lille, or wherever it was."

"You would have left me?"

"We must leave each other. And it is worse if I stay here."

"Then I won't leave you, Halka. Ah, my little Halka, my little witch, don't send me away from you."

"Haven't we gone over all that? If you save Lisette for my sake, then you will have saved me, too. When I see that miracle, then I will believe again and I will begin to live again."

"Yes; and then it will be too late for us," he said.

"It will be too late for the happiness of which your Uncle Egan is always talking, but not for peace. Even if we never see each other again we shall have this to believe in and it will give us faith. Never again will the executioners and the whole night of chaos have power over me," she went on. "Against all the torture and hate and vindictiveness I will have that one great miracle of fraternity to set up. I will have you forever; and I shall never again despair."

They walked on. Below them in the almost dry river-bed the small pools of water turned red in the sunset among the grey pebbles and boulders. He took her hand.

"I will give my life for you, for that is what it is. I lay it down for you," he said.

CHAPTER XVI

IN THE GRAVEYARD

THE *LAISSEZ-PASSER* DID not come. Since the affair of Descoux, the details of which they heard from Paula, who in her turn had overheard all in the bathroom, Dominic did not dare go to Captain Renier. He felt a reluctance to let himself in for possible questioning, to have to see the sharp glance of the Captain's small blue eyes fixed on him, turning him into a suspect, making him feel in all his bones the secret shame of the hunted. It was a strange thing, but however he might know himself innocent of any real crime, of any crime of the heart, as soon as he was in the presence of Renier or the other officers, even when applying for a permit, he had this sense of half-guilt.

He discussed with Halka what was best to do.

"Don't go to Renier," she said. "He knows very well that it was Lisette that Descoux took to Basel the second time on his wife's pass. That man knows everything, everything! And in his quiet, prim way he will make your very heart wither."

"Yet he is good. His ideas are sound," said Dominic. All the same, he did not go to him.

"And very likely it is he who is holding up the *laissez-passer*, waiting for you to go to him," Halka went on. "You must go without it. With your Uncle Egan, it shouldn't be so difficult. Half the time, anyhow, there is no control, and once over the frontier you won't have any trouble."

"We will wait another few days," Dominic said.

But Lisette was getting weaker. Although she had now fewer hæmorrhages, she lost weight and her small face became ghostlike, her eyes growing larger and darker as she lay, day after day on her pillows, waiting for Dominic to tell her that they were going.

Dominic knew that they must go, even without the papers. Not so much for the sake of Lisette, because the fate of

Lisette was not what moved him in the last depths of his soul. But for Halka's sake, because he must not let her think that he hesitated. And for his own sake, too; it was too much to bear, this long-drawn-out anguish. Let them get into the train—it hardly mattered to him what train—and be carried away, away from Halka, from the one sun that shone for him in the midst of the night. Ah, he remembered that evening of his release: how he had got on the tram and been borne back to her, been borne to the well-spring of his earthly joy through the night of freedom in which all had been magic, entranced! And now he must get on a train and let himself be carried far, far away, into the outer darkness where she was not.

So be it. But he dare not contemplate it closely. He must do it blindly, quickly, now that the hour was come.

He went round to Frau Arnheim with some idea of saying goodbye to her, though more to speak to her about Halka. At the last she was the one he turned to, strangely enough, in spite of all the irritation she caused him. He found her in her tiny kitchen in the midst of boiling fruit for the winter. And even this was a source of minor annoyance to him, this eternal storing up, putting away. He had brought a packet of American cigarettes, one of the many that Uncle Egan had brought with him, and he offered this to Frau Arnheim, knowing that while she could smoke to her heart's content she would be ready to listen to him endlessly.

But, after all, what was there to say that could set up some real contact between them? She would be here in the same place where Halka was when he was far away. That was what brought her close to him. He looked at this rather statuesque, white-haired woman avidly lighting a cigarette and saw her for the first time. She was, for all her stupidity, her petty calculations and her ridiculous snobbishness and false pathos, capable of easing his anguish of heart. Ah, how weak he was! What need he had for someone with whom to share a drop of the bitter cup that he must drink!

He told her of his intention to leave the next day with Lisette and his Uncle Egan.

"When Halka is alone, you will keep an eye on her, Aunty?

You will go and see her and have her here with you sometimes? I will send her parcels so that there will be always enough to eat and I'll manage to smuggle in some cigarettes for you," he said.

"Of course I will see her and ask her here. But you know she is not always easy to get on with, this Halka. I sometimes have a feeling that she doesn't like me."

"That is her way. She is suspicious of everyone, but it is not so hard to win her trust. She will come here to you when I tell her that I count on her doing so. She will be glad to come in her heart; and even if you find her sometimes difficult to get on with, only be patient with her. For my sake, Aunty."

Frau Arnheim looked at him curiously.

"You know," she said, "I am glad for your sake you are going home. This was no life for you there in that one room with the two Mayersky girls. What does your uncle say to your marriage?"

"He says nothing. He is only glad that I am going back with him. As for Lisette, he hardly notices her."

"At one time I was afraid it was Halka you meant to marry," said Frau Arnheim.

Dominic said nothing.

"Lisette at least was innocent," she went on.

"Ah, Aunty, can we really go on speaking of innocence any more?" Dominic exclaimed. "That might have had some meaning when life was so sheltered and secure that the only way a woman had to express innocence of heart was by her modesty and virginity. But innocence has a more real sense than that. Aren't they innocent who have suffered without guilt, who bear the marks of violence on their flesh? The flesh and blood of women, Aunty, is capable of more than a negative innocence. The bodies of women that have been purified in the · fire of prison camps, of torment, of bombings, of hunger and cold, they have achieved an innocence that goes far deeper than the old one. That is the innocence of Halka, Aunty."

"It's true, I don't understand the world any more," Frau Arnheim said. "All these people; I try to do what I can for them, but I can't help feeling they are all demoralised. You

194

were the only one among them all who was still a gentleman. And now you are going and I am going to be left here, without a soul, amongst a pack of thieves and whores!"

She lay her head with its stately crown of white hair on her arms on the table in front of her and began to weep. Dominic laid his hand on her shoulder uneasily. He could not take her tears very seriously. He felt uncomfortable and wished he had not come. And her praise of himself only added to his sense of the falsity of the situation: because he knew very well that it was only his outward behaviour, his reticence and good manners, that appealed to Frau Arnheim. Had she been able to see into his heart, she would have been as deeply shocked by him as by all the others.

But she stopped crying as quickly as she had begun. She sat up again with her hair coming down and the pale, sagging skin of her face blotched with tears.

"When I was a girl, I had many admirers," she said, patting her hair back into shape and relighting the damp cigarette on to which a tear had fallen. "There was a naval captain who used to come sailing with my father and me on Lake Constance. He was a member of a very old Rhineland family and he was killed afterwards at the Battle of Jutland. But what I wanted to say was that with such men around them women had an incentive to be true and modest. In the end it is the men in each generation who set the standard by which the women behave. The Mayersky girls—what men have they known? Only the riff-raff among refugees and Black-Marketeers; they never saw a gentleman till they met you."

"Ladies and gentlemen," said Dominic. "The very words are already rather ridiculous, and soon one will never meet them any more except written up above the entrance to lavatories in the few old cafés that have remained."

He felt a resentment against this old woman with her endless stupidity, as it seemed to him. For a moment he thought he even saw how the great cataclysm had to come, how all the old pretence and *faux sublime*, the false idealism, had to be swept away in blood and tears. So much blood and tears had had to flow until all that old civilisation had been shaken and undermined, and he felt a bitter anger against Frau Arnheim as one of those who had played the old, insidious game, who had gone on marrying and giving in marriage, attending church services and listening to the words of the professional moralists about the idealistic God who from His secure Heaven smiled down complacently on a more or less secure world. Ah, all that complacency and mediocrity! Even Christ they had made complacent on His Cross—a smug little crucified God secure on His Cross! "I am on my Cross, and all's right with the world!" All the blood and tears it was taking to make the Cross a real Cross again, and he did not know if it ever would be done. He did not know.

He got up. There was no use staying here any more. But she laid her hand on his arm.

"I used to think it was Halka you were going to marry," she said to him. She kept going back to this. So much was not clear to her and she wanted to understand him.

He said nothing.

"I will do what I can for her when you are gone," Frau Arnheim went on. "You need not worry about her. I will look after her as far as lies in my power."

"Thank you, Aunty. You are good. But now I must go. I must really go, because there is so much to do."

"And I suppose we shall never meet again," said Frau Arnheim.

"No. It is hardly likely. But I will write to you and I will send you things, too."

She came with him to the door. There seemed to be something she wanted to say to him—something perhaps that might have comforted them both a little or that might have bridged the void that she felt was between them in spite of her looking on him as, of them all, the one that was nearest to her. But she did not find anything to say. She stood at the top of the stairs with her air of forlorn stateliness and he pressed the packet of cigarettes into her hand and a second packet that he found in his pocket.

"Well, Aunty, *auf Wiedersehen*," he said, feeling, too, the emptiness, knowing that there was nothing to pretend any more, no real understanding between them. "Not *auf Wiedersehen*; but it doesn't matter. Remember Aunty sometimes when you are back at home in your peace and prosperity," she said. But there was something false, some falsity of heart in these last words. She would never, never be completely simple, without pathos and without pretence.

When he got back to their room he found Uncle Egan awaiting him impatiently. Halka was out somewhere and Uncle Egan had stayed with Lisette. But he found it very hard to talk to her. He could not look at the small, suffering face with the dark eyes that looked at him with a kind of obstinacy. There was this burning look in them that he could not bear. It was not just her illness. There had been the Doyle girl at home whose funeral had taken place shortly before his departure. He had still to tell Dominic about it. It had been a very solemn and moving event, one of the funerals at which he and Hand and another old crony of his, a Colonel Partridge, had drunk solemnly and with that heavy, emotional gloom flooding not unpleasantly through their breasts. The Doyle girl. She had been a light girl, a girl notorious in the little community; long ago she had, Uncle Egan thought, been a friend of Dominic's. He had gone to see her during her illness and had talked to her; she had asked about Dominic. But this Lisette, she was quite different. He wondered what had ever made Dominic marry her. She was such a little slut. Her hair was always in her eyes, and her eyes were always staring out of her tangle of hair with such an obstinate look in them. She never responded to any of his overtures, to his telling her of how it would be when they got her home to Ireland and she was stronger. He had even promised her to take her out on the lake. But she had only looked and looked at him until he had lit a cigarette to break the tension. He did not know that for Lisette the lake was a holy place, the place of her dreams, and that when he spoke of it she was in a trance, a kind of obsession that held her in its grip, making it even harder for her to breathe. She longed for that lake, she longed for it more than for life; or perhaps it was to her the image of life, the life of that other world. She wanted it obstinately, with all the strength of her burning will.

When Dominic came in she smiled, her expression softened, and he went over to her and bent down and kissed her tenderly. He divined her a little. Ever since their bridal night, he had had a glimpse of her, and he felt very humble towards her. It was her innocence before which he was humbled and through which he was purified and redeemed.

In the last weeks, since his journey to Basel and his engagement to her, he knew that at last the final traces of his old blindness had been lifted from him. All that he had suffered had been the beginning of his redemption of heart, but Lisette had been its consummation.

Dominic sent Uncle Egan out to buy their tickets. On his papers he could buy the three tickets to Paris. The train left early in the morning. He hoped that Halka would return before Uncle Egan so that he could be alone with her a little for the last time. But Uncle Egan came back with the tickets and still Halka had not returned.

Lisette lay with closed eyes, but he knew she would not sleep for excitement. She was too exhausted to move or to speak or listen any more to what he said to her, but she could not sleep. She lay half comatose, and images took hold of her with an avidity that drained the last dregs of strength out of her breast.

At last, when it had already begun to grow dusk, Dominic could wait no longer. He got up and with some excuse to Uncle Egan left the house. Once in the street, he did not know whither to turn, where to look for her. But after walking aimlessly for a time he turned away from the centre of the town, passed the Cathedral and plunged into the labyrinth of tracks beyond it that cut through the mounds of brick and jagged rocks of cement. He passed through the waste of ruins and came out into the leafy, suburban streets beyond. He went on, until he came to the wall of the old churchyard, and at the small gate that gave into it he stopped.

He waited a few moments at the gate. If she was not here, then he felt he was lost. He turned in through the gate and into an alley that was like a dark tunnel under the thick leaves of the chestnut trees that hung over the wall. It was a deep, warm dusk full of the breath of summer and very still. The birds had stopped singing. He walked along the alley and past two or three benches that were empty. But they were not the benches on which they had sat. He passed the ruined chapel and just beyond it on the bench that he remembered he saw the figure of a woman sitting, and he knew before he could recognise her that it was Halka.

He sat down beside her without speaking and she turned to him. She raised her arms softly and pushed back her hair from her neck and cheeks, coming back out of her solitary thoughts.

"It is so close," she said.

"Have you been here long?"

She did not answer. She let her arms fall back as she bent forward, her forearms resting on her lap. That, too, was a familiar gesture.

"Before it got too dark I was reading the names and dates on the tombstones," she said. "Such a short time to be in the flesh and have names, and then to be bodiless forever and have no name."

As she spoke, he was conscious of the shadow of the trees and of the gathering darkness as he had not been since a child. There was again something awful about the dusk that dissolved away the earth. He knew again the dread of bodilessness and namelessness creeping up out of the darkness, out of the shadows.

She put her arms round him, not with the soft movement with which she raised them to brush back her hair, but drawing him to her with violence. He felt her arms like thin bands of steel. He put his hand under her, feeling the living warmth of her flanks and the back of her thighs that had warmed the old planks of the seat. It was a soft radiation that seemed to come from the sun of her belly and would have warmed, he thought, even the cold stone of the tombstones that glimmered pale in the shadows.

But he withdrew his hand and did not caress her any more, And she took her arms from around him. They sat on, speaking of many things, but not of what had just been.

199

To that they would not add a word. They left it untouched in its perfect darkness. They must not touch or examine it or bring it out into the other time, into the common light of day or the common darkness of night.

When they got back, Uncle Egan was finishing his packing. He had given up his room at the hotel and was spending the last night with them in the room to simplify the departure early in the morning. He was just rearranging his flies in the book of flies that he had brought with him and never used.

He looked up at them with a slight flicker in his grey eyes that Dominic caught. He knew then that nothing was hidden from him. In the closeness of their blood there passed between them this flash; as between father and son, in whom the deep blood-bond has not been broken, there must pass that which for others can remain hidden.

But nothing was said. Uncle Egan did not even ask them where they had been. He told him that Lisette had at last fallen into a restless sleep. Once or twice he had lifted her gently back on to the pillow when, in tossing, she had fallen into a cramped, contorted position in the bed.

He had brought a bottle of cognac with him from the hotel for the journey. He had also sandwiches for the journey, as well as what remained of the food he had brought with him, which he was leaving for Halka. And there were some extra things he had managed to get hold of for her in his hotel.

"You should be able to manage on that until you get the first parcel from home," he said to her.

Dominic knew that Uncle Egan said this, and was concerned about her, because of the flash that had passed between him and Dominic at the moment of his return with her. His hand had been dipped in the secret spring of her living warmth. For a moment the spring of her blood had touched him and radiated through him and his uncle knew it through the mysterious paternal bond. Quite without reasoning, Uncle Egan wanted to do for Halka the little he could. He looked at her with a slight sense of trouble, of anxiety.

"What will you do all alone here, Halka?" he asked, addressing her by her name for the first time.

She smiled and shrugged her shoulders. To such a question she did not suppose he expected any answer.

They did not sleep. Uncle Egan opened the bottle of cognac and they drank it, keeping only a little in the bottle in case Lisette should need it on the journey.

In the morning at an early hour, Halka woke her sister and began to help her to dress. She helped her into her clothes, doing all with a tenderness that Dominic had never seen in her towards her sister before.

When all was ready, they set off for the station, burdened with their odds and ends of battered luggage. Uncle Egan had had his suitcase taken to the station the evening before. The way was long. Dominic thought it would have no end. As he trudged through the well-known streets in which the traffic was just beginning to flow again, he was aware of how great a part of his life had come to fruit here. Here had been his life, the abundance of life that had been given to him, in fear and trembling, in hunger and cold, in peace and fulfilment, in the final ripening of his heart.

At the station there was the impinging of the world of noise and crowds, of many faces set in their own wills, passing and repassing, crowding and streaming slowly towards the ticket offices, towards the platforms. He felt the strength go out of him. He felt himself turn ghostly and dead in the press of the men and women around him.

It came about quietly, stealthily, as the worst things nearly always happened. Under the bright lights and with a movement of strange people around them he took farewell of Halka. Her pale witch's face was before him for the last time. Or so he believed, because he had little faith in the reassurances of Uncle Egan about getting her over next year or the year after. And then there was the chance of another war, another cataclysm and that they would not be together when it came. Standing there beside her on the roofless, burnt-out platform, there was nothing to say. All had been cast away, they had cast their bread on the waters and the waters had turned into the dark flood of chaos.

"This is the worst of all," Halka said. He had to listen

intently to catch her words above the train noises. "Worse than the leather whip in the camp and the electro-shock and all the other horrors."

"They went over and this will go over and life will go on," he said.

"Oh, life," she repeated, as though it was something of no more use. "If I had not loved you so much I should not have asked you to do this," she added. "Because it was not nearly so much out of love for Lisette as out of love for you. To be as you would have me be."

He nodded. He knew that he would have to think over these words in the time to come.

The movement around them indicated that the train was about to depart. Behind him towered the long grey coach smelling of dirty steam. It was like a great steel hearse into which he must climb, a deathly machine that would swallow him up and bear him away.

"Well, little witch, goodbye," he said. He kissed her quickly. He would not say any other words or use any of the phrases of farewell. For a moment he felt her arms round him, steely with strength as they had been in the graveyard, but then she let them fall quickly to her side. He climbed into the train. He stood at the window of the corridor and she was below him on the dirty, grey platform in her old summer dress.

"Let my right hand wither if I forget thee." The words came to him from one of the psalms that he had sometimes read in the evenings in their room on his couch in the corner.

The train began to move. He stared down at her. He kept looking back until there was nothing to see but the lines and the broken walls of the collapsed signal-box and wisps of blowing steam. Then he shut the window and turned into the carriage, in one corner of which Lisette was settled and where Uncle Egan was keeping a seat for him.

CHAPTER XVII

AT THE FRONTIER

AFTER A TIME Dominic was aware of his neighbour on the right. On his left in the corner by the window was Uncle Egan and opposite in the other corner, Lisette. His fellow traveller had already made some efforts to engage him in conversation. When Dominic began to notice him, he saw a dark little fellow regarding him out of a single bright eye from under the brim of an old felt hat.

"Excuse me. I didn't catch what you said."

"Oh, nothing of importance. I was wondering whether you could tell me if one can get a meal on this train."

"I don't know."

The other went on talking and Dominic listened only cursorily until a sentence or two caught his interest. He was explaining that that very morning he had been released from the Neuberg Asylum.

"How long had you been there?" Dominic asked.

"A long time, sir. More than four years."

"Then perhaps you remember a friend of mine, a Fräulein Mayersky?"

The little man considered. He sat slumped back, his shoulders drawn up and his hat forward, half hiding his face. A scar was seared across his temples and over one eyelid to the bridge of his nose, and under the half-dropped eyelid there gazed a dull, unseeing eye.

"What did she look like?" he asked. Dominic described Halka. There was both a fascination and a great pain in doing so. The little man listened to him.

"Yes. I seem to remember her," he said. "But she did not stay with us long." He went on to speak of himself again. But now Dominic began to listen to him. He was not just a stranger, another passenger on the crowded train that was carrying him away. He was someone who had set eyes on Halka before he himself had ever seen her.

"I am not going very far," he said. He mentioned the last station before the French frontier. "Whereas I see from your luggage that you are making a long journey. But I can't say I envy you. Wherever you go it is all very much the same. It is all known. There is nowhere to travel to where it is really any different. This world of ours is all mapped out; every inch of it is measured. It's too small, that's what it is. It's too small and we are too many. And there's no getting anywhere really worth going to by taking a train or an aeroplane. With me it's different. You see, I was blown up, or blown away, if you like to say so. Blown right out of our orbit into another one, on to another planet, inhabited by other beings. If you had the dreams that I do about this other star—it is always the same one I dream of—you would understand how very small and dull I find this earth of ours. For instance, just now before you got in I had dozed off and dreamt I was there again. When I am there I am always a child. All is new to me there, you see, and I make the most exciting discoveries. Just now they were showing me a picture-book. It was a book about that planet and they were showing it to me as you show a child here pictures of life in this world, the deserts of Africa, sheep-farming in Australia or the cotton-mills of Lancashire.

"But the pictures in this book were in colours like no colours on earth. I could only marvel at them. There was a picture that was completely grey, but this greyness was nothing like the greyness to which we are used, this greyness, for instance," he went on, nodding toward the window of the carriage, outside of which the summer dawn was just beginning to creep into the sky.

"In the foreground there were a few mounds or bushes, wreathed in the grey mist and a gate or something like that; it had the air of being at the end of the world. But not the end of this world which has no end any more. Why, they have a twice-weekly air service now, I hear, that flies over the Pole! This picture was called 'Winter in . . .' and then came the name of one of the countries on that planet. And, I can tell you, even from the picture, I had the feel of a great, almost endless winter, nothing like our little winters, but something that we have no idea of—a new kind of weather far beyond our monotonous alternations of sun, rain, snow, sun. There was such a stillness in the picture as you can't imagine. I could not have imagined it had I not seen it. But not our stillness; that is dead. This was a stillness as of needles—soft needles neither of rain or frost or sunshine. Needles of stillness, if that means anything to you, and the bushes were not frozen into solid mounds by frost but by stillness."

The little fellow stared up at Dominic from under his hat with his scarred face, his one bright eye gleaming.

He went on talking, describing other pictures from this book of his. It was always the colours that obsessed him and which he tried in vain to give an idea of.

"There was a picture of an ocean: it was nothing but an ocean of colours, so deep that I could hardly bear to look at it. It blinded me at the first glance, but then I noticed in the lower part of the picture there was something like a sluice, or the gates of a kind of lock. The whole ocean was being let through this sluice, foaming and pouring through the lock-gates in some vast industrial enterprise. Under it was written 'To the . . .' and another of those words that they had to explain to me. It meant, as I had thought, power-house, or something like that.

"When I read of our modern inventions I can afford to smile, because I know that in this power-house a force was being conserved that makes our atomic experiments a joke.

"As a matter of fact, there are several of these immense power-houses on the planet, though their exact purpose I have yet to learn. But, mind you, I shall find out. You must understand that I actually spend more time there than I do here. I may say there is a part of me there—the essential part. Here is one eye, but my other eye is there. It happened at the moment I was blown up on the Russian front. There is a small knot within us, I must explain to you, that ties all together, body and soul, mind, spirit and senses. This knot was loosened in me by the force of the explosion. It was loosened as one loosens a knot in a piece of string, but it was not severed, you understand. I flew apart, so to speak, like

205

a split atom, one might say, though I don't pretend to know much about the atoms. And one part flew out across space until it came to that star and was hooked on into the orbit of that other solar system and there it remained while the rest of me, rather battered, as you see, remained here."

Dominic listened. It was easier for him to listen to the talk of this shell-shocked German ex-soldier than to have talked to Uncle Egan. And he intended to bring the conversation back to the asylum when the other had finished speaking about his delusions. He wanted to hear him say something about Halka, if only a few words. Ah, how he longed to hear a few words about her as she was before he, Dominic, had yet laid eyes on her. Let the other go on about his precious planet to his heart's content so long as he came back, before his journey's end, to that.

He did come back to it. Prompted by Dominic, he appeared to be meditating, his one living eye closed and his other under its mis-shaped lid fixed in its sightless stare.

"I can recall her," he said after a few moments, "but she is like a dream to me. I had the job of carrying around the soup buckets to the women's stables, as we called them. Your little friend had a peculiar smile; that is how I remember her. She smiled at me even when she couldn't hold out her mug for soup because her hands were strapped into the canvas jacket that they put on us sometimes."

His one eye had lit on Lisette, who leaned back with her eyes shut in the corner opposite.

"There she is, isn't she?" the little fellow went on, "I'd know her again anywhere."

Dominic said nothing. The other's mistake surprised him because he had never noticed much similarity between the two sisters.

As they approached the frontier, he began to go over the plan he had made for getting himself and Lisette through. Often, he had heard, there was only a very peremptory control. He had his passport and one of Uncle Egan's papers, the one with the signature of a French general. Although it was not a *laissez-passer*—Uncle Egan himself had to show his *laissez-passer*—he hoped that with his passport it might suffice.

The name on it was, of course, the same, and Dominic would point to Lisette as his wife. If it worked, it worked, and if not there was no more that he could do. He relied mostly on the effect of Uncle Egan with his specially stamped pass, his indefinable air of worthiness, of solidity, with his fishing-rod in the rack and his immaculate grey flannel suit. They must slip through in the general reassurance that Uncle Egan would surely create in the mind of the French official.

At the last German station the little ex-soldier took down his rucksack and got out. He shook hands with Dominic and his twisted mouth flickered for a moment in a fleeting smile as his one eye regarded Lisette huddled with closed eyes in her corner. Her face really seemed to bring back some memory to him.

The compartment had emptied and Dominic sat beside Lisette. She opened her eyes and asked where they were, if they had yet passed the frontier.

"No. Not yet."

"But we'll manage all right, yes?"

"Oh, yes."

He did not believe that they could alter the shape that things took, not anyhow by ruses and plans. Existence took its form from within; in one's own centre was contained all that would happen to one as the tree in the acorn. Nothing was haphazard, nothing took its shape on the spur of the moment. What would happen at the frontier depended on something already in process of developing within them, a thrusting of their beings along their own path. This movement conditioned the outer shape that existence took. He could hold out the paper and passport and thus give things a chance to move thus if the other fateful impetus was at work at the deeper level.

"I prayed to Ste. Thérèse," Lisette said.

Funny, thought Dominic, that she should speak of prayer.

The only way that might perhaps alter the shape of things was prayer. If you went on praying long enough until the prayer became perfect, then he knew it had that power. But this "perfect" prayer, what was it, really? It was almost no prayer at all. It was a detached prayer—a prayer in which you saw that what happened was good, and it was not a prayer for the shaping of events so much as for the understanding of them.

"I didn't know you ever prayed," he said.

"Oh yes, especially lately that there has been so little for me to do. But only to Ste. Thérèse, like I used to long ago. I pray to Ste. Thérèse, but it is Halka that I see.

"Do you know," she went on, "I see now that it makes no difference that Halka was actually in the asylum when I thought it was a convent. Convent or asylum, it was holy because she was there. And I see how little I understood then to have been so upset. Now it is like it was again between us that time when I was six or seven and we lived in Lodz."

Lisette talked on about Halka. She did not realise that it was unlikely she would see her again for a very long time. She took it for granted that it was a short separation and that Halka would soon be able to follow them to Ireland.

At the frontier station on the Rhine there were gendarmes on the platform and some French military police. Dominic heard the police coming along the corridor from compartment to compartment, the doors sliding open, then a pause as the papers were examined and the doors sliding shut again. For those whose papers won't bear a very close inspection, for those with false papers or invalid papers, these are moments of almost intolerable suspense, he thought. They listen and listen, missing no sound, while pretending to be reading or looking out of the window. They are like animals cowering motionless in a thicket while the sound of the hunters comes nearer.

But Uncle Egan, coming from an island well beyond the European mainland, from a little world untouched by the cataclysm and its aftermath, sat unconcernedly in his corner. Even for Dominic and Lisette he had no great anxiety. He still had faith in God being in his heaven and all being right with the world, in the guilty being punished and the innocent unmolested.

An officer of the gendarmes slid back the door of the compartment. He examined the papers of the couple sitting in the corner by the door. Then he took Uncle Egan's *laissez-*

passer and looked at it, and Dominic knew that they would not get through. It was a quick, subtle flash of animal instinct, based on he hardly knew what, on the expression on the face of the officer, on his way of examining the paper, on the very attitude of the military policeman standing outside in the corridor.

The gendarme handed Uncle Egan back his papers and took the document that Dominic handed him with his passport. He read the recommendation with the General's signature.

"*Laissez-passer?*" he said.

"That's in place of a *laissez-passer*." Dominic spoke the words he had prepared. "My wife's very ill and I had no time to wait for the formalities to be completed. I understood this letter from your general would be sufficient."

The gendarme folded the document and put it between the pages of the passport. He did this with a kind of tenderness, as though sensuously relishing the drawing out of the moment. Then, as he handed the passport back to Dominic, he said:

"*Venez;* get off the train."

He turned to the military policeman in the corridor and spoke to him and then went on into the next compartment.

"We must get out," Dominic said to Uncle Egan, who had not understood what had passed. Lisette had grasped it. She stood up. She was very pale and without a word, without any fuss, began getting together her few things.

In that moment Dominic's heart went out to her as never before. He had never felt so close to her. She had made no fuss, no protest, asked no questions. She knew that there was nothing to be done but submit.

When Uncle Egan heard what had happened, he wanted to get out, too, but Dominic dissuaded him.

"That won't do any good. You can be more help to us in Paris. Go on to Paris and speak to your general," he said. "That's the only way you can do anything."

They got down on to the platform with their luggage and the military policeman escorted them into a hut that stood between two partially demolished station buildings. Dominic had a glimpse of heads at the carriage windows watching them.

There was a long delay while they sat in the hut. They heard the train move off, and for a long time after that they sat on there.

"Forgive me, little Lisette," Dominic said. "I made a mess of it. I might have known it wouldn't work."

"It's I who should ask for forgiveness," she said; "being such a burden. You've done all for me. Whether it worked or not, that's not the main thing."

"Not the main thing." But doesn't she know that it's her life or death? He thought she did know.

"What will they do with us?" she asked.

"Wait a minute. I will go and speak with the policeman," he said.

He went to the door where the military policeman was leaning in the sun, smoking a cigarette. He spoke to him, telling him of Lisette's condition and asking for a doctor to be brought to examine her if they did not believe him.

"The Captain will be here in a couple of minutes," the man said.

After a bit, the gendarme officer came with another officer, a captain. Dominic spoke to them and took out the letter from the general and gave it to the captain. He was a small, dark, harassed-looking Frenchman. Not bad, not corrupted by his power, not a bully, Dominic thought. He read the letter and glanced at Dominic's passport.

"My wife must be got at once to a sanatorium," he said. "If you don't believe me, you can get a doctor to come here and examine her."

The dark, little Captain glanced at Lisette.

"She is very pale," he said. He was affected by Lisette as many Frenchmen are affected by women, and his tone was at once less official.

"Do you know of a sanatorium?" he asked.

Dominic knew the name of a sanatorium that Frau Arnheim had told him of in the early days of Lisette's illness. He even had the address and telephone number in his pocket-book. It was somewhere up in the mountains behind Marheim.

"If you would ring them up, Captain, and ask them to send an ambulance to meet the train at Marheim, they will take her."

The Captain had gone over to Lisette, telling her not to worry, offering her a cigarette. His rather handsome, harassed face had a moment in which it relaxed into a quick smile. It was the recognition of her as a woman. For the French, thought Dominic, women are still women even when they are suspects. That was something that kept them human, many of them, even in the service of the machine.

But then again they were left in uncertainty. They sat on alone in the hut for a long time. At last a train came in which was going back in the direction from which they had come, and they were put on to it with an escort of two gendarmes.

It seemed an endless journey back to Marheim. Lisette spoke very little; mostly she sat with her eyes closed, her hand in Dominic's.

They reached Marheim in the late afternoon and there was another delay while one gendarme stood with them on the platform and the other wandered about, had a long conversation with another Frenchman and, at the end of it, appeared to ask him quite incidentally about his two prisoners. Then both went off somewhere and there was another wait.

How well Dominic knew all this waiting, this sudden, sinister alteration in the flow of time! As soon as you fell into the hands of the police, all became a long, interminable waiting. Finally, the gendarme came back and spoke to them. It turned out that there was actually an ambulance from the sanatorium waiting for Lisette.

When it came to getting into it, she did not want to. She looked despairingly at Dominic, her dark eyes full of fear. The light in the pupils was as though shattered; it came to him at that moment how fear seemed to break up the light of the eye, which was the light of the heart, into an incoherence.

"I want to stay with you," she said. "I want to go with you to prison."

"You've got to get better as soon as possible," he said. "That's what you've got to do."

211

He saw her being driven off in the ambulance, her small face at the narrow window in the door at the back. Then he was marched off by one of the gendarmes. He was taken through the familiar streets and across the bridge. He soon saw that he was being taken to the Nietzschestrasse and he walked on, the gendarme beside him, under what at first he thought was a cloud of darkness. But the darkness was luminous and he was astonished at remarking in himself none of the familiar signs of pain. He did not feel any trace of horror at the thought of the dungeon that awaited him. On the contrary, his steps were light, the way was beautiful that led him to it. He had been brought back to the place where Halka was. He had lost her and she had been given back to him as Isaac had been given back to Abraham.

The wait in the kitchen of the villa, the turning out of his pockets, the being led down the stone stairs into the dim recesses of the cellar had lost all their terror for him. Never had he thought it possible that he could experience these things again and have to take care to hide the lambent little flame of joy in his heart.

When he descended the two steps into the cellar, he stood still and listened to the door being locked on him, and the sound of the key turning was sweet.

He saw he was not alone in the cellar. Another prisoner was sitting on the edge of one of the beds. He himself took possession of another, the same that he had had the last time he had been here. He exchanged a few words with his fellow prisoner and lay down on his bed.

The cellar was for him like a pool of past time. The tide of time, in ebbing away, had left this small pool and here he was in it again, with the past touching him; the smell of the straw mattress, the feel of the rough blanket, the marks on the cement walls belonged to that past time. Here all had remained without movement and the air seemed to be charged with the scent of the past. Now he had come back and found this little bit of the past left like a pool. It was the same; he could almost have been back there again in those days of his first knowing of Halka, when she had come every day and they had sat for a few minutes in the upstairs office, and then, at the end of his interrogation, he had been brought down here again each evening and had lain on his bunk as he now did, remembering her. But it was also not the same. Then, in the midst of the flow of that time, he had not been so conscious of its atmosphere as he was now. It had matured and grown in body like wine; he could taste it now as he had not before.

Ah, to be here, in this blessed place, and not to be there, somewhere on the way to Paris! Even the fact of Lisette could not diminish the secret beatitude of being back here in the cellar. He was back here not through the following of his own will. He had cast his bread on the waters, and more quickly than he could have dreamt it had been brought back to him.

He had asked the German policeman, while he had been turning out his pockets in the kitchen, to let Halka know what had happened, and the policeman, who remembered them both, had promised to do so. Perhaps she would be allowed to see him, but that was of lesser importance. He was here where she was, and once he would be let out, they could not keep him very long, and he could go to her. The main thing was that she should go to see Lisette, who, he knew, would be eating her heart out alone up there in the sanatorium.

"What did they grab you for, if one may enquire?" asked his fellow prisoner.

Dominic told him. His was not a very interesting case. "And you?" he asked, not because of much curiosity, but because it was the way that prisoners began that contact with each other that relieved the loneliness of incarceration.

"They accuse me of being a guard in a concentration camp during the war," the man said. "They want to make out that I am a certain Karl Radek, who seems to have been a rather bloodthirsty customer; whereas my name happens to be Bergmann, Karl Bergmann, and I was never near any camp. I spent the war working in a factory in Frankfurt, as my papers show."

Dominic was aware of the grey face of the other, of the expression of his eyes, fearful and without repose.

"They grabbed me and locked me up here simply on the

testimony of a Jew who says he recognises me and who I never laid eyes on before in my life!"

"Who has charge of your case?" Dominic asked.

"A big, fair fellow, a captain. I don't know his name."

The other went on talking in that way he had, as though wanting to accuse some principle of justice or some god for what had happened to him, but being unable to, because he did not believe in any.

"There is no justice. There never was and there never will be," he said.

"Would you like there to be?" asked Dominic.

"I don't follow you."

"How many of us would really dare to ask to be dealt with by a pure spirit of justice? No. I don't think it's pure justice that we want."

"And if you are innocent, then what?"

This assumption of innocence by his fellow prisoner weighed on Dominic. He was oppressed and almost brought out of his state of peace by the presence of this restless spirit who spent hours on end pacing up and down the cellar, a blanket thrown over his shoulders. He was never quiet. He was continually bending down and trying to look through the keyhole in the door to catch a glimpse of someone going up or down the stone stairs, or climbing up on the small table to try to look out of the barred window. And at other times he would talk and talk, always coming back to the subject of justice and innocence.

"They won't condemn you on the evidence of the Jew alone," Dominic said to him.

"But what prevents them raking out someone else? There are plenty of people only too ready to make accusations in exchange for something to eat? The Captain has already threatened to bring some woman to testify against me who I am supposed to have beaten."

Dominic lay down on his bunk and pretended to read. He wanted to escape from the flow of talk, of going back over and over the same event in all its aspects.

He saw again the old graveyard and the huge dark trees standing in their stillness, that was another stillness to the

214

stillness of buildings. And below them here and there the half-hidden tombstones, grey and old with the ivy and moss creeping over them. And there was Halka close to him, her breasts bare before him, the skin pale and almost luminous, not contradicting the tombstones, but completing them, both part of the one strange world, emblems of that called love and of that called death. And across her breasts the thin white thread of scar, winding from the bluish white under-part of one across the very centre of the other, passing just below the pink nipple set in its brown corona.

When the door was unlocked and the policeman stood at it with the soup bucket and the slices of dry bread in his big hand, he told Dominic that he had delivered his message, that the Fräulein was going up at once to the sanatorium, and that as soon as she got back to-morrow she would come here and try to see him.

When the door was re-locked and they were eating their meagre supper, Dominic's fellow prisoner remarked: "You seem to be on good terms with the warder. Did you know him before?"

"Yes. I was here before."

Dominic looked at the other as he spoke to him. He regarded him with a peculiar curiosity, looking specially at his hands, and then back at his face. But he did without seeming to, so that the man did not notice. Dominic did not eat his slice of dry bread, and when he saw the other, who had quickly eaten up his, looking at it, he got up and went over to him and gave it to him. As he gave it, he glanced closely into his face, and for a moment met his eyes. There was a fascination for Dominic in thus approaching him and looking into his face. It was as though he expected to see there something that would be a revelation to him, a sign. But he saw nothing. Only the surprised, grateful glance of the dark, restless eyes as the man took the piece of proffered bread.

And there had been another reason for making him want to go over and feel the close presence of this other. He wanted to stand beside him, if only for a moment, as Halka must have once been close to him, naked and with her hands tied

215

behind her back to the leg of a table, as she had told him. He wanted to look into this face as Halka had looked into it as it had bent over her.

He went back to his bunk and lay down on it. He felt very tired; suddenly the whole stress of the long, too eventful day overcame him. And in the midst of his exhaustion he was aware of the other. He was conscious of the presence of the other in the cell with the same instinctive consciousness that he had sometimes had of the presence of a woman in a room. As certain Catholics may be conscious of the Presence in the tabernacle on the altar. He turned to the cement wall and pulled the dirty blanket over his head to shut out the cell and the other. What astonished him was that he did not feel the hate that he had expected to feel. Only an intense consciousness of the other's presence. He had looked into his face and he had not seen what he had expected to see, no profound and evil revelation; only a kind of mean and frightened restlessness in the dark eyes. One could neither love nor hate according to any plan, to any logic. The conscious love of Christ that was preached was really no love, not the real thing, but a sterile striving of will, a trick. And hatred—one could not hate to order either. The breath of love and hate blew where it listed. He lay in his great weariness, hearing the other beginning to tramp backwards and forwards, up and down the cellar. But in the very centre of the weariness still glowed the little core of rest, of home-coming.

CHAPTER XVIII

GUILT AND INNOCENCE

THE NEXT DAY WAS a Sunday, a day when nothing happened to prisoners, when the stagnation of time was more oppressive than ever. But Dominic was no longer conscious of this. At the end of the day, Halka would come;

even if she could not see him, she was near him; he might even hear her footsteps on the gravel.

At breakfast, although he was by then hungry, he gave Bergmann one of his two slices of dry bread. Again as he handed it to him, he looked into his face, but again he did not find there any reflection of what he half hoped to see. He wanted to see the shadow of evil with his own eyes. To be able to hate and to exult in his hatred.

When Bergmann went to the bucket in the corner and let down his trousers and sat down on it, his long, hairy thighs sticking out in front of him, Dominic thought: Now is the moment to hate him. And instead of looking away out of delicacy, as he would normally have done, he stared at his grey face, at the grey, pointed muzzle of this monster intent on evacuating.

But then he turned away, disgusted with himself, disgusted at the fascination which Bergmann, or Radek, could have for him. And even when he felt the beginning of hate in him, he did not exult. He did not want any more to feel hatred. When at midday he again shared some of his food with him, Bergmann said: "Don't be a fool. Eat it yourself."

"I wish to be a fool," said Dominic.

The other looked at him perplexed.

"If I really knew what being a fool consisted in and what wisdom consisted in, but I don't!" he went on. Suddenly he wanted to talk to his fellow prisoner. The other was only too glad to listen, to have a break in the long, silent monotony.

"One must experiment," said Dominic. "And what a good time this is to experiment and learn. No one can say: don't be a fool, don't risk doing something new or different when you have the example before you of the success of the well-worn paths of behaviour. No one can say that any more because the well-worn paths of behaviour have proved disastrous enough. That is at least something.

"Never has there been a time that gave such an opportunity for all sorts of experimenters in behaviour," Dominic went on. "First for people like this Radek that you tell me of. His lust was that of inflicting torture, perhaps specially on the bodies of women. And perhaps even, let us suppose, the more innocent his victims the greater was his pleasure. And there seem to have been many men like this Radek, and I dare say there always have and always will be. It is only at certain times like that of the last ten or fifteen years that these people have had an opportunity of behaving openly as they desired. But they are there, they are always there. And that is the really astounding thought: the concrete presence of so much evil always on the earth, either constrained and partly frustrated, or active. And the only thought that is capable of balancing it, so to speak, is the belief that at the same time there is another force at work on earth, another potency, equally concrete and living. I mean that side by side with your Radeks there are those whose hearts are full of such innocence that if you have been given a glimpse into one of them then your astonishment is greater than the astonishment at the Radeks. Oh yes; that is the double marvel. The marvel that such pure evil exists in the human heart, and the second marvel, which is actually a greater one, that there is such an unfathomable innocence in others."

Dominic stopped speaking. He was sitting on the edge of his bunk and he looked over to Bergmann, who was sitting on his own bunk opposite. He looked again at his hands. It was true what he had said. He could marvel at the thought that those hands before him, joined on the patched knees of the other's trousers, had been the living instruments of so much torture. Bergmann was watching him suspiciously.

"What is this Radek to you?" he asked. "For all I know, he doesn't even exist."

"Oh yes; he exists. Both *he* exists and his victims exist. That is the significant fact. Both exist—both exist perhaps here in this very town. We are not speaking of possibilities, of monsters and angels, but of beings whom we can see and touch."

"Well, and what if he does exist? What if you were to meet him, what would you do to him?" asked Bergmann.

"Nothing. That is not my business. It is not for me to either punish him or forgive him. Only his victims can forgive him."

218

"Do you really suppose that a single one of them would forgive him?" said Bergmann. "That would be quite impossible."

"What is possible to commit is possible to forgive. Not for many, for the extreme potency of evil and of good is limited to a few people. I could neither commit nor forgive such things. But I live between the great poles. I live like the mass of men vaguely aware of these two huge polarities which determine the shape of the world and of time, and in me neither has its centre," said Dominic. He talked to Bergmann, and at the same time it was not to his fellow prisoner he talked. He spoke without thinking very much of his solitary listener, groping towards some further understanding.

At the time when their evening meal of soup and two slices of dry bread was brought, Dominic enquired from the policeman whether, when Halka came, he thought she would get permission to speak to him.

"There is no one here. They have all gone off as usual on Sunday," the policeman said.

"Couldn't you let her see me for a moment?" Dominic asked. "You remember when I was here last I was allowed to see her every day."

The policeman scratched his head. He took up the can of thin soup and poured some into the dish that Dominic held out for it. "I don't know. I can't promise," he said. "I don't want to get into any trouble with the French."

Dominic left it at that. When the door was locked again, he went back to his bunk without any sense of being a prisoner. He lay on his bed and the evening deepened outside the small barred window under the lime tree. But time had no more horror in it as it had had these last weeks. Now it had stopped flowing, carrying him away with it. It was still, a pool of stillness, and in it lay all that he desired. He had no impatience. If she did not come this evening, she would come to-morrow or the next day. But he knew she would come soon, as soon as she got back from visiting Lisette in the sanatorium.

Bergmann would gladly have begun a conversation again. It was just the dusky silence in which Dominic found his tranquillity that to the other was unbearable. This hour of evening in the cellar was for him haunted. The whole day he could cut himself off from the past. He could be Bergmann and talk about and believe in the injustice that was being done to him, but at the hour of dusk-fall he felt a change; he was always at that hour in danger of becoming Radek again and being haunted by the past and by the future. So he made a great effort to start the conversation that had lapsed since the interruption of their evening meal. But Dominic pretended to be sleepy and answered only in monosyllables, and after a time the silence the other dreaded descended on the cellar.

After a time there was again the grating of the key in the lock. The door opened and there stood Halka in the doorway at the top of the two steps with the lit outer cellar and the stone stairs behind her. The policeman peered in, his long face over her shoulder.

"Ten minutes. Not more," he said and locked the door after her as she descended into the cellar.

Dominic had jumped from his bunk and they stood together on the cement floor in the dusk. Out of some deference, perhaps, the policeman had not switched on the light.

"I did what I could. I had the note from the General, but it was no good," Dominic said.

"I heard all from Lisette. Ah, you couldn't have done more."

"Is she very ill?" he asked.

"Yes. But the doctor up there told me that in any case she couldn't have stood the journey. It was already too late."

He was silent. He took Halka by the hand and led her to his bunk. As they sat down together she was facing Bergmann across the cellar and they saw each other's faces for the first time. Dominic felt a tremor go through her body beside him as she recognised her "executioner." She stared at him for a moment, and he stared back at her, and then he jumped up and walked over to the far wall under the small high window and stood there with his back to them.

He knew that face. It was one of the many faces that came

back to him, especially at this hour of evening when he was alone shut up and there was no one to talk to, nothing to do. He did not want to see those faces, none of them. The bodies, when he thought of them, the bodies with the blood oozing heavy and dark out of the thin slits made by his special whip, that still stirred him. The bleeding bodies were beautiful, but it was horrible that they had faces that could appear to him and look at him and accuse him. He was afraid of faces, of all new faces. And now this one had appeared before him in the dusk of the cellar, the woman, no doubt, that the French Captain had threatened him with; the one who would come and testify against him.

Again Dominic felt her arms round him, steely as they had been that evening in the graveyard. And now he didn't hold himself back from her; he let himself fall towards her, down on to the straw mattress. And again he felt the dark, radiant warmth of her thighs and her flanks. He felt the quick, decisive movement of her hand between their bodies, loosening her dress.

"Is it really he?" he asked.

"Yes," she said. She was trembling, but he did not know whether from fearful memories or desire. Then there were no more words between them. She was laid bare to him; to the final depths of her body she was exposed and laid bare. This last exposure must be silent, like the silence of death, because there is no word that does not ring false or mean in face of it.

Bergmann had gone to a bunk in the corner and lay on it, turned to the wall. He knew that she had recognised him. He lay with the dusky wall just in front of his eyes, staring at it, and not even hearing the rustling of the straw from the other bunk. He stared at the wall, staring, but not seeing it, seeing the face of this woman in the agonised grimace that he had once had the power to put on it.

Halka lay still in Dominic's arms, falling back into the quiet dusk of the cellar. The wave that with a flash had spread through her, like a soft explosion within her, flashing through her, melting her very bones, died out in her and she came back to the dusk and it was quieter and deeper than before. Never before had she felt like this. There had always been fear and a residue of horror at the bottom of her heart. Even that evening with Dominic in the old graveyard she had not been quite freed from it. Now she lay beside him on the straw and felt secure and at rest. It was a new, new experience for her. He saw her face, pale beside him and, as he kissed it, it was damp with tears. The tender, damp flesh was like something newly opened, or newly broken out of its shell; like a cluster of primroses in the damp spring grass. He lay and was conscious of the deep stillness of the cellar and of her moist cheek beside his and of the smell of the straw through the sacking.

Then it was time that they roused themselves. The policeman would be coming back. Halka sat up and arranged her clothes; she raised her arms and lifted back her hair from her shoulders.

"To-morrow I will go up again to Lisette and in the evening I will come here again."

"Captain Renier will probably send for you, anyhow. He will want you to testify against him," and he nodded over to the figure on the far bunk who had not stirred.

"But, you know, I won't testify," she said.

"No?"

"Let them do what they like with him, but I don't want to take part in it."

"Captain Renier will tell you that it is your duty to give evidence, your duty to all the other victims who can't speak, who are dead," Dominic said. "And not only to them, but to others whom, if he is not convicted and executed, might become his victims in some future war or revolution."

"All the same, I won't testify," she said. "Because I forgive him."

Dominic was silent. He was almost shocked at her words, as he had been almost shocked at how she had managed everything so simply and directly since she had come into the cellar. Nothing had weighed with her, neither the thought of Lisette in the sanatorium, nor the presence of Bergmann, nor the uncertain moment of the policeman's return. Yet he knew that she was right, in all she was right, without false

222

sentiment, false shame and without one drop of vindictiveness or malice. Hers was the innocence of which he had spoken, the unfathomable innocence that was on the earth to set over against the monstrous evil.

The policeman appeared at the door; he stood at the top of the steps and switched on the light and looked down at them with his long, impassive face that reminded Dominic somewhat of Petrov's.

Next morning he was brought up to Renier's office. Renier was sitting at his desk, looking prim and scrubbed with a shine on his big, pinkish face and his crisp fair hair. Under the desk the Pomeranian was curled up at his feet.

"Why did you let yourself in for that stupid business at the frontier?" he asked Dominic when he had taken a chair at the other side of the desk.

"Because my wife was dying and we couldn't wait any longer for the *laissez-passer*."

"Why didn't you come to me about it? I told you long ago to come to me if you were in any difficulty."

Dominic was silent and the other went on: "But I know very well why you didn't come. Because of that business of Descoux. You were afraid of getting that girl you married mixed up in it. That was it, wasn't it? You were afraid that I knew that it was she he took with him to Basel on his wife's papers."

"That's true," said Dominic. "I probably should have come to you, but I thought I could manage it without."

Captain Renier regarded him with his small blue eyes, that glance that made Dominic always feel uneasy.

"I don't know why you ever married her," Captain Renier said. "But that's not our business."

He looked through some papers on his desk. Dominic knew that, although he would not ask, he was curious about this point. Captain Renier always wanted to get to the bottom of everything, he felt, not merely because it was his profession, but because of a passion he had for facts. For facts of the most private and personal kind. What he must know! thought Dominic; this queer fellow with his cold little eyes and his prim mouth of a spinster must have an appalling factual knowledge of the hidden life of this town. What an amount of factual knowledge of depravity of all sorts he must have!

When he was away from him and thought of him, he felt a distaste for him and even a kind of fear, but as soon as he was face to face with him he could not help liking him.

He explained very shortly why he had married Lisette. It was something that he would have told no one else. Not even to Uncle Egan had he even hinted at it. But in one sense he did not look on Renier as an ordinary man. He was like a confessor to whom it was possible to say everything and to be sure that, in so far as what he said had no political significance, it would never be breathed again.

Renier listened. When Dominic had finished, he said nothing. He rubbed the Pomeranian gently with the toe of his shoe.

"There is no need to keep you here," he said after a moment.

"Will I be released?" Dominic asked. Strangely, the question of his release had scarcely been in his thoughts. He had not yet come to be fully aware of the fact that he was a prisoner.

Renier nodded. "I hear they put you in a cell with the prisoner Radek," he said.

"Yes. Though he calls himself Bergmann."

"That was an oversight, putting you in with him. Do you know who he is?"

"Yes."

"How do you know? Because you had a visit from Mademoiselle Mayersky, eh? That policeman let her in to you yesterday, I suppose?"

Dominic smiled and Renier went on:

"He'll lose his job if he's not careful. She recognised Radek, did she?"

"I don't know," said Dominic.

Renier was silent. He turned over the papers on his desk. Then he said:

"She won't testify against him, is that it?"

"I don't know. Probably not."

"Why not?"

"Perhaps she was not quite sure that she recognised him or perhaps because she thinks that executions don't achieve anything," said Dominic.

"They were never meant to achieve anything," said Renier. "They are merely an antiseptic measure. They don't cure the wound, but they sterilise it; they eliminate the germs and prevent the disease spreading further."

"No one is really fit to deal with the great criminals but the innocent," Dominic said. "We others, in judging and punishing them, become corrupted by our power over them. And one can't just simplify the problem away by regarding them as germs. They are men capable of repentance."

"I don't believe it," said Renier. "Have you been twenty-four hours in a cell with Radek without finding out the reality? Didn't he speak to you? Wasn't he full of his innocence, of the injustice of keeping him? Didn't you see that he was quite pleased with himself? Or did he show any trace of repentance? Or, leaving aside repentance, any trace of being capable of seeing himself as he is?"

But Dominic was not going to argue with Renier. He had no argument to put up against the other's words. And in the end neither he nor Captain Renier were the ones to pronounce the last word. It was Halka who had that right.

"Not that it matters so very much," Renier went on. "Even without her, we shall have enough evidence. But all the same I shall bring her here and face him with her. By the way," he went on, "I was almost forgetting to ask you Did you go and see my friend in Basel?"

"Yes. I had a talk with him."

"What did you think of him?"

"There is something in him, some power. That sort of power that a few men seem to have, prophets and leaders. But they seldom make anything out of it but an additional confusion, a little more chaos added to the huge chaos. Still, there was a great deal in what he said. There was all in what he said, excepting the last essential word, that was left unsaid. And that is how it always is. In books, in speeches and articles. So much wisdom and understanding for the ills of the world, and yet in the end, at the very last, there is something wanting; the final word that we long to hear is never said."

"What is that?" asked Renier, curiously.

"I don't know. I only know I long to hear it and I don't hear it, not from all these people, not even from your old man in Basel."

"Well, be off with you, and God be with you," said Renier, suddenly smiling, his lips momentarily losing their look of being pressed one against the other, his blue eyes twinkling in a momentary glance of friendliness. Dominic was touched, as in some way he always was by this man. They shook hands and Dominic went downstairs and out of the villa into the sunny, leafy street.

Halka was not in their room. He had not expected her to be, as he knew she was up at the sanatorium and could not be back until towards evening. It was sunny in their room and he opened the two windows wide over the trees and the river and sat down in his corner on the couch.

Ah, how beautiful it was to be here and to be waiting for her! To-morrow they would go together to see Lisette and they would go every day, either together or one of them.

He began to prepare himself a meal. There were still the things that Uncle Egan had got and left with Halka. But he had not finished eating when he heard the door of the flat being opened and Halka came in.

She said his name and came over and sat beside him. She sat for a moment in silence, her hands in her lap.

"Lisette is dead?" he asked.

Halka nodded.

"Were you not there?"

"Yes. I was there. She died an hour or so after I came. She was very ill in the night. They thought in the night she must die, but she would not die without me. She wanted you too, but when it could not be you she had to have me. She had had many hæmorrhages, but afterwards she was too weak to have any more. She was lying there with only a very small breath of life left in her lungs. The doctor was astonished that she remained alive."

226

She told him about the death of Lisette, sitting beside him on the couch in their sunny room. Not that there was much to tell. Lisette had seen her and known her with the last light of her eyes. Halka had sat by her with her hands in hers and had spoken to her, leaning close over her. But what she had said, she did not tell Dominic, and he did not press her to tell him. Perhaps, he thought, it would sound banal if she were to repeat it to me here in this room.

"I spoke of you," said Halka. "I spoke of you, because that is what she wanted to hear, and of other things. Of a dream I once had. And a little of the old, old days. But for the most part of you. I told her, too, of my coming into the cell to you yesterday evening and of our being together in it."

"Did you dare to tell her that?"

"Oh yes. It was no secret from her. And it did not give her pain. She had never the conventional, mediocre standards. Otherwise she wouldn't have gone to Basel with Descoux. She was completely innocent. Or some might say completely depraved. But you know how she was, I don't have to tell you."

"No," said Dominic; "though I never really knew her, not as you did."

"She lay there, and then, after I had come and been with her a little, there was no good to keep the life in her by the force of her will. I saw that she let go at last, and let that fierce little will of hers at last relax. And then she died."

They stayed all the rest of the day in their room. They had to accept what had happened and get a little close to it, this death, opening themselves to it, letting it begin to become part of their life. And that couldn't happen all in a moment. At first it was a shock, a blow like others, like being arrested or other misfortunes. But then that first stage of shock had to recede a little and the thing in itself had to begin to take root in them. Because it had roots. This death had the power, not only to shock them, but also to touch them, and then to begin to take root in them and become, in some way, a part of them, of their life. And so, Dominic knew, it had to be. Death was loss, but it was not pure loss. He began to feel that which before he had only suspected. It was also a

227

commencement of something that was not pure loss. Lisette was lost to them; in one way, she was cast away and destroyed. But there was a way in which her death was not pure destruction, but was like the dropping of a seed into the very bottom of their consciousness.

But this they could not speak of. On this first day there was still the death before them that is emptiness and destructiveness. Only they had an instinct to let this go over them, to let the horror of it sink into them, and to know at the same time that it was not the end, the final shadow that they would be left with.

On the evening of the next day there was the funeral to the small churchyard of the village high up in the mountains.

They took the train up into the mountains. The little Paula met them at the station and went with them. She had come round the evening before with a letter she had had from Descoux, and when she heard of Lisette's death she had asked to be allowed to come to the funeral with them.

They did not mind her with them. They did not want someone like Aunty or even Petrov, people who would in some way have impinged on them, who would have been mourners and would have put on an air of mourning. (Because, since his finding of Marianne, Dominic was no longer sure even of Petrov.) But Paula had no idea of trying to show anything. She had brought the letter of Descoux with her again, because the evening before, in face of the news about Lisette, she had forgotten to show it to them. It was a short letter written from Arras, saying that one day he hoped to return to Marheim. He sent his greetings to Halka and "to Monsieur *et* Madame Malone." "It is a little dull here," he wrote, "and nothing happens. The girls think only of money. Everyone thinks of money and the prices are exorbitant. Send me a line with news of you and the others. I suppose they have put some *petit fonctionnaire* into my old flat. Perhaps Marheim, too, will become serious. It would, if Captain Renier had his way. *Moi, je n'aime pas ce type.*"

There was nothing at all in the letter, but it brought back Descoux to them.

"When we were in Basel, at the Hôtel Helvetia," Paula

said, "he bought me this," and she unloosened her blouse to show them a corner of the pink *brassiere* she was wearing over her small olive breast. "And the knickers I have on, too," she said. "I put these things on to-day especially."

It was her way of wearing mourning. These precious gifts from the fairy-land of Basel and the Hôtel Helvetia which she kept carefully wrapped up in a drawer, she had put on to-day to honour the memory of Lisette. It was a little gesture from her heart, Dominic reflected, more convincing than black vestments and wreaths.

"You must get that nightdress of Lisette's," Dominic told her, "that she once meant to give you and didn't. She would like you to have it."

The black reptilian-like eyes glowed in the round face of Paula. She had a large, blank, olive-coloured forehead and under it her black little eyes like a lizard's.

The train climbed up through the dark, heavy curtains of fir-trees that covered the mountains. Dominic had always hated this scenery, the crowd of black, monotonous pine trees, and he hated the small villages with their chalet-like houses and wooden balconies. This Black Forest with its dreary picturesqueness had always oppressed him. But to-day he found that it had changed for him. Because Lisette had died here and was being buried here in the midst of the black crowd of trees it was no longer inimical to him. Her bones would lie here under the dark, pine-wrapped mountains. Her bones lying in this earth would endear the dark landscape to him, so that it, too, would become for him one part of the earth where he would have a sense of home. The other was the sand-hills and, above all, the lake where he had spent the years of his early man-hood.

The sanatorium was a big building of white stucco and grey weather-boarding above a small village with a yellowish, long-spired church. It was not one of the tourist villages, and there were no large hotels; only a small *gasthaus* in which Halka had stayed on her first visit.

The coffin was open in the small room at the sanatorium used as a mortuary. They had not wanted to screw on the lid until Dominic came, one of the nuns told him. He had

229

not expected this. He had not expected ever again to look at Lisette's face and he did not want to. But the nun was there, standing beside him with her hands clasped, waiting for him to do so—waiting, it seemed to him, to begin to say a short, silent prayer while he looked at the dead face of his wife.

He went to the coffin and looked into it. Lisette lay there in the nightdress he had promised Paula. That was the first thing that he noticed. Her face was withered and dead; he did not want to look at it—it was something that he was almost ashamed to do, to peer at the dead, exposed face that should be veiled and buried in darkness.

They followed the hearse down to the village, and the coffin was carried into the tall, narrow little church. During the short service, Dominic knelt between Halka and Paula and made a prayer that was no prayer. It was simply that he saw the short arc that the life of Lisette had been against the dark background of the night in which she had lived. He saw the purity of the line of her flight through the darkness; he had a glimpse of her being and then again it was lost to him in details.

But for a moment, as he had a glimpse of her rising and setting, he saw her as she had been, shining with her own fleeting light. And he was touched in his spirit and humbled before her. He knelt there and for a moment knew Lisette and knew himself with a pure flash of knowledge, and it was before her he was kneeling, at her feet.

CHAPTER XIX

THE FALLING STAR

DOMINIC AND HALKA began to prepare for the winter in their room. Parcels began to come from Uncle Egan, and he wrote long letters about the possibility of Dominic bringing her home. Dominic answered a little vaguely. The only thing he did was to warn him not to mention in any official circles in Ireland the death of Lisette. With great trouble, he had had her added to his passport, and if once they wanted to go to Ireland he could bring Halka there as his wife. He was not going to go into any more of the formalities and red tape of which he had a loathing beyond words. But for the moment he did not propose them moving from where they were.

They had an iron stove installed in their room for which they exchanged some coffee from the parcels of Uncle Egan. Then they went out to the forest to cut their allotment of wood. It took them two or three days, and on the last day Dominic worked late into the evening to finish chopping the last of the logs.

It was already dark as they walked back down the road through the steep valley.

"How I look forward to the winter!" Halka exclaimed. "Never before have I looked forward to anything, to any time. We have our room with a stove and the parcels. We have all! If it wasn't for the others, I'd say: Let the winter be long and dark. Let it go on and on!"

He, too, was moved at the thought of the winter before them and they together in their room, shut into it together alone and without immediate threats of change of any kind.

They had come through fire and were tempered. She first and then, in his degree, he too. They had not sought to save themselves in the world, to save their lives, and life was being given to them. They felt it being poured into them, into their bosoms from a measure full and running over. It was something that they could not speak about. They each, in their own way, felt this fullness of life in them. It was something which they could never touch or examine but they were conscious of it. They felt themselves like the field in which it was hidden, this pearl. Or sometimes it was the room in which it was hidden; at least it was somewhere, in the air, in themselves, that they felt day by day, this hidden balm of life. It was in all that they did, under all that they did. Her body was luminous with this lambent glow to him; in her breasts and in her belly it burnt. But it passed from her body into a thought; what they read together sometimes was the vessel, the measure in which the balm was measured and poured out on them. Or in other ways, in other things. In a simple meal that they shared together, opening a tin, slicing the bread. All was a measure that held the balm, or the field in which the treasure lay buried. There was no division into sensual and spiritual. There was no division or weighing or measure. The measure in which life was given to them was running over, always full and overflowing so that they were filled and fulfilled.

Walking back from the forest, Dominic contemplated this. He knew that when she spoke about the winter and wished it long and dark, it was this, too, that she meant; but neither of them could ever come directly to saying it. They could only marvel at it in silence, and sometimes in reading they would come on some passage that seemed to refer to this that had happened to them, and these passages they re-read and marked, but even then they did not definitely compare their own state to what they read. That was something that they did not dare to do; they had both an instinct against trying to speak of it.

The night was clear and over the black silhouette of the hills the stars were shining. Halka stopped on the road.

"You know, long ago Lisette had a picture of a saint, a young girl, to whom she used to pray. And afterwards she told me that it was half to me that she prayed, because for a long time I was a kind of guardian angel to her. And now the roles are reversed. Only I don't know if I dare speak to her. If I could speak to her I would say: 'Lisette, give me a sign, only one sign that in the midst of all the darkness you hear me.'"

Dominic was silent. They stood on the track, and below them there was the sound of the stream flowing over pebbles. Then there was a fleeting stream of vivid light across the sky as a star fell. They waited a moment longer and then they walked on down the road towards the village, from where they would get a tram home.

October 9th, 1947.

AFTERWORD

I finished *The Pillar of Cloud* in October, 1947 in Freiburg in Germany, the first novel I wrote after World War II which I spent in that country.

It is a personal chronicle of the collapse into ruin of an era in European history but also, I like to think, a prophecy which all such chronicles of intense experience in some degree are. In *The Pillar of Cloud* I quoted from a poem of Benjamin Fondane, a Frenchman who had been in Auschwitz until September, 1944, since when he was not heard of.

> *Know, then, that I had a face like yours*
> *A Mouth which prayed as yours,*
> *If a speck of dust or dream entered the eye*
> *The eye wept a little salt. And when*
> *A thorn pierced my flesh*
> *It dripped a blood as red as yours!*
> *Certainly, just as you, I was cruel, I had*
> *A thirst for tenderness, for power,*
> *For gold, for pleasure and for grief . . .*
> *Yes, I have been a man like other men*
> *Nourished on bread, on dreams, on despair. Oh, yes*
> *I have loved, I have wept, I have hated, I have suffered,*
> *I have bought flowers, and I have not always*
> *Paid my debts.*
> *And yet, no!*
> *I was not a man like you. . .*
> *You have not strayed from city to city*
> *Tracked by the police,*
> *You have not known disasters at dawn,*
> *The cattle trucks*
> *And the bitter sigh of humiliation. . .*

I have known disasters at dawn (in some moods I imagine I have seldom known anything else) and cattle trucks (or police cars) and the sigh of humiliation.

"They (the narrator and his companion) *had come through fire and were tempered. She first, then he in his degree. They have not sought to save themselves in the world, to save their lives and life was being given them."*

Of course, it is not yet saved, nothing is saved until doomsday. But we must learn to listen to the secret language of the New Testament (all vital communications are in a secret language, those between lovers included).

I suppose a central impulse in compiling *The Pillar of Cloud* and *Redemption* was to record my conviction – vision is too presumptuous a term – that pain and anguish are great evolutionary forces through which mind and heart, nervous system and psyche, mature and develop in complexity.

When such experiences are shared by two people, as in war, the first step is taken outside the private and personal. In *The Pillar of Cloud,* the central character, repatriated to Paris en route for Ireland, stands at the Arc de Triomphe and is appalled to see the droves of cars circling it (even in the same direction) as if nothing had happened.

Having shared so much with Halka in Berlin he imagines in his innocence, and, of course, guilt too, that if he writes to his wife at home she will in the new dispensation, welcome them both to live as a "ménage à trois". And, indeed, I actually did write to my first wife, Iseult, in Ireland with this proposition.

As we know half a century later there was no universal change of heart. Not that my conviction has been shown as entirely mistaken. Vast changes, as in Russia, have taken place and new currents of thought and feeling are flowing against the polluted tide.

Francis Stuart,
Dublin,
July, 1994